The Fall of the Prodigal

The Fall of the Prodigal

Michelle Lindo-Rice

www.urbanchristianonline.com

Urban Books, LLC
97 N18th Street
Wyandanch, NY 11798

The Fall of the Prodigal Copyright © 2015
Michelle Lindo-Rice

ISBN 13: 978-1-60162-698-1
ISBN 10: 1-60162-698-3

First Trade Paperback Printing February 2015
Printed in the United States of America

10 9 8 7 6 5 4 3 2 1

This is a work of fiction. Any references or similarities to actual events, real people, living or dead, or to real locales are intended to give the novel a sense of reality. Any similarity in other names, characters, places, and incidents is entirely coincidental.

Distributed by Kensington Corp.
Submit Wholesale Orders to:
Kensington Publishing Corp.
C/O Penguin Group (USA) Inc.
Attention: Order Processing
405 Murray Hill Parkway
East Rutherford, NJ 07073-2316
Phone: 1-800-526-0275
Fax: 1-800-227-9604

The Fall of the Prodigal

He had it all. Will he have to lose everything
in order to save his soul?

A condemned man. His two brides. One untimely death.

The Third Installment of the
"On the Right Path" Series

Michelle Lindo-Rice
mlindorice@gmail.com

What readers are saying about *Sing a New Song:*

"Ms. Lindo-Rice writes with heart, humor, and honesty."
—Shana Burton, author of *Flawless,*
and Flaws and All

"Michelle Lindo-Rice has written a sweet story of the power of love despite the main character (Tiffany's) sordid past."
—Michelle Stimpson, bestselling author of
Falling Into Grace

"The author's writing is crisp and her character's emotions are authentic."
—Pat Simmons, award-winning and
bestselling author of the *Guilty* series.

"The author did a phenomenal job in drawing reader's heart and spirit into the characters . . . Ms. Lindo-Rice developed an endearing, engaging, multi-layered story with realism and redemption."
—Norma Jarrett, *Essence* bestselling
author of *Sunday Brunch*

What readers are saying about *Walk a Straight Line:*

"I could feel the breeze and smell the scent of the flower garden the wind was carrying with it; that's how fresh this story is . . . I loved how the story flowed."
—Blessedselling author E.N. Joy
of the *New Day Divas* series

What Readers Are Saying

"The message of resilience in Colleen's story is powerful and important . . . as is the message of commitment, love, and friendship that come through."
—Rhonda McKnight, bestselling author
of *An Inconvenient Friend* and
What Kind of Fool

To my nephew
Mark Anthony Lindo
A truly gifted mind. I love you!

*A man's heart deviseth his way but the
Lord directeth his steps.*
—Proverbs 16:9

*Though he fall, he shall not be utterly cast down:
for the Lord upholdeth him with his hand.*
—Psalm 37:24

Acknowledgments

I begin by thanking my Lord and Savior Jesus Christ. He makes all things possible and I'm thankful He's using me for His purpose and to bring Him glory.

I now take the moment to mention some special people in my life:

My sisters who support me through this crazy process: Sobi-Dee Lindo & Zara Anderson.

My parents, Pauline & Clive and my sons, Eric Michael and Jordan Elijah.

My cousin, Kashief and my Uncle Willie for getting me on some radio stations to talk about my work. Much love!

This time around I'm going to mention my special male friends in my life for over twenty years:

A shout out to one of my best friends. Ever. Even though we barely talk: Linden 'Lin' Millwood.

Another big hail up to John Millwood. He read half of my first ever written work in one night and told me I had a gift. If only I had listened from way back then when he told me I needed to write for God.

My friends at work who listen to my nonstop diatribe about what's going on with my books: Annemarie Maynard, Maryann Morehouse, Olive Pryce, Lisa Craig and Stacey Horstkamp are just a few. My boss lady: Linda Apple. Thanks for giving me my wings and allowing me to fly. To Jane Adams, Love you.

My editor and talented writer, Rhonda McKnight, who has a heart of gold and is one of my biggest supporters. Thank you.

Acknowledgments

Felicia Murrell, copyeditor. Her work ethic is above par. She had her work cut out for her helping with this project, and I am grateful for her diligence.

The super gifted acquisitions editor, Joylynn M. Ross who is the blessed-selling author known as E.N. Joy. Thank you so much for believing in me.

Thank you to the Mr. Weber and the Urban Books crew. They work behind the scenes and deal with my neurosis: Natalie Weber, Smiley, Karen, the copyeditor, proofreader and others I may not know about.

I'd like to thank every single new reader who has reached out to me through e-mail. I'd like to thank bloggers and reviewers, Teresa Beasley, Paulette Harper, Faith Simone, Orsayor Simmons, Tiffany Tyler, Tan-ishia Pearson-Jones, Patricia Markham-Woodside and Kimyatta Walker—hope I'm not forgetting anyone—Forgive me, if I haven't mentioned you.

And, to loyal readers who took a chance on a new author and one-clicked, God bless you. Now strap on your seat belts and enjoy the ride.

A Note to My Readers

The Fall of the Prodigal is my most ambitious project yet. It features some sensitive subject matter. However, my aim is to deliver the content tastefully, and with artistry. I could only do that through the direct leading of the Holy Spirit.

Yes, this is a work of fiction, and some events may seem farfetched, but the overall theme of love and forgiveness is true. It is my hope that after reading *The Fall of the Prodigal,* you'll view everyone the way God sees them.

When God looks at us, He sees us beautifully and wonderfully made. We are all precious in His sight. Our circumstances set us on a path to accept the gift of salvation, which is our Lord Jesus Christ.

You have not chosen *The Fall of the Prodigal* by chance. May it inspire you and complete the purpose for which God intended.

Sincerely,
Michelle Lindo-Rice

Chapter One

Rape.

What an ugly four-letter word. The very idea was preposterous. He had been arrested for rape. Michael Ward shook his head, remembering the charges written under his mug shot. He did not have to take any woman by force. Look at him.

He was at the top of his game. He began as an architectural designer. Then he moved into real estate where he purchased, rebuilt, and resold properties. It took some time, but his name meant something in the hotel resort business. Patrons knew any building bearing the MJW seal signified quality and topnotch service, for a price, of course. He had two MJW hotels in New York City, three in Atlanta, two in London, and one in Dubai. He had spa resorts sprinkled across Florida, Texas, and Chicago, all with the MJW stamp of approval.

Now, after all his hard work to build his empire, Michael could not imagine a nineteen-year-old bringing him to his knees.

Last week, he had been cracking open a bottle of champagne, celebrating his newest property acquisition in Colorado. This week, he was squatting in the corner of a four-foot cell, waiting on Verona "Tiger" Stachs to post his bail and negotiate the terms of his release.

How had he gotten here?

He had been booked on multiple sex and assault charges and had almost lost his cool at his arraignment.

The fact that it was September 11 was not lost on him either.

Someone had set him up, and once he was out of here, he intended to find that person and make him pay. For the past few years of his life, Michael had become an expert at payback.

"It's all set," Verona stated from the more desirable side of the bars. "You'll be home within the hour."

"Took you long enough." He did not say thank you. He paid her an annual salary to the tune of $700,000 and felt she should be thanking him. Michael walked to the entrance of the cell. "Did you bring it?"

Verona wrinkled her nose at his rudeness. She reached inside her briefcase and retrieved a handkerchief and wipes and thrust them at him. "As you ordered."

Michael wiped his face and hands. He couldn't wait to take a shower and let the water run for days. He doubted he'd ever feel clean again. The stench of jail would remain with him. "What about the press?"

"The hounds are barking," came the wry reply.

He glared. "Is this amusing to you? Do you know what it's like to sit in this squalor inhaling the stink of dried urine and other body fluids I refuse to dwell on?"

She shook her head. "I'm sorry. It was bad taste. It won't happen again."

Michael took pity on her. He was good-natured, but his reputation and life were on the line. This was no laughing matter. Verona had worked through the night to find a judge to grant his bail hearing. Thanks to her, he would spend the night in his own bed. He could cut her some slack. "I'm sure I'll laugh about this at some point in my life," he said in a gentler tone, "but for now, I want to get home."

Verona yawned and stretched, but her eyes were still sharp. "Let me go over the terms of your release."

The guard on duty unlocked his cell. Michael used the handkerchief to touch the iron door as he came out. His first stop was the restroom. Next, Verona led him to a small meeting room. On the table, he saw Chinese food, juice, and coffee. The aroma of chicken lo mein and beef with broccoli filled the room. His stomach growled and his mouth watered. Michael twirled some of the noodles around the small plastic fork and took a bite. He smiled. "Thank you."

"With your estate, the judge sees you as a flight risk. Therefore, your business assets, bank accounts, and credit card accounts have all been frozen. You must surrender your passport."

Michael munched as he processed Verona's words. He felt like punching a wall but took another bite of his food instead. He was not a criminal. It was debasing to be treated as such, but what choice did he have?

He wiped his mouth. "Where do I sign the papers?"

"The press is camped outside the police station. You're worldwide news. The chief of police agreed to shuttle you home in an unmarked police car. I've arranged for a stand-in to lead them off your trail."

"I like the way you think." Michael arched his eyebrow in appreciation. She was smart, cunning, and deserved every dollar he was paying her.

"There's one other thing. I can't represent you. I specialized in criminal trial in law school and I practiced for a short time so I was able to fill in tonight. But you need the best. I have some referrals."

"No, I have someone in mind." Michael tapped his fingers on the table. He knew the perfect person. It had been years since Michael had spoken to him. There was no time like the present.

"Great! Who is he? Give me his name. I need to brief him."

4 Michelle Lindo-Rice

"I'll have to handle this one myself." He did not relish begging, but he needed someone with tenacity and a proven track record of winning hard-to-prove cases. There was only one man who fit that bill.

"Do I know him?" Verona asked.

"Yes, as a matter of fact you do." Michael said. "Do you remember when you handled my paternity case?" He referred to the time when he had pursued custody of the two children from his previous marriage. Michael knew they were not his, but he had wanted them. It was selfish. In his defense, he had been on a different track then.

"Oh, yes, I remember. If memory serves me right, didn't you drop that case? Wait a minute, wasn't it against—"

He cut her off. "I sure did after I found out—"

"What happened? What aren't you telling me?" Perched on the edge of the seat, Verona's eyes shone with curiosity.

Michael clammed up when he saw the interest in Verona's eyes. He knew she was curious to know why he had suddenly dropped the custody case three years ago. He had not told her then, and he did not intend to now.

Michael dropped the case when he learned he had fathered his own children. No one but his mother knew about his fraternal two-year-old twins. Twins he had never seen.

Old hurt surfaced. Michael hardened his heart. He did not share too much of himself anymore. Not after he had been burned by love.

He said, "What you may not remember is my ex-wife's husband, Keith, is a former attorney. I plan to ask him to lead my defense if we go to trial. Note the word 'if.'"

"The likelihood is one hundred percent," she said. "Wait. Are you talking about the same Keith I'm thinking of? Minister and host of *Second Chances* you put on blast on national television, when you revealed he'd slept with your ex-wife and fathered her two children? That Keith?" She looked at him like he was crazy.

Michael dared her to say something. He had not gotten where he was in business by being a coward. When he wanted something, he went after it with dogged tenacity. Right now, he wanted—no, needed—Pastor Keith Ward.

The man who had stolen his wife.

His brother.

Chapter Two

"You can't be serious about representing him! You haven't practiced law in years. Have you forgotten what that man did to you, me, and our children on live television? And, did you forget he was a no-show at his own mother's funeral?"

"How can I? You've been reminding me about it for weeks. He's my brother. I'm going to take the case." Keith Ward addressed Gina Ward, his wife of three years, with as much patience as he could muster.

Gina jutted her chin. "And, what about the church? Did you forget the four thousand members of Zion's Hill who depend on you every week?"

"Did you forget I have several qualified people like Bishop Combs and Deacon Broderson who are more than capable of delivering the Word? I'm not abandoning the television show or the church. I'm taking a hiatus while I help Michael. He's my blood. I have to help him."

Gina's face crumbled. "He's your brother but he's also the one who put Trey and Epiphany through hell. You might be able to forgive, but I won't ever forget, and you're all kinds of foolish for even talking to him. Michael is not the man you knew as a child. He's bitter and evil. For all we know, he could've staged this whole thing to get close to you."

Keith looked up from his law journals. This time she had call him foolish, which was better than stubborn mule, ox head, buffoon, or, his personal favorite, nincompoop.

"Not even Michael is that diabolical. He could spend the rest of his life in jail," Keith said.

Her chocolate eyes darkened. "You mean to tell me after three years of excommunicating you, all he has to do is come begging and you jump to do his bidding? Some things never change."

"He's my brother and your ex-husband!" Keith said.

Gina clutched her chest. "Don't remind me. You don't think I regret marrying Michael because of guilt? You don't think I regret walking down that aisle, all the while knowing I was in love with you?"

"I was making a point that Michael—"

"That Michael's what?" she interrupted. "He's not the same! He's cold, unfeeling, and heartless."

Keith glared. "How would you know?"

"Don't you read the papers? He holds his employees to an exceptionally high standard. Any little mistake and they're fired."

"Don't believe everything you read."

"Ha!" she scoffed. "It's true. He bragged about it on CNN, said his clientele is particular and he prides himself on delivering the absolute best."

"That's business. This rape charge is personal. Even if he's tough and demanding, it doesn't mean he's a monster," Keith said.

"Quit defending him!" Gina yelled.

The woman was exasperating! "I'm taking the job." He injected a note of finality.

Gina changed tactics. "Well, make sure you charge him four times whatever your retainer used to be," she demanded.

Keith played with his tie. "I'm not accepting any money."

"You mean to tell me you're willing to bring this monster into our lives and disrupt our household for free?"

Her chest heaved. "I'm not having it. Michael makes an obscene amount of money. You need to make him pay."

Keith shook his head. "Gina, this isn't about money for me. I make enough money from my stocks and investments to live a comfortable life. Plus, the church is more than generous."

Her lip poked. "Yes, but you refused their money at first. If I hadn't . . ."

"Honey, we both know you don't care about money. This isn't about finances. You're holding on to a grudge, which will fester and rot if you don't give it to God," Keith said.

Gina clenched her fists. "He pays."

Keith leaned farther into his chair and looked at her. How he loved this woman: his little spitfire. He could not believe she was his. Even when she aggravated him he had to smile. He could not help it.

"Don't go showing me those pretty teeth of yours, 'cause they won't distract me." She rolled her eyes. "You think all you have to do is flash your dimples and I'm putty at your feet. Well, it's not happening this time. I'm not caving."

Before she was finished speaking, Keith was on his feet. He moved toward her. Gina read his intent and retreated. "Stay away from me, Keith Ward. If you come any closer, I'll . . . I'll scream."

"You wouldn't." Like a lion, he cornered her until she was flush against the door of his office. He stooped to bite her ear. "Hmm. You're wearing my favorite scent. Could it be you've planned this whole seduction?" He peeked under her shirt. Eyeing the lacy camisole Gina had on confirmed his suspicions.

"Well, is it working?"

He laughed. "Yes, your strategy is proving to be most successful." Keith scanned the rest of her getup. "Are the kids awake?"

She shook her head. Her labored breathing clued him in that she was as excited as he was.

"Well, let's make the most of it. Shall we?" he asked.

Gina batted her lashes. "Does this mean you've changed your mind?"

He poked her on the nose. "No, it means I'm going to assure my wife she doesn't have anything to worry about. There's no need to fear anyone but God."

She pushed against his chest. "Too late. I am afraid. I'm afraid of Michael Ward and his malicious ways."

"You leave my brother to me," Keith said. "I know how to deal with him. I've been praying for years for God to lead Michael home and put him back on the straight and narrow. This may be the means through which God is answering my prayer. It took a lot for Michael to call and ask for help. Believe me. I can't turn my back on him."

Gina's face showed she did not follow his logic. Keith did not bother to explain. It would take too long, and he had a much better way to bring in Monday morning. He lowered his voice. "How about you let me give you a good morning welcome, before you take off for one of your ministries and leave me here all by my lonesome?"

She undressed with speed, a sure sign she was more than ready for some good loving.

Keith scooped Gina into his arms and headed for a small door. It opened to a sparse room, boasting a queen-sized bed. When they designed their home, Gina had the room built in. "For emergencies," she'd said, slyly.

He had caught on and agreed. Making love to his wife was an emergency. One that required his immediate attention.

Later that day, Keith reviewed the court files and police report. Evidence and motive were both there. The accuser, Mindy Laurelton, was the daughter of one of Michael's business partners, William "Bill" Laurelton. As Keith examined the statements, he could not picture the Michael the young lady described. Nor could he see his brother dating one so young, although there was an intriguing e-mail exchange.

Keith cupped his chin. Michael could be described as many things. A rapist was not one of them.

"Mr. Ward? Your brother's here."

Keith looked up and flashed his Jamaican housekeeper, Josephine "Josie" Smalls, a weary smile. He rubbed his eyes. "Okay, can you bring him back here?"

"I'll go get him. I made oxtail and rice and peas if you're hungry," Josie offered, wiping her hands on the apron she always wore.

Keith looked at his watch, noting it was about three in the afternoon. "Thanks, Josie. I'll wait for Gina to get home."

Gina was out with Epiphany at Nassau Coliseum. *Dora the Explorer* was in town and Epiphany was ecstatic to go see her live. Trey was at basketball practice. Josie would pick him up and take him out for ice cream before bringing him home. Keith had it all planned down to a tee to avoid any run-ins with his brother and Gina and the kids.

He supposed he could've set up the meeting at the church, but Michael was his brother. He could not remain impersonal.

"Thanks for taking my case. The grand jury returned with an indictment and now I'll have to stand trial. But I suppose you know all that."

Keith looked up toward the voice and his eyes widened. It had been three years since the brothers had seen each other. Michael looked cold and hard, and he had lost weight. He looked lean, more like a runner, than the football player he had been throughout high school and college. Michael had shaved his head and his signature goatee. The new him would take some getting used to.

Keith rested his palms on his cherry oak wooden desk and stood. He extended his hand, knowing a hug would not be welcomed. "It's been awhile. Sorry it took something so tragic to reunite us."

Michael returned the handshake but didn't waste time. "I'm here because I need you. You're the only one I can trust."

Keith arched an eyebrow. Trust. He never thought he would hear his brother use that word to describe him; "traitor," "hypocrite," were two that sprung to mind.

"I know what you're thinking," Michael said. "But, it's true. My life is at stake and you're the best. Name your fee. My freedom is worth any price."

So, he was making this all business. Keith gritted his teeth. "You don't have to pay me, *brother*. We're family. I love you and I'm happy to use my skills to help your case." He hunched his shoulders waiting for the venom to spew at his family comment.

Michael scoffed, slid into a chair and clasped his hands. "How are my ex-wife and my ex-children doing?"

Keith took a deep breath. *Lord, give me strength. Lead me and guide me. Help me keep my cool.* "My wife and children are well," he emphasized in a brittle tone.

This was the first and last time he would invite Michael to his home, for now. He had relocated from his previous residence in Jamaica Estates to Garden City. His home was close to his church, which was an added bonus. Zion's Hill was about twenty minutes away in the neighboring town of Hempstead.

Keith shuffled the papers on his desk to get down to business. "I've been looking over your file, and the evidence is damning. This is going to be a tough case."

Michael followed his lead. "That's your specialty, isn't it?"

Keith saw the confidence reflected in his brother's eyes and cautioned, "I'm going to do my best but it's been years since I've practiced. I'll need to do some research and I'll have to hire an assistant. I definitely have my work cut out for me. I'll need your full cooperation."

Michael gave a dismissive wave. "You won't need to hire an assistant. Verona will help."

"Who's Verona?"

"You remember the attorney I hired for the custody case?"

Oh, yes. How could he forget Verona Stachs? Michael had sued to take his children from him and Gina, their rightful parents.

"Yes. I do remember her." He couldn't disguise the edge in his voice. *Maybe Gina was right. Maybe this wasn't such a good idea.* He felt resentment rise, along with his own guilt, and silently prayed, *I rebuke this feeling, in Jesus' name.* God had delivered him, given him a second chance, and Keith wasn't about to dwell in the past.

He knew God had a hand in all this. Somehow, his brother would be led to Christ. Michael would find the right path.

"What do you need from me?" Michael asked.

The question brought Keith back to the present. "I need you to tell me everything. I need to know every contact you've ever made with Mindy Laurelton. Leave nothing out. Tell me the whole sordid truth."

"There's no sordid truth to tell more than I didn't do it." Michael's voice was firm but his eyes pleaded with Keith's. "You've got to believe me. I know how it looks, but I'm innocent."

For the first time since he entered, Keith saw humanity in his brother's demeanor. Underneath that tough guy cloak was a scared man, afraid of losing it all.

"I believe you. Tell me everything that happened," Keith said.

Michael exhaled. "I don't even know where to begin."

"How about you start with Mindy and the e-mails? Start by telling me why you made it very clear in your note you had no problem taking her by force."

Chapter Three

"That man is infuriating!" Verona plopped her Burberry satchel on the white Samoa Italian leather sofa she'd snagged at 30 percent off for $9,000. She yanked her teal blouse out of her white pencil skirt and sank into the couch, ignoring the panoramic view of Central Park from her penthouse. Well, it was not really hers. She lived in the five-bedroom penthouse courtesy of Michael Ward.

In her haste, Verona twisted her ankle, almost breaking her five-inch red bottoms. "Awww!" she screamed. "Michael Ward is going to pay for these Louboutins." She snatched the offensive shoe and its partner off her feet and tossed them across the floor.

Her cell phone buzzed. She did not feel like talking to anyone. *I ought to let it go to voicemail.* Nevertheless, she dug inside her bag until she had located it.

Nigel Lattimore's face filled her screen. Verona pressed the answer button. "What do you want?"

"I hear you'll be working with my former client," he drawled.

Verona rolled her eyes. "And what of it?"

"Didn't you tell me you were quitting Ward Enterprises? So, what gives?"

"Nigel, I don't have time for you," Verona screamed. "And, I certainly don't owe you any explanations! Why are you calling anyway? I only answered because I knew you'd keep calling until I picked up. Ugh, you're so annoying!"

Again, he did not take the bait. "To offer my services as I know this isn't your specialty. I told you we should start our own firm."

"As if . . ." Verona heaved a long sigh. She heard his chuckle and cursed herself for allowing Nigel to get to her. He needled her on purpose, and when it came to him, she was an easy target. "I don't need your help. Besides, I wouldn't open a firm with you no matter how you plead. You don't have the capital," she bragged.

"Not everyone can be as lucky as you to score such a cushy retainer."

She grinned before serving a jab of her own. "How's Rupert?"

"His name is Raymond. How many times do I have to tell you that?"

Verona snickered; pleased she had gotten under his skin. Nigel was a preacher's kid, hailing from Tampa, Florida. He had moved to New York, away from his father's prying eyes, to live with his life partner. No one knew. Except for her. She had found out by accident when they were back at Stanford.

She and Nigel had dated for a year and a half. He was the perfect gentleman, saying he did not believe in sex before marriage. Verona had been charmed by his old-fashioned ways until she caught him with his pants down.

Needless to say they were through after that.

He turned the tables on her. "Does Michael know you're in love with him? Have you confessed your true feelings, yet?"

In a swift move, Verona cut the line. *Take that, you creep.* One lonely night at the bar they had bumped into each other and she had blabbed. Big mistake.

Her cell phone buzzed again. This time she saw Michael's face. She answered the phone. "I made it clear I wasn't going to continue on your case. I did specialize in criminal law but . . . it wasn't for me."

"For what I'm paying you, I own you."

Verona snarled. "Listen, you might sign my checks, but you don't own me. No one owns me. The fact that you'd fix your mouth to say something like that is offensive." She paused for a second. "Is this what you do to women? Treat them like your property? No wonder you have a rape charge."

Verona sucked in her breath and covered her mouth. Had she uttered those dreadful words to her boss? "Michael, I'm sorry. I didn't mean to say that."

He was not rattled by her accusation. "Why are you angry? Hundreds of attorneys would jump at the chance to work with the legendary Keith Ward."

Because I'm in love with you. Because I can't watch you lose this case.

"Because you need the best and it's not like you can't afford it. I'll be more than happy to write a check on your behalf," Verona said.

"Quit being modest. It doesn't suit you. You're ruthless, you're vicious, and you know the law."

There was a time when Michael's words would have been enough for her. But words were not a warm blanket at night. She was ready to fall in love and settle down. She wanted the babies, the pacifiers, the . . . everything.

"You're right. I am the best. But, there's more to me. I'm more than all that." *I'm also a woman. Why can't he see me?* Every day men hollered at her about her translucent brown eyes, her long, luscious curls, her body, her style; but not Michael Ward. He remained impervious, seeing her as one of the boys.

He continued, "Oh, wait. I forgot to mention your culinary skills. Is there anything you don't do well, Verona?"

Yes, there was. She changed the subject. "Fine. You win. As usual. I'll consult with Keith, tomorrow." Verona let out a yawn on purpose, wanting to get him off the phone.

"You'd better not be yawning tomorrow," Michael warned. "I need you here on your A game. Equipped with boxing gloves."

"Wait!"

"Yes?"

Verona bit her lip. There was something she really needed to ask. She took a deep breath. "Were you in love with Mindy?"

"What?" His voice raised an octave.

"As your attorney, I need to know." She lied. The woman in her needed the truth.

"No," he sputtered. "Where's your good sense? Mindy's a kid for crying out loud. What do I look like? A pedophile?"

Verona's heart sang. "I had to ask."

"I value my privacy," Michael mumbled. "I guess my life will now be up for public debate and scrutiny. If you must know, there's only one woman for me."

"Gina?" Her heart pounded as she anticipated his response.

"No, Gina is history. It's Lauren. Or did you forget about her?"

How could she? Michael mentioned Lauren Goodman at least twice a week. Lauren had been the reporter who helped him expose Keith as the real father of Gina's two children on national television. During that time, Michael and Lauren had a brief tryst.

"She's dead," Verona said. "Why are you harping on a ghost?"

She heard his sharp intake. Verona could have bit her tongue at her insensitivity.

"I don't care what the obituary says. Lauren is very much alive and I won't rest until I find her," Michael said.

Verona repeated gently, "She's gone, Michael. You have to accept that. I showed you the death notice myself."

Lauren had been killed instantly in a bad car wreck in Alabama. The car caught fire upon impact. According to the report, Lauren suffered serious burns. Her mother, alive at the time but now deceased, decided to cremate her daughter's remains.

"Never! I don't believe one word written on that paper." He disconnected the call.

"Lauren's gone," Verona whispered. "Why can't you accept that?" She clenched her fists. "But, I'm here. I'm here."

Chapter Four

I should fire her. Verona's impertinent and her demeanor isn't befitting an employee. Michael gripped his iPhone. Lauren was not dead. He refused to accept that. He had read the obituary and hired investigators to visit Alabama. How convenient Lauren had been cremated. If her mother, Leslie Goodman, were alive, he could have probed deeper.

Michael tapped his chin. If Lauren died, then where were his children? Verona did not know about John and Olivia. He did. Yet, they were not mentioned. That was more than odd. That was significant. Nope. Until he saw the ashes, Michael would not accept Lauren's death.

Michael wandered around his Park Avenue penthouse suite. The silence maddened him and he was sick of the beige and mint green walls. He owned another penthouse suite near Central Park, and he kept personal suites in his own hotels, but this was the one he called home. However, it was empty.

Michael remembered a time when he had a family. A son he adored, whom he showered with everything a boy could ever want. He sighed. That was eons ago, before he singlehandedly destroyed his life.

Keith now had it all. But, didn't he always?

When they were boys, Keith excelled at everything. He had what was known as the Midas touch. Everyone flocked to Keith. Everyone loved him. Including Michael. He had idolized his big brother.

Deep down, Michael believed Keith had been his mother's, Geraldine "Gerry" Ward's, favorite. He wanted to ask Gerry on many occasions. But, Michael was not about to ask a question when he was not sure he could handle the answer.

Michael made his way into the kitchen for a glass of water.

For the first time in over thirty years, Michael thought of his and Keith's father, Vincent Ward. Vincent had been a cold man, hard to please. A welder, Vincent worked hard, but kept to himself. There was no denying Keith was his favorite. "My boy," Vincent called Keith. Michael stayed by Gerry's side. He quaked if his father even looked his way.

Michael leaned on the counter and rested his chin on his hand. He strove to remember if his father ever smiled. If Vincent ever laughed, it was because of Keith. "I'm proud of you, son," his father would puff out his chest and say.

With effort, Michael shrugged away the past. Why he bothered to drudge up those memories was beyond him. He strode outside to the balcony to look down at the crowds of people moving about their business.

It was October and Halloween was two days away. He thought of John and Olivia. His children were named for Olivia Newton-John and John Travolta, the lead actors from Lauren's favorite movie, *Grease*. He wondered what costumes they would be wearing and smiled.

Reality returned. His smile wavered. He was a potential convicted rapist. Yet here he was daydreaming when his life hung in the balance. Michael flashed back to Keith putting him through the wringer with questions about Mindy.

When he first met Mindy, she was a tall, gawky seventeen-year-old with braces and pimples. Then overnight, she blossomed into a swan, with a crush. On him. Michael humored Mindy, seeing her as sweet and shy. Until that day in September.

It was the same night Verona delivered the bombshell about Lauren being deceased. Grief-stricken, he drank himself into a stupor. He had never been a big drinker. The last time he overindulged he had ended up in a fight with his brother. When would he learn to leave the bottle alone?

Granted, Keith had deserved to be sucker punched for sleeping with Gina. But that was not the point. This time his drinking precipitated the most serious consequence of all. Michael faced possible life imprisonment, or death on the streets, for a crime he had not committed. The evidence, though circumstantial, condemned him.

Michael rubbed his bald head and groaned. He left the balcony and wandered into his office. Switching his MacBook Pro on, he liked how fast it sprung to life. With quick taps, he read the e-mail dated September 10.

Her: Hi, Michael. I'm here all by my lonesome. Would you like to come over? Better yet, why don't you give me your number? I'll make it worth your time.

When he read the text, Michael had been rip-roaring drunk. So when Mindy signed her name, all he saw was her e-mail address: Laurelton.m@LE.com. One person sprang to mind. Lauren.

Michael's heart leapt. Lauren was finally reaching out to him. His fingers flew across the keyboard. I can't believe you're e-mailing me. What took you so long? I've been waiting for this moment, and now, I intend to get what I want: you. *He hit* send.

Her: You want me? How do you want me? Ooh, I'm feeling giddy with excitement right now. I can't believe it! This is the best night of my life.

He was in full flirt mode. Baby, I want you, and when I want something I'm not above taking it by force.

Her: Come meet me at the Ritz-Carlton.

Michael pumped his fists. He was in. Be there in one hour.

Still in a daze, Michael hailed a cab and met "Lauren" at their designated spot. He whistled.

Or, was he singing? Michael shook his head. *Whatever.* He had been happy, happy enough to tip the taxi driver well. He did remember that.

Once Michael arrived in the suite, the sight he saw made him stone-cold sober. Red blood. White sheets. Mindy dressed in sexy gear, wailing. Her body writhing in pain.

"Mindy? What are you doing here?" Michael asked. The answer slapped him in the face. He hadn't been e-mailing Lauren.

Michael paused. He scrunched his nose in thought. He remembered being caught off guard by Mindy's brash words in the e-mail. She appeared unassuming. Her written words, however, showed a daring woman.

He flashed back to the scene. If he closed his eyes, he could see the pain.

There was pain in Mindy's eyes. "Help," she whimpered. Her fingers stretched toward him.

Michael called 911, sped to her side, and grabbed her hand to offer comfort. Then he called Bill. Once the cops and Bill arrived, mayhem ensued.

Inconsolable, Mindy moaned. "Michael, Michael. I was meeting Michael," she said, implicating him.

Michael's gut wrenched. His blood chilled.

Thrashing about, she asked, "Why? Why did you do it? You hurt me and all I did was love you."

Frozen with horror, Michael's mouth hung open. Wide-eyed, he shook his head at the eyes pinned on him. The words, "I didn't do it," were stuck in his mouth.

Police swooped in, threw him to the floor and smashed his face into the carpet. That was the beginning of his out-of-body experience.

Handcuffs clamped his wrists. Miranda rights recited. He was shoved into the police car. Questioned at the station. The charges. The arraignment. Numerous indictments.

Michael barely recalled any of it. His mind was stuck on that repulsive accusation. No matter how he explained he thought he was talking to Lauren, no one listened.

He walked that road to the jail cell alone.

As Michael reminisced, his mother, Gerry, sprang to his mind. She had died the year before. Michael had not gone to her funeral. He had been submerged in a huge business deal in Singapore when the news of Gerry's stroke reached him.

"She's in stable condition," the nurse told him when he called long distance.

"We're certain she'll recover," the doctor reassured him.

Upon hearing that, Michael had finished his business. "I'll be home in a week," Michael said to himself. "I'll go see her then."

He would regret that decision for the rest of his life. Guilt ate at him and tore at his being. He had pushed everyone away except for his mother. Gerry had been his rock, standing by his side. Now she was gone. All he had left were memories and pain.

Keith never broached the topic of their mother, which surprised him. He suspected his brother wanted to know why he had not attended Gerry's funeral. Michael had tensed when Keith said, "Michael, before you go, I need to talk with you."

He had removed his hand from the doorknob and turned to face Keith, fighting the urge to wipe his sweaty palms on his trousers.

"This situation needs the ultimate advocate. One who's well equipped to handle the case," Keith said.

Keith's quiet, confident tone made Michael ask, "Who?"

"Jesus. Pray with me, brother." Keith extended his hand in Michael's direction. "You don't have to go through this alone."

Michael stiffened his spine. "Do me a favor. Keep your prayers and your 'come to Jesus' speeches to yourself. I know the real you."

Keith dropped his hand.

Michael turned up his nose. "I know you. Underneath that holier-than-thou exterior lies a cheat. I do need your help but I won't be subjected to your hypocrisy. Let's keep this strictly business."

Keith chose not to argue, to Michael's surprise. "Fair enough. I won't preach at you, but God has done too much for me for me not to talk about Him. I refuse to eliminate Him from my conversations. I won't deny Him."

A chill swept over him, but Michael was stubborn. He made sure to have the last word. "Well, I'm not God."

Chapter Five

"Are you telling me you had that man up in my house? Why didn't you go to his place or even the church? Why'd you have to bring him here?" Gina's chest heaved. "I mean I almost fainted when Josie asked if Michael Ward was coming back for dinner."

Gina had not even taken off her jacket. She must have stormed right into his office once Josie told her about Michael's visit.

A soft answer turns away wrath.

Keith held up his hand to get a word in.. "I thought it would make it less impersonal if Michael came here. So he would know he had family."

"Family?" Her head swung left and right as she scanned the office. "If this is about family, where are all the pictures? Huh? Why did you move them?"

Keith snapped his fingers. He had forgotten to put them back. He pulled open the bottom drawer of his desk and took out the three pictures of him and Gina with the children. He placed them back in their rightful place. "I didn't want Michael feeling uncomfortable so I put them out of sight."

Gina placed one hand on her hip. "Are you ashamed of me and your children?"

Keith moved to her side and held her stiff body close to his. "Of course I'm not ashamed. How can you even think such a thing? You, Trey, and Epiphany are my life. I love you all, more than anything in this world."

When Gina gave a little nod against his chest, he relaxed. In a moment of panic, Keith had packed the pictures away. He had not wanted Michael making any offhanded remarks that would have them at each other's throats.

To be honest, a small part of him sometimes felt he had stolen Michael's happiness.

Gina pulled out of his arms and looked into his eyes. "I know you were protecting us, but you don't have to. We've come too far with our love and with God to fall under your brother's thumb. I know Michael feels betrayed because of our affair. But we were destined to be together, and he didn't love me the way you do."

Keith nodded. She was right about that. He cradled Gina in his arms, contented to remain there forever. Then there was a knock at the door.

"Come in," he yelled. Gina stepped out of his arms.

The door cracked wide open and Epiphany "E.J." bounced in the room. At six, she was already a beauty. She had twin dimples and a light in her eyes that melted Keith's heart every time he looked at her. She had him wrapped around her finger and she probably knew it.

Imagine that for the first three years of her life, Keith had not known Epiphany existed. Now he could not imagine his life before her.

"What's up, pumpkin?" he asked, pulling her curls.

"Did you do your homework?" Gina wanted to know.

E.J.'s little head tilted up to look at Gina. "Yes, Mommy. I colored inside the lines, too, as you said." His daughter turned to him. "Daddy, are we still going to have ice cream?"

Ignoring Gina's arched brow, Keith bent down to whisper to his daughter. "That was supposed to be our secret, remember?"

"Oh yeah," E.J. replied, with wide-eyed innocence. She faced Gina and with a loud whisper, said, "Mommy, could you please cover your ears?"

In spite of himself, Keith laughed. "It's okay, E.J., we'll have a small scoop another time. For now, get ready for your bath. Where's your brother?"

"Trey's playing video games and it's a school night," E.J. announced.

Gina scooted her daughter to the door. "E.J., let's go. Daddy has to work."

Grateful, Keith threw Gina an air kiss. "I'll be up to pray with you and Trey in a few minutes."

E.J. poked her lip. "What about my ice cream?"

Gina spoke up. "None for you, missy. Your daddy didn't know you didn't eat your broccoli and carrots at dinner. So, no treat."

Keith could hear his daughter's entreaties as they went down the hallway. He smiled. Epiphany was going to make a good attorney or politician one day.

He gathered the papers for Michael's case and sank into the small plush couch in the corner of the room. He needed a character witness. Someone, besides him, who knew Michael on an intimate level. Someone who knew his brother's generous, softer side. Someone like Gina, his brother's ex-wife.

"Are you serious?" Gina punched him in the chest after he'd posed the question to her as they lay in bed. "You're asking me to take the stand to defend that creep? You have a lot of nerve even voicing those words. I don't even have to think about it. My answer is no."

Keith turned on his side. "Gina, I hate to remind you, but you loved Michael enough to marry him at one point. For the first seven years of his life, Trey thought he was his dad. Michael was a rock when Trey was ill, remember?"

"Yes, I know. I was there." Gina rolled her eyes. "I was there when he treated Epiphany like dirt."

Since Michael knew Epiphany was not his biological child, he shunned her. He barely spoke to her. He even made Trey choose between him and Epiphany.

"That may be true but Michael's not all bad," Keith said. "You have to forgive him as God has forgiven you."

"I don't want to."

Keith chuckled at her childish pout. "I understand, but you know we must forgive others, especially those who don't deserve it."

"You're right. There are those who don't deserve it," she returned, twisting his words. "I'm not going to testify on Michael's behalf. You can't make me."

"I'll pray on it." He patted her hand.

Gina snickered. "Go ahead, set God on me. I'm still not going to testify."

Chapter Six

"Mousie! Mousie!"

Mousie listened to the cheers of the crowd and gave them a knowing smile. Like a cat, she crawled up the pole and arched her back with the grace of a ballerina dancer. Her white bloomers elicited an even greater roar.

She opened her legs, waiting for the precise moment when her audience saw the gaping hole and registered she might not be wearing any underwear.

As expected, a crescendo ensued. Bills were tossed in every direction. Mousie flipped her body in a deft move and executed a split.

More bills.

Her burgundy, spiced lips widened with approval. She twitched her ears causing her signature super-sized ears to wiggle up and down. Then she lowered the top half of her frame and wiggled. Her red and black tassels jiggled suggestively.

More bills.

With superior adeptness, she stood from her split. The men knew what that meant. She reveled in the cries, "Don't go, Mousie! Show us the cheese!"

Finn Morrison, the announcer and owner of the joint, prompted them. "Cheese, please. Cheese, please."

Mousie grinned. Imagine that when she had approached Finn with the idea, he had said, "They'll laugh you to scorn." But, she had persisted.

And, oh how right she had been. Her act had been a rousing success. Mousie was in big demand. So big in fact that she could afford to be eclectic. She came when she pleased, whenever the mood struck. Men flocked, not knowing when she would show up.

Finn basked in the rewards of having a packed house. "Sheer genius," he said when she got offthe stage that first night, right before he smacked her on the lips.

Mousie had grabbed the front of his pants and squeezed until he jumped back with a yelp.

"Never touch me again." She took the stack of bills in her hand and threw them at him. "Here's your money."

Finn's mouth popped open. "You don't want it?"

"No, it's dirty," Mousie spat. "I don't want it."

He squinted his eyes. "Then, why are you doing this?" This he asked while scooping up the cash. She watched him flick the bills as he counted. Then he looked at her wide-eyed. "Do you know how much this is?"

"Like I said, I don't care."

Finn grabbed his head. "Three thousand dollars! Who makes three thousand dollars their first night? And, an amateur at that."

Mousie shrugged and turned to leave the room. She wanted to go home. Her tail swished hitting his leg. "Ouch!"

He did not see her vicious smile. She had done it on purpose of course on her way to the door. Mousie intended to practice using it as a whip. So many needed a spanking, and she was happy to oblige. With a mouse-like voice, she said, "I'll be back," before slipping through the door.

"When? When?" Finn asked.

"Whenever."

That had been a year ago.

Mousie zoned in on the crowd and spoke into the microphone attached to her ear. Another perk. She used her signature voice to ask, "You want a slice of my cheese?"

"Yes! Yes!" the men chanted.

More bills.

She sighed. Really this was getting old. It did not take much for her to get paid—well Finn. She still didn't want the money.

She counted to three before she tore off the special-made bloomers with a big swoop. Her gold-encrusted scrap underwear sparkled. She arched her back bending her body until both her hands and feet were flat on the floor.

Even more bills.

The lights went out. The bouncers gathered the cash. Mousie retreated.

"They keep paying me!" she screamed at Finn. "Why are they paying me?"

Finn pushed a bottled water into her hands and wiped her face with a hand towel. Mousie lifted her face and allowed him to perform the father-like task. It'd been six months before she'd taken water, and another two before she had permitted him to wipe her face.

"Mousie, please calm down."

She grabbed the towel and threw it to the floor. Then, she stomped on it as a child would when throwing a tantrum.

"Gentle," Finn stated. "I'll count to three. One, two, three."

Mousie relaxed and plastered a cherubic smile on her face. Her hand gave his paw-sized hand a pat. "Thanks, Finn, you take such good care of me." Then, she straightened her spine. "I'll be back."

"When?"

"Whenever." With a flick of the wrist, she was gone.

Until next time.

Chapter Seven

How dare she look at him like he had no right to be in his own establishment?

Inside the MJW Conglomerate, located in Midtown, blocks away from the Empire State Building, Michael met the front desk clerk stare for stare. She had the good sense to look away. His company signed her check. She had better keep her censure to herself.

Michael adjusted the top button of his Brioni navy pinstripe suit and walked across the marble floor to the elevator. He glanced at his Jorg Gray 6500 watch. He had bought one when he learned it was among President Obama's watches of choice. Michael had chosen his outfit with care. He wanted his board of directors to see he was very much the boss. In charge.

Twelve committee members, nine men and three women, waited for him. Some faces held frowns and others pity. He squared his shoulders and took his position at the head of the table. "Let's have it," he dared.

Following his words, Verona entered the room. He eyed her black pants suit and burgundy stilettos. She made her way to "her" chair next to him.

Leonard Paulson, his VP, said, "Michael, we feel it's in the best interest of the company if you stepped down until your personal life—"

He glared at his VP. "No."

"Our stocks nosedived and—"

"No," he repeated. Then he eyed Patti Mourer. "How are the resort plans going for our L.A. expansion?"

She sputtered, "It's on hold. One of the key players is friends with Bill Laurelton and he's . . ."

Michael nodded. Evidently, the contractors were picking sides already. He had been found guilty among his peers. "I see." He arched an eyebrow. "What's his name?"

"I don't think . . ." Patti trailed off. It was obvious she was afraid to mention a name. Michael's ruthlessness to those who crossed him was well known.

Eyes shifted. Pencils drummed the table. No one would look him in the eye. These were people he had handpicked for his company. He was tough, but generous and now when he needed their support . . .

Verona spoke up. "Patti, perhaps you can work on revising the specifics of the plans?"

"Why are we speaking in such generic terms?" Michael said. "Patti, if Steven Cummings wants to pull out of the deal because he thinks I'm a rapist, find someone else."

"I have been trying," Patti said. "You know how fast a reputation can bring a company down. Look at Paula Deen."

"Each of the resorts has been inundated with cancellations. A father defaced one of the Atlanta resorts with the word 'rapist' by your insignia. It's a mess," someone said.

Michael froze. He knew what the board members were after. "You want my resignation."

"If you don't resign, then I'm leaving. I have a nineteen-year-old daughter," Nelson Phillips, his Cuisine and Caterer CEO said.

Nelson's challenge seemed to give the others a voice:

"I'm not staying on a sinking ship."

"I won't work for a tarnished company."

Verona jumped in to defend his position. From a business aspect, he knew they were right. Michael swiveled his chair to face the wall, tuning them out. If it were any of them, he would have fired them already. But MJW Conglomerate was his life. He had nothing else of substance. He could not let it go that easy.

He turned to the chief financial officer, Walter Stein. "What's the damage?"

The older man sighed like the world was on his chest. "It's worse than we feared. Stocks are now at pennies on the dollar. Our days as a Fortune 500 company are at an end."

"Can we recover?"

Walter shook his head. "Possibly. Take a leave of absence and put Leonard in charge."

Leonard leaned forward. "It would be in name only. You can still work behind the scenes but we have to show the public something. How will we look if we turned a blind eye to an accused rapist?" He pointed to the only other empty chair in the room, which belonged to Bill Laurelton. "Because I know he isn't."

Michael redirected the conversation to Verona. "Draw up the papers."

She touched his arm. "Give yourself a day or two."

"No. Do it," he whispered.

"I've taken the liberty of drafting your press statement. Take a moment to look it over." Antoinette Myers, his Publications and Advertising CEO, stood. She walked up to him with the paper in hand. "I'll notify the press and release a statement announcing your resignation. It's a good call, Michael."

Verona jumped to her feet. She raged at each of them. "You all should be ashamed. Imagine you're putting Michael's head on a platter to deliver up to the masses. Not one of you came to his defense!"

Antoinette gave Verona a nasty glare. "If it were any of us, Michael would do the same thing."

Michael did not comment. He knew Antoinette spoke the truth.

With a wave of the hand, he gestured for both women to quiet down. Then he dismissed the board. All twelve of his executives scurried out of the conference room, their relief palpable. Michael sunk into his chair. Only Verona remained.

"If it's any consolation, your personal assets are still intact. You're a wealthy man and can live multiple lifetimes on what you have."

Michael knew she meant to appease him. Instead, her words made him feel hollow. "Leave me. I need to be alone."

Verona came to sit across from him. "You don't have to be alone. I'm here."

Michael saw sincerity in Verona's eyes. Her words could mean many different things. He wasn't ready to hear that. "I want to be alone."

Verona gathered her belongings in silence. Michael purposely turned his chair away. He didn't need anyone. He didn't need anything.

Out of the blue, a phone conversation he had with his mother jarred his memory:

"I wondered when you'd get around to calling me."

"Of course I'd call. Michael, you're my son, even when I disagree with your actions."

"I lost her, Mother," Michael moaned.

Gerry exhaled. "I wish you would move on. You're too fixated on your ex-wife. Honey, you have to let Gina go."

"I am not talking about Gina, Mother."

"Then, who?"

"I'm talking about Lauren Goodman, my reporter friend," Michael said. *"I took her for granted. My behavior ran her off. She quit her job, took off, and no one knows where she is. Now all I can think of is how I reacted when*

she told me she was pregnant with my child. I did not believe her. I called her a liar. Threw her out. She is gone and all I can do is sit here." Michael rambled, letting out his secrets in one whoosh of air.

"Whoa! Slow down, son. Start from the beginning." Her calmness soothed him.

"Lauren came to me. She told me she was four months pregnant and I was the father. I didn't believe her. She pressed me not to go after Keith and Gina for custody of the children. I thought it was a scheme. So, I grabbed her. Hard. I know I hurt her," Michael said. "She told me she loved me, Mom, and it meant nothing. I was wrapped up in my revenge. I was too bitter."

Gerry said, "Now I'm going to tell you point blank I've got a big problem with a man, especially a son of mine, putting his hands on a woman. But, I love you and you've got no one. You've managed to push everybody out of your life. Since you don't need money, I'm going to give you what you don't have, but surely need. Prayer. Pray with me, son."

"I don't deserve it." Michael groaned.

"That's the beauty of forgiveness. We never deserve it. God hasn't forgotten you, son. The doctors said you were infertile. God said no to that. He made the devil a liar. You have to find Lauren. Michael, if she loves you, she will forgive you, too."

Michael scoffed. Goes to show, God was partial to certain prayers. Like Keith's. His brother had been given a second chance; he had gotten the girl and a talk show to boot.

And, what had he gotten?

Nothing.

His heart hardened.

Michael made a fist. Well, that would change. One day, he'd have it all.

Michael had done it, too. He did have it all and now because of Mindy Laurelton, he was about to lose everything. His reputation and his businesses. He jutted his jaw. Maybe it was time he did some digging into Bill Laurelton's past. To the world, Bill was the distraught father of an innocent nineteen-year-old.

Michael rubbed his chin. Everyone had some old bones dangling in their closet. Everyone. And he would find them. He knew the person for the task. Frank Armadillo. He'd been using Frank for years for special jobs. If Bill had dirt, even a speck, Frank would find it.

Chapter Eight

"He's their uncle, their blood. Nothing can change that. We keep returning to this same argument and frankly, it's tired."

Gina smacked her teeth. This argument had started in their bedroom and spilled over into the kitchen. Keith headed to his office. She was right behind him. "No, it's not tired. It's relevant, now. Your taking Michael's case is disrupting our lives."

Now seated behind his desk, Keith exhaled. "Sweetheart, I'm trying here. I wish you'd meet me halfway."

"You know what? We've never argued like this, ever. And your brother is to blame because you decided to represent a rapist."

He puffed his chest and looked up to the heavens. "God, give me strength!" Then he pinned Gina with a stern gaze. "Michael's not a rapist, and forgive me but you of all people should know that." After all, she had been married to Michael first. Keith raged, "You're so stubborn. I mean you won't bend."

Gina pointed to the carpeted floor with emphasis. "You're calling me stubborn? Against my distinct wishes, you took this case. Now you want my children around him? Not going to happen."

He jumped to his feet. Within seconds he was in her face. "I'm the head of this home and—"

"Don't you pull that head of the home nonsense with me, Keith Ward. I know the scriptures and I'm not following you blindly in your wrongdoings."

"Wrongdoings? How is defending an innocent man wrong? He's family and his life is at stake." He rested a hand on her shoulder.

She shrugged him off.

Keith grabbed her and pulled her close. "I'm done fighting," he said. Gina's chest heaved against him.

"Whatever."

Keith tucked his finger under her chin. "Michael is still worthy in God's eyes. He's still deserving of salvation."

"You're right," she answered begrudgingly. Then she changed topics. "Are you going to Trey's game? Because I'm meeting with the board of trustees about the T.K. Cancer Ball next Monday. The meeting was supposed to be yesterday on the eleventh, but they moved it to today because of Veterans Day."

Gina referred to the foundation they'd established to help children facing leukemia. Trey had survived the debilitating disease because Gina's father, Jeff Price, had been a donor. Since then, she'd been led to this ministry. She volunteered to assist single or low-income parents at the hospital.

Keith couldn't meet her eyes. He had been bogged down in Michael's case and it had slipped his mind. He had a Post-it with November 12 on his computer. He had recorded it in his iPhone. Yet, he still had not remembered. Keith knew better than to admit that to Gina, though. "I forgot I needed to use your car."

"Where's your car?"

For a moment he considered lying. But the Ten Commandments were too ingrained in him. "I left it at the church. Michael gave me a ride because we drove by the hotel as he recapped that night for me."

"Michael came back to our house? Did he come inside?"

The woman had a one-track mind. "No, honey. Michael hasn't been back here since exactly two Tuesdays ago when you made it clear you don't want him here."

Gina closed her eyes and drew a deep breath. She opened her eyes and whispered, "Keith, I'm not the bad guy. I'm protecting my children, my home."

He strove for patience. *Lord, I need you, now.* "I understand, believe me. No one will hurt you or our children ever again. Not while I'm alive and breathing. Plus, we've got God on our side. We have no worries because He's got us covered."

She relaxed. "Giving my life to God was the best decision I've ever made. I don't regret it one bit."

"No one who is saved and changed by God regrets it. I wish the same for my brother. Honey, Michael needs Jesus and he's entitled to salvation like everyone else."

He had said those words at least a hundred times. However, for the first time, Gina softened. Pointing to her head, she whispered, "Up here, I know it and I agree." Next, she touched her heart. "But here, I'm not ready to welcome Michael home like he's the prodigal son. I'm not about to throw a feast or party like there's no tomorrow."

Keith nodded. "I get it. My advice is to pray on those feelings. We'll take baby steps. I won't push, but Michael needs family. He needs our support." Then he said, "Michael needs you, too."

Gina broke eye contact and glanced at her watch. "I'll drive you to your car. Make sure you videotape Trey's game for me."

"I will," he promised.

She strode out of the room to grab her coat and wallet.

Keith's cell phone rang. He swiped to answer once he saw Natalie Henderson's face. Dubbed "The Hawk," Keith had hired Natalie as his assistant years ago when he was an evangelist with Zion's Hill television ministry.

Natalie supported him through the fateful interview where Michael revealed Keith as Trey and Epiphany's biological father. The interview became an instant YouTube hit and ended Keith's days as a televangelist. But after an outpouring of letters from the viewing audience, the network had offered Keith the show *Second Chances*. *Second Chances* featured people who needed a second chance, just as he had been given. It aired on BET every Thursday night.

Keith promoted Natalie to operations manager. She spearheaded the TK Foundation and its Cancer Ball. Natalie was a beauty with sharp green eyes and an even sharper tongue.

"What's wrong?" Keith asked.

"Hello to you too, boss," she said. "Everything's fine with *Second Chances*. It's the foundation's Cancer Ball. We have a situation with funds appropriation. I need to meet with you ASAP. Big trouble."

From Natalie's dire tone, he knew he was not going to like it. "How about I meet you after Trey's game?" Efficient, Natalie would have already checked his schedule and known his whereabouts.

"That sounds great. Your wife is on her way here. Should I discuss this with her?"

"No, don't say anything to Gina yet. I'd rather you speak with me first. I'll text you later."

Keith was about to end the call when Natalie said something of interest. "By the way, your brother's been calling some committee members inquiring about the foundation."

Why was his brother sniffing around? Keith whispered a prayer for guidance. "I'll ask him about that. Is there anything else?" He gathered his papers and his camera, listening with half an ear.

"I know you won't want to hear this, but I think representing your brother might hurt the foundation. Commitments have been somewhat lackluster this year. I'll know if we have sold all our seats in a few hours."

Keith dismissed Natalie's concerns. "I don't think one thing has to do with the other. I anticipate another sold-out event." He heard her cluck in his ear. "We'll talk."

Forty minutes later, Keith strolled by the field toward the bleachers. He saw Michael sitting there. With Verona.

What was his brother doing here? How did he know about Trey's game?

Thank God Gina was not with him. There would have been a major showdown. Keith walked to where Michael was sitting. *Don't make a big deal of it.*

Nevertheless Keith's parent radar had been activated. He zoned in on Trey to assure himself his son was all right.

"Hi. I called your secretary and she told me you'd be here. After the day I had, I decided to swing by. I hope you don't mind, *brother?*" Michael's weary eyes held a challenge. Michael knew Keith would not be pleased to see him here, but he had come. Without an invite. With company.

Was Michael trying to stir up trouble?

"The game's about to start," Keith said, choosing a seat where he could watch the game and keep an eye on his brother.

Michael squinted his eyes and pointed to a tall, lanky boy. "Is that Trey?"

Despite his slight uneasiness, Keith could not hold his proud grin. "Yes, that's him. He's the best on the team." Like him and Michael, Trey was a natural-born athlete.

Michael lowered his cap farther on his head. *Maybe he doesn't want Trey recognizing him.*

Keith saw Trey scan the crowd. When Trey spotted him, he lifted his hand in a slight wave and shouted, "Dad!"

Keith knew the exact moment Trey recognized Michael. Almost in slow motion, Trey's eyes widened. With eyes glued to Michael, Trey stood frozen until the coach called out to him. He turned and ran to join his teammates as the gaem was beginning.

Keith glanced Michael's way to gage his reaction. Michael's eyes were pinned on Trey. Gina's warnings echoed.

"Michael?" he queried.

Keith did not think Michael heard him until he turned. Michael had tears in his eyes.

"He's grown so much. I didn't know how much I missed him and loved him until this moment."

Uh-oh. What did that mean?

Twenty minutes into the game, Michael patted Keith's arm. "You're doing an amazing job with my nephew. He looks great."

Keith heaved an invisible sigh of relief. "Thanks, Gina and I are impressed with him. He's so put together. We are blessed."

Verona looked around the men to address Keith. "Trey's also very good. He just hit a homerun."

Keith smiled. He noted Verona's hand was on Michael's arm. He saw his brother shift to break contact. Troubled, Keith wondered, would Michael let anyone close to him ever again? He was wrapped tight with anger, envy, and malice. All the hurt and pain made Michael's heart like granite.

Keith whispered a quiet prayer to God. "Loose him, Lord. Loose my brother from the agony binding him. Loose him and set him free."

Chapter Nine

"The numbers aren't adding up." Sitting across from Keith in the conference room, Natalie gave him a worried glance.

"I see that," he said.

He bit into his turkey sandwich and studied the spreadsheets. As soon as the game ended, he had dropped Trey off at home and driven into Manhattan. At first glance, it appeared everything was in order. On closer inspection, Keith could see there had been a subtle shifting of funds. His event was sold out and funds collected. Yet, by the look of things, they would not be able to pay the caterers or pay for the venue.

"Besides myself, the only people who have access to the account are you, Gina, and the two trustees."

Keith pictured Bishop Combs and Deacon Broderson. "No way!" he said, with a wide sweep of his hands. "I refuse to believe that of either of them."

"Well something's amiss," Natalie said. "Funds have been misappropriated and if this gets out . . ."

"We're ruined," Keith finished for her.

"You need to tell Gina," Natalie said.

"She's going to be heartbroken. I'll tell her tonight. Or," he massaged his temples, "I could use my personal funds to cover the missing amount."

"No." Natalie shook her head. "I wouldn't advise you to do that. That's tantamount to admission of guilt—embezzlement. It could mark the end of your career."

Lord, what do I do?

"As luck would have it, we do have an anonymous benefactor who offered a sizeable donation."

Keith perked up. "I like the sound of that!" A benefactor would solve their immediate problems. He would still have to find out if there was an Achan in the camp. He referenced the Bible history of Achan. Achan had stolen a vessel and hidden it causing God's wrath on the people.

"I did some serious digging. I think I might know who he is. The problem is he's an alleged rape convict. He even had his attorney purchase two plates."

Michael. Irritation seeped through him. It seemed as if everywhere Keith turned, Michael was invading his life.

"Let's hold for now," he told Natalie. "Let me pray, consult with God, and talk to Gina. In that order. I'll have an answer for you in a couple days."

"Wait. I almost forgot to mention, Bill Laurelton is on the list of attendees. Both he and Michael will be there. I've beefed up security and placed them at opposite ends of the room. I doubt they'll run into each other."

Keith looked heavenward. "When it rains . . ."

He said his good-byes and went through the door. As soon as he arrived home, he went into his office to pray. Then he sought the word on how to deal with Bishop Combs. Keith knew the appropriate scripture for this occasion.

He read Galatians 6:1, which said:

> *Brethren, if a man be overtaken in a fault, ye which are spiritual, restore such a one in the spirit of meekness; considering thyself, lest thou also be tempted.*

The Word was true. If he were in the bishop's position, he would want to be treated with love. He would want some measure of mercy.

Keith called his secretary, Dianne Hupert, at Zion's Hill. "Can you set up a meeting with Bishop Combs and Deacon Broderson?"

"The bishop is out on a cruise. He and his wife left a couple days ago. I can set up your meeting when he returns."

Rocks lined his insides at that new information. Bits of conversations with Bishop Combs came back to him.

"I'd like a raise."

"My wife wants to shop at Neiman Marcus three times a week. She doesn't understand why I can't afford her lifestyle."

Bishop Combs owned Combs Consulting, which oversaw the foundation's funds and allocations. He had shocked the congregation when he married a twenty-six-year-old waitress, Suzette Hodge. The younger woman had been nothing short of demanding.

Keith rang the bishop's cell phone, again. He left a voicemail message on the odd chance Bishop Combs checked his messages while he was on the cruise.

He called the deacon next. However, Natalie had beaten him to it. Broderson was already meeting with her the next morning. Satisfied with that phone call, Keith then went to seek out his wife.

Gina was in the computer room. Programs and other paraphernalia associated with the foundation were spread out around her.

He dove right into the conversation. "Gina, there's a problem with the Cancer Ball. Funds are missing."

"Missing? What do you mean funds are missing? I was just at the meeting. No one mentioned any money troubles."

"Natalie met with me." He picked his way across the stuff lying across the floor and sat on the couch in the corner. "She and I are talking with Deacon Broderson tomorrow. We suspect it might be the bishop."

Gina's mouth hung agape. Her eyes were the size of saucers. "The bishop? As in Bishop Combs?" Shaking her head, she said, "I don't believe it."

"I'm having a hard time processing it myself. He and Suzette are off on an extended cruise."

She shook her head. "That doesn't sound good."

"We might have a benefactor."

She tilted her head. "Who?"

"Michael."

Gina jumped to her feet. Papers flew this way and the other. She didn't appear to care. "No way! The man is ingratiating his way into our lives. I want nothing to do with his money."

Keith defended Michael. "You're forgetting he loves Trey. He bought two plates, so expect to see him."

She wrapped her arms about her. "Why? Why won't he leave us alone? He probably orchestrated the whole money fiasco so he can swoop in to save the day."

Keith raised his eyebrows. If there were rain clouds, Gina would find a way to blame Michael. He was convinced of that. Keith returned to the previous topic. "I plan on confronting the bishop as soon as he returns. In the meantime, we'll proceed with the plans."

She touched his arm. "Please fix it. This can't get out. This organization was formed to benefit others. We can't afford any scandals or bad press."

Keith nodded. His stomach knotted. *God, only you can turn this situation around for your good.*

Chapter Ten

"I'm not your lackey, Michael Ward," Verona spat at him.

Standing on the edge of the curb outside his penthouse, Michael eyed Verona. She was in the driver seat of his corvette and insulting him. Can you imagine? Verona owned an SUV, but preferred his smaller, faster vehicle.

Even though it was after nine-thirty p.m., cars whizzed by and pedestrians bustled past him on their way to the theater or some other diversion. Used to New York's active nightlife, Michael tuned them out.

Michael hunched over and asked, "Did you get the tickets? Did you make the donation?"

"Yes, I bought two tickets in your name. But, there is a holdup with the donation."

At that moment, a driver honked, momentarily distracting him. Michael shook his head and gestured for the man to go around. Ignoring the crude finger and disgruntled look from the driver, Michael returned to his conversation. He narrowed his eyes. "What holdup?"

"They refused to accept it." That was all the explanation she offered.

"Make them."

He could see Verona tapping her foot inside the car. Too bad. He wasn't finished. "I need you here tomorrow at eight a.m. Leonard is coming with the papers for me to sign and things could sour fast."

She nodded, then rolled her eyes at him before tearing off. Michael waited until his car disappeared around the bend.

What is eating her? Verona had been unusually quiet at the game. She declined his dinner invite, citing a headache. Was she dating someone?

What did he care? Michael shrugged and entered his building. Verona didn't need a boyfriend, or any distraction but him. He made his way to the elevator that whisked him up to the penthouse suite. By the time Michael reached the door, thoughts of Verona had left his mind. Instead, he was filled with thoughts of Trey.

Seeing his nephew shook him. Michael had not known what it would feel like to see Trey again. He had raised Trey as his son for seven years. To his surprise, he had shed tears. Tears of joy, not pain.

Michael wandered into his study. It was the first time he had felt an emotional connection to anyone besides his mother.

He welcomed it.

He feared it.

However, seeing Trey out there on the field made Michael question his past actions and current decisions. After his marriage to Gina ended, he vowed to avoid any emotional entanglements. Michael liked not feeling or caring. It made him feel invincible.

Then Lauren dropped the news she loved him and was pregnant. That was his chance to grab on to what she offered. A family of his own. However, Michael had not seen it that way. Instead, he had kicked Lauren out the door and out of his life, and he had not been nice about it. Michael could not believe God had given him the miracle of fathering his own children. When he finally realized the truth, it had been too late. Lauren had left him for good.

If he found her, he could set things right. He could have a part two, a do-over. Michael closed his eyes and imagined holding John and Olivia in each of his arms. Oh, how he yearned for it.

His cell phone buzzed snapping him out of fantasyland. "Did you forget something?" Michael asked.

"I can't come at eight in the morning. I have a dentist appointment," Verona said.

"Listen, it's a no-brainer. You need to reschedule."

Michael made his way into his walk-in closet and pulled out his gray suit and light blue shirt. He could hear Verona fussing but tuned out her words.

"Michael, are you listening to me?"

"Of course."

Verona emitted a huge sigh. "I can't reschedule. If I do, it'll be months before they can fit me in."

"I'm not following your thinking." He snagged two ties. Which should he choose? He used his phone's camera to snap a picture of the ties. Verona continued her explanation but he interrupted. "I'm texting you two pics of my ties. Tell me which one I should wear."

"What do I look like to you?"

"I'll personally get you a new appointment." Now if she would just answer his question about the tie.

"Personally?"

"Okay, I meant my secretary. I will guarantee you the whitest teeth on this side of the bridge," he said. "Now, can you answer my question? Please? Checkered or print."

Verona released another dramatic sigh followed by an ungracious, "Fine. Send them," before he heard the dead end of the line.

Michael texted the pictures. It didn't take two seconds before he saw Checkered appear on the screen. He studied her choice before agreeing. Thx, he responded.

Michael replaced the other tie. If there was one thing he could appreciate about Verona, it was her fine taste. She knew how to put herself together.

Is she seeing someone? The question popped into his mind. He hoped not. His life was at stake. She had better not be seeing anybody especially on his time.

Why should I care if she has a boyfriend?

Verona could have a hundred men for all he cared. As long as she made sure she was there when he needed her.

Michael scoffed. Why was he dwelling on a non-issue? If Verona had a man, she would've told him. Wouldn't she?

Michael searched his pants pocket to call Verona and demand to know why she had declined his dinner invite. Then, common sense prevailed and he shoved his phone back into his pocket.

"I'm not going to call her. Verona might get the ridiculous idea I care if she has a man. And I don't. I don't care at all." All this Michael mumbled as he speed dialed Verona. If she did not answer, then . . .

"What now, Michael Ward? Do you need help zipping your pants?"

Relief seeped into his spine. She was not out on a date.

Michael panicked. He could not tell Verona the real reason for his call. "I need you here at seven-thirty, instead, to review everything. I want to ensure there'll be no mismanagement of my funds."

"Leonard Paulson is your VP and pretty adept at handling your affairs. And, he's loyal. I told you when you hired him, he was a good choice."

"That's all well and good. Be here," Michael insisted. "Need I remind you who's the boss?"

He's the boss but he couldn't decide on a tie.

Verona hung up on Michael. If she didn't know better, she would think he was calling just to be calling. Michael called her for everything: ties, shoes, food; you name it; he had called her for it. What did he do without her before?

Verona went to gather items for her bath. Of all the men in the world, she couldn't understand why him? She loved him, yes. But, he was insufferable. Hard to please. Demanding. Yet her heart flip-flopped upon seeing him. Every.Single.Time.

Verona had believed herself a smart woman until she had been dumb enough to fall in love with Michael Jason Ward. Before him, she had been all about progress and carving her name on a judge's bench. Now, she had visions of baby booties and pacifiers, complete with a ring on her left hand.

Verona rested her hand over her flat stomach. She had lied to Michael. Her appointment was with an OB/GYN. She had skipped a year and was due for an annual visit. She hoped they would be able to reschedule soon.

The next morning Verona used her key card to enter Michael's suite and headed to the kitchen. Of course, he was already there. She put the coffee on to percolate. He dropped bagels in the toaster. She reached into the cupboard for two large mugs.

The two met by the refrigerator: Michael to reach for the cream cheese; and she for the creamer. Their hands met briefly. Verona inhaled. Her insides fluttered. Her knees wobbled. While she strove to breathe normally, Michael appeared unaffected. The oaf.

"Someone's in a funk," Michael said.

Verona cut her eyes at him. Let him think whatever he wanted. She would speak to him only when necessary. She wasn't on the clock, yet.

The bagels popped and Michael retrieved two plates. He lathered the bagels with a generous amount of cream cheese.

"You know I prefer a small amount."

"Someone's grumpy." He smiled, while removing some of the excess.

Verona yanked open the kitchen drawer and fetched the Santoku knife. Grabbing some fruit, she made a fruit salad for them to enjoy with their meal. They had done this ritual many times before when consulting on cases, but now that Verona knew how she felt about Michael, it was hard to keep up the pretense of normalcy. It strained her nerves to the max.

They slid into chairs and commenced their meal.

Michael tasted his coffee. "Ahhh . . . it's perfect."

"Thanks for getting my whole wheat bagel this time," she begrudgingly said.

"Still doesn't beat cinnamon raisin."

Verona couldn't take it anymore. She placed her half-eaten bagel back into her plate. "Michael, what's this meeting about? Please, let's quit the pretense of domestic bliss."

"Okay, fine. Just before Leonard comes, I have a special request. I need you to befriend Gina." Gone was the agreeable man from minutes ago. He was now every inch the astute businessman, known for his cutthroat deals.

In a swift move, Verona scraped her chair back and stood. Through gritted teeth, she asked, "You want me to make nice with your ex-wife? You don't pay me enough to handpick my friends."

"This is different. It's business," he said, with clipped tones. "Keith told me Gina refused to be a character witness. I can pay people to say whatever I want, and I will if I have to, but having my ex-wife present me in a positive light would help. I thought if you were able to get close to her, you might use your persuasive powers and she'd change her mind."

She blinked. Michael was asking for too much. "Character witnesses aren't generally used in criminal cases, but I can understand using Gina for this case. Now, I like to win, believe me, but this leaves a bad taste in my mouth. You did put her on blast on live television."

The truth was Verona was not above playing friends to suit her purpose. But, she could not abide being in the same vicinity with someone who had slept with Michael. Jealousy tore at her core. She would not be able to laugh with Gina knowing she wanted to rip out Gina's hair.

"I need you, Verona." Michael abandoned his food. His long hands reached over to grasp hers.

Oh, how she longed to hear those words, under much different circumstances, of course.

"I'm going to be in jail for the rest of my life. You have the power to help set me free. Please don't say no. At least tell me you'll think about it."

Verona opened her mouth to turn him down. She surprised herself when she said, "I'll do it."

Chapter Eleven

"This whole thing is going to blow up in your face. Mark my words." Gina stomped into her closet and wiggled into her form-fitting gown.

"We're going to be late. Hurry up, woman." Keith reached into his drawer for his cuff links.

Gina finished applying her lipstick and smoothed her hands down her Alexander McQueen dress. "Don't ignore me. Trey told me all about his Uncle Michael coming to his game. Not cool."

"FYI, I didn't invite him. I was going to tell you, but Trey beat me to it. Michael is blood. You can't deny your blood. No matter what. When Christ returns, He's looking for people who are covered under Jesus' blood. When God sent the death angel through Egypt, those who had the blood on their doorposts were spared. That's how important blood is, and Michael and I share the same blood."

"Don't preach at me. Save it for your audience. By the way, with you working on the court case, how will you still manage the *Second Chances* tapings?" Gina asked.

Keith eyed Gina's curves outlined in her black gown shimmering with silver polka dots. He spotted the killer shoes on her feet and gave his watch a quick glance. "I've got that covered. Do we have time for a . . ." He wagged his eyebrows suggestively.

In spite of herself, Gina laughed. "No, we don't have time. Is that all you ever think about? What you can do

60   Michelle Lindo-Rice

is answer my original question." She left their room in search of her coat.

"Yes, that's all I think about." Keith said. "Can I help it if I have a hot wife?" He followed her to grab his coat as well. "*Second Chances* is in syndication, so the network agreed to do a six-week special featuring my highest-rated shows. It'll be during November and December—holiday season. After that time, I'll have guest speakers. I'll fit it in, somehow with God's help."

"You would have the time if you weren't fixated on Michael's case. How do you know he didn't do it?"

Keith's neck popped back. "He didn't. You know that. Now, let's get going or they'll start without us."

"They wouldn't dare. It's our foundation."

Gina chaired the Trey Keith Foundation established in their son's honor after Trey battled leukemia and won. The foundation assisted other families with whatever they needed—money, food, clothing, shelter—so they could focus on what mattered: fighting cancer. Gina volunteered her time and often read stories and tutored the children in the cancer ward.

When Gina and Keith arrived, Keith was ecstatic to see the crowd of professionals in attendance. What started out as a venture with 150 people now boasted 1,000 participants at $10,000 per plate. Keith's celebrity status was a draw. He tapped his pocket for the small speech he'd prepared.

He scanned the crowd and smiled at Natalie who was being chummy with Dexter Greene, NFL quarterback. That's one hookup he could not see happening. Keith tilted his head at Natalie, summoning her.

"Has the bishop shown up yet? Or are you too busy swooning over Dexter Greene?" he asked once she had made it over to him. Bishop Combs had returned from his cruise but had been avoiding a meeting. Keith intended to pin him down tonight.

"No, the Bishop hasn't shown up. I'm keeping an eye out for him." She did a couple of dance steps and turned to rejoin the football star.

"Let me know when he does," Keith said.

Natalie nodded and pointed in another direction. Following her finger, Keith saw the back of his brother's head. Of course, he had Verona with him.

With a hand on Gina's back, Keith guided her through the throng over to where Michael and Verona stood. Since Gina was short, she had not seen Michael until they were in close proximity.

Too late now.

Gina gripped his hand in a tight squeeze to communicate her vast displeasure. Through a forced smile, she said, "I can't believe you invited him."

Keith knew she would not act out in public, but he would catch heat for it later.

"Verona, you look lovely." Keith kept his eyes away from his wife's, feeling the heat of Gina's indignant glare. Good thing he wasn't made out of ice.

Verona wore a cream A-line gown with a generous slit in the front. She blushed at Keith's compliment. "Thanks so much for having us," she said.

Keith nudged Gina to say something.

"You do look amazing," she finally said. Her good manners won out and she addressed Michael. "How've you been?" Despite her question, her demeanor said, "I really don't care," but Keith was glad she had spoken.

"I've been better," Michael stated. Keith saw him eye Gina's gown. "You look good, Gina."

Gina didn't acknowledge Michael's compliment. "I must go greet the other guests and check to see if Colleen and Terence have arrived." Gina referenced her best friend since high school, Colleen Hayworth, and her husband, Terence. She excused herself. Keith knew Gina couldn't abide being in Michael's presence for too long.

Keith noticed Verona's facial expression when Michael eyed Gina's outfit. He knew that look well. *Poor girl.* Jealousy was depicted all over her face. Did Michael know? Keith doubted it. Michael could be clueless when it came to women.

Keith spared Verona by changing the subject. "Our court hearing is set for two weeks."

"I know. Verona told me." Michael hung his head. "At times, I can't believe this is happening to me. How did I get here? How did I manage going from the top of my game to the lowest of the low? Could somebody explain that to me?"

Keith shook his head. "I may not be able to answer that question, brother, but God has His reasons. You might feel like Joseph now, but God has a way of working things out, when you least expect Him."

Keith could see Michael was listening. His brother squinted his eyes. "Who's Joseph?" he asked.

Verona chimed in, before he could answer. "Mr. Preacher Man is talking about Joseph from the Bible. His father, Jacob, had twelve sons. Of the twelve, Joseph was the treasured son. His brothers were so jealous they sold him into slavery. A lot of things happened but basically, Joseph went from prison to become the second in command of the entire nation of Egypt."

"You know the Bible?" Michael swung his head to face her, like he'd never seen her before.

Keith saw Verona blush. "I grew up in church," she stammered. "There's a lot you don't know about me."

"I'm seeing that," Michael agreed, touching his chin in thought.

Watching their interaction, Keith felt like he was intruding on a private moment.

"Verona, let's meet up tomorrow to go through the case," Keith suggested.

"I'll be there too, and she goes by Tiger," Michael rushed in.

"You don't have to come," Verona assured his brother with a small pat.

"I'll be there, I said," Michael insisted as he faced her. "It's my case, and I'm paying you. I want to ensure you're doing the best for me."

"You can always fire me," she shot back. "I don't know why I continue to work for such an insufferable . . ."

Some serious bickering between the couple started. He suppressed a knowing grin. Michael had feelings for Verona, even if Michael didn't realize it. They sounded and acted like an old married couple. Speaking of married, Keith sought out his wife.

Tuning them out, Keith scanned the crowd until he located her schmoozing with Ned and Penelope Winthrop: his boss and his boss's wife. As he left Michael and Verona to their own musings, he wondered why Michael had insisted on coming. Was it that Michael didn't trust Keith around any woman?

Chapter Twelve

"Did you forget already why we're here?" Michael gripped Verona's arm.

She shrugged out of his grasp. "Ease up, will you? I saw Gina head toward the ladies' room. I'm on it." She sashayed toward her destination.

Michael watched the sway of Verona's hips and swallowed. Why did she look so appealing all of a sudden? When she arrived to get him, he had not been prepared to see such a vision before him. Michael had taken in her upswept hairdo and the sheath gown hugging her curves like it was glued on and forgotten how to breathe. To cover his discomfort, Michael had been gruff. "You're late. I don't pay you to be late."

Verona growled at him but he hadn't cared. He didn't need her looking so . . . good. It was a distraction, and one he didn't need.

A hand burrowed deep into his shoulder blades.

Michael whipped around. It was Bill Laurelton, his former partner and his accuser's father.

"What a shame I didn't bring my bug spray." Bill jabbed his finger into Michael's chest. "You've got guts showing your face in public after what you did to my daughter."

Bill's gnarly breath hit him with full force. Michael retreated several steps. "Trey's my nephew and this is a foundation in his honor. I'm here to support him. I don't want any trouble. But, I didn't do anything to your daughter."

Bill raised his voice. "Yes, you did. You raped my little girl." He tried to take a swing but staggered.

Michael felt the stares of a few onlookers. He did not relish the attention. He whispered, "Bill, please, this is not the time or place. If you want us to talk, we can. Remember, we're friends and partners."

"Friend! You're no friend of mine. You're a rapist and when I'm done with you, you'll be penniless and eating with swine." Bill's loudly slurred words quieted the room.

Michael saw a flash in his peripheral vision and recalled the press was present. Michael turned to leave.

Men pulled their women behind them, giving him confrontational glances. There was not one friendly face. Michael broke into a light run. In a childish move, someone stuck a foot out. He tripped and stumbled. *Oh, no.* His body catapulted. Michael was going down face first. Then a strong pair of hands grabbed him.

"It's all right. I've got you."

Michael gave Keith a grateful look. Once he had been righted, Michael flung himself into his brother's arms. For the first time, in a long time, he felt at peace. He felt at home.

Verona's bravado vanished as soon as the door closed. She scanned the stalls until she located Gina's shoes. Those silver stilettos were must-haves. Verona entered the stall and hurried to relieve herself before Gina exited hers.

Okay, here goes. "I can't believe there's no paper in here." She groaned, and then waited.

"I hate when that happens. Do you need me to pass you some?" Gina offered.

Bingo. "Would you?"

She heard a chuckle. "Look out for my hand." Their hands met between the stalls.

"Thank you so much."

Seconds later, Verona heard the flush and telltale lock unclick. She took care of her business and rushed out to join Gina at the sink. "I must say I love your shoes." Gina's smile faltered once she recognized her. The smaller woman nodded and then moved to dry her hands. It was obvious Gina could not get out of there fast enough. Verona knew she had to talk fast. "Gina! Wait, don't go. Please."

Gina turned. Deadpanned, she asked, "What can I do for you?"

Verona looked Gina square in the eyes. "I was doing my job. I don't always have to agree with my client's wishes. In fact, I'm glad you have your children. They belong with you."

She referenced the court case of three years prior, when Michael hired her to pursue custody of Trey and Epiphany. He did it to punish Keith and Gina for their betrayal. Michael knew he didn't have a chance to win but he wanted to make them pay.

"Really? Forgive me if I don't believe that. I think it's all about money for you. Just like the hefty donation made on behalf of Tiger Trust for Cancer Kids? What was that about?"

Now Verona sounded like a money-hungry she didn't know what. "No, it isn't about money. I have to earn a living. I worked hard to get where I am. The donation I made will help children in need."

Gina snorted. "Or, it will help assuage your guilt for not caring about anyone or anything." Her words hurt, but Verona didn't respond. Gina shrugged. "Okay, I've heard you out, and forgive me when I say I hope I never see you again anytime soon."

Verona wasn't one to give up easy. "I hope you're referring to not seeing me in court, because my real reason for

seeking you out is that I want to learn more about God."
Where had that come from? She knew she had to think
on her feet, but now she'd put her foot in her mouth. She
couldn't tell when she'd last been to church.

Ever the pastor's wife, Gina's tone changed. "You're
interested in Bible Study?"

No, Verona really wasn't. *The things I do for Michael
Ward who doesn't even know I'm a woman, or I exist,
or I'm in love with him.* "Yes, I am. Believe it or not, I've
seen your husband's show. I've listened to his sermons
and he's really inspiring." Well, she had listened in an
attempt to discredit him, but Verona wouldn't mention
that tidbit. Verona had to admit he was eloquent and
could sway a crowd. However, that didn't mean Keith still
possessed the skills to sway a jury.

Gina wife beamed at Verona's compliment. Aha! Keith
was her ticket into Gina's good graces.

"He is inspiring. Keith's conversion is genuine. He
truly cares about people's souls. That's why he's taken
Michael's case. Keith thinks this is God's way of leading
Michael home." Gina snickered. "Keith seems to be
under the mistaken impression we'll experience another
prodigal return home sappy story."

Verona crooked her head. This time she wasn't pretending her interest. She wanted to know what Gina
thought. "You don't think Michael's life mirrors the story
of the prodigal? I mean he is about to lose everything.
He's signed over his business. His assets are frozen. His
freedom's on the line," she rattled off. "Your ex-husband
is in a bad place. Michael had to return, reunite with
Keith, and seek his help."

By tacit agreement the women left the restroom when
other occupants entered.

Gina arched her eyebrow at her. "You sure you need Bible Study? Because it seems to me you know your Bible pretty well."

Busted. "True. But, knowing the Word isn't the same as living the Word." Gina nodded.

Silence ensued.

At that moment, Verona and Gina heard shouting. Gina's hand covered her mouth in shock. Verona clutched her chest. They heard Bill Laurelton eviscerating Michael before the massive crowd. They saw Michael's ashen face and his attempt to run.

Without realizing it, their hands connected upon seeing the well-placed foot that precipitated his fall.

"Looks like the fall of the prodigal." Gina smirked. Her sense of humor wasn't welcomed or acknowledged.

They're going to stampede him, Verona realized. She had to help Michael. "No!" Verona stepped forward, but Gina pulled on her hand.

Verona and Gina watched as Keith pressed through the crowd to lunge and save Michael from falling. Every one watched the embrace knowing they had front row seats to brothers who had found their way back to each other. Cameras flashed in rapid succession. The reporters in the crowd pulled out their pens, glad to have found something newsworthy.

Verona found her voice once her heart slowed. "Looks more like the return of the prodigal to me," she said, enjoying the verbal sparring. Was she starting to like Gina a little bit?

Gina rolled her eyes. "Bible Study. Wednesday night. Seven p.m. Don't be late."

She was in! Verona kept her features cool but she wanted to dance a jig. "I'll be there. On time."

Yes, Verona admitted, in spite of her jealous notions, she liked Gina. In fact, Verona applauded Gina knowing how difficult this must be for her. She would be scared too if she had faced the possibility of losing her children. Even if it was farfetched, it was still scary. "I'll be there," Verona responded with her most humble tone.

Gina took a couple steps then turned. "Oh, and, Verona, you can bring your Bible, but don't bring that face with you." She swirled her index finger in circles as she commented.

"What face?" Verona creased her forehead.

"The face of a woman in love with her boss." With a click of her heels, the shorter woman left Verona standing there to pick her face up off the floor.

She did not appreciate that barb. So what if the barb had hit its mark? Verona swung her head from left to right paranoid her face reflected her emotions like a light bulb. She touched her cheeks in a self-protective gesture, feeling like all eyes were on her.

Common sense spoke to her brain. She was being dramatic. No one was paying her any attention. No one could tell. Her eyes connected with Gina.

She was wrong. Gina Ward could tell. Gina knew Verona was in love with her ex-husband.

Chapter Thirteen

The Preacher and the Prisoner!
One Brother for the Pulpit, Another for the Prison!
No Second Chances for him!
From Prosper to Pauper!

"Blah, blah, blah. They're all the same." Verona read the headlines as she plopped one paper after another on the on the kitchen table in Michael's penthouse. "The press is marching in a grand parade with this." She pointed to a picture of Michael and Keith embracing. Outraged, she exclaimed, "They're making a mockery of a tender moment."

"As they should."

Verona had not been prepared for Michael's response. "Don't you care what they are saying?"

"Not if it's the truth," he said. "Look at me. I look like a wuss having to clutch my brother for help. My old business partners must be enjoying a laugh at my expense." Michael snatched the paper to examine the picture before slinging it to the floor in disgust. "I wish they hadn't captured me at that exact moment. I look—"

"Vulnerable?" Verona filled in. *And cute, and hot, and human.*

Michael shoulders slumped. "Yes, vulnerable." He grabbed his head. "I hate it! For years I've prided myself on not needing anyone. I climbed to the highest rung on the proverbial ladder of success and now look at me. I'm practically on my knees."

If only he would get on his knees. "Humility never killed anyone. It's pride that goes before destruction and a haughty spirit before a fall," Verona said.

With a question in his eyes, Michael asked, "Did you quote the Bible?"

She gulped. "I did."

He looked at her with suspicion. "I didn't know you were into the Bible and stuff like that. I don't ever recall hearing you say you go to church."

"That's 'cause I don't." Verona's voice sounded as edgy as she felt. Michael was treading into dangerous territory.

"But you used to be in church," he pushed. It was as if Michael sensed something and he could not resist digging. "I mean, no one quotes scriptures like that unless they grew up at the altar."

Fine. She would admit to the obvious. "Yes, I used to go to church. Used to; as in not anymore." Folding her arms, she injected steel in her voice. "I don't want to talk about it."

Michael glided into her space. "You don't want to talk? Or, you won't?"

She blinked. "Either one, pick your choice."

He held his hands up. "Prickly, aren't we?"

"Very. Now leave it alone."

Michael touched his chin before tilting his head. "I see there are many more facets to you I still haven't discovered."

What an understatement. Verona was wading in the river of denial and she liked it. "What you see is what you get."

He tapped her chin. "Somehow I doubt that."

She was shaken from his touch, but Verona refused to take the bait. If it killed her, she wouldn't show how moved she was by his proximity. She lifted an eyebrow at Michael and said, "Can we get to work please? Your brother will be here in an hour and we have things to discuss."

Taking purposeful steps, Verona walked into Michael's study. Once he had entered and was seated, she took a deep breath. "Even though you've resigned, the company is still in trouble. The stocks plunged. Investors and contractors are dropping our business faster than I can count. After Bill's stunt last night, we're on our face."

Michael clenched his fists at her words. Concerned, her body propelled toward him of its own will. She touched his arm. "Say something," she whispered.

Michael remained mute.

Helpless, she, a master manipulator of words, was speechless. Then Verona saw it. A single tear rolling from one eye. She gulped, moved in a way she had never been before.

"Michael," Verona said.

Nothing. Not a single, solitary word flowed from his lips—lips, which looked luscious and inviting.

In slow motion, Verona closed her eyes and bent her body toward him. Her hair swooped into her face but she was not concerned with her wayward curls. She opened her mouth and released her tongue as the tear reached Michael's cheek, capturing the crystal drop before it could slide into oblivion.

When she opened her eyes, her hazel ones encountered a pair of befuddled brown orbs with the question, "What just happened?"

Chapter Fourteen

"For your reading pleasure!" Gina swung her arms with dramatic flair.

Keith felt the whoosh as papers landed by his breakfast. His head popped up. "What's this?" he asked though his eyes scanned the headlines.

"I don't know how much more of this I can take," Gina admitted. "What does the network have to say about your standing next to a rapist?"

"He's not a rapist," Keith defended. "And the network has my back. The show is about giving people a second chance."

She released a plume of air. "I've got to take E.J. and Trey to school since I promised I'd let them sleep late, but we must talk."

Keith stood and snatched her hand. "Take it easy, worker bee. Give your husband a kiss."

Gina turned her body away from him. "I don't have time." She yelled, "E.J.! Trey! Get a move on!"

Her powerful voice rang in his ears but Keith would not be swayed. He pulled her close and kissed the top of her head. "I love you."

Gina lifted her face to his. "I love you too."

Within seconds, they were embroiled in a passionate foray of major lip locking.

"You guys are disgusting."

Keith and Gina broke apart at Trey's voice. "Don't knock it 'til you try it, son," Keith ribbed.

"Never." Trey put a finger down his mouth for effect.

Keith gave Trey an affectionate pat. "I'll make sure to remind you of those same words in a few years."

Keith made short work of getting dressed and drove across the bridge to the penthouse suite. He parked in the guest spot and entered the building making his way to the elevators. He had been given an access card and swiped it before heading inside the suite.

He stopped at the sight of Verona's tongue licking Michael's cheek. He would have been happy for them if it weren't for . . . Keith cleared his throat.

Michael and Verona jumped apart. They acknowledged his presence with an awkward greeting. Verona composed herself and held open the files.

For the first time since Keith could remember, his brother gave him a halfway decent welcome. "Have you seen the papers?" Michael asked.

Keith nodded. "Gina did too. She wasn't amused."

"Has she agreed to be a character witness?"

He stammered. "Ugh, well, Gina needs more time. However, I'm sure she'll do it when the time comes." He saw disbelief written on both their faces and felt compelled to defend his wife. "She will. Michael, you know Gina. Do you think she'll be able to live with herself if she didn't at least try to help you?"

"The Gina I knew wouldn't. But, I'm a prime example of how a person can change," Michael said.

Keith nodded. "True. People and feelings can change like the weather. But, when God changes you, it's permanent. Gina is a child of God. He'll speak to her heart."

Keith saw Michael mull over his words and was grateful he hadn't been given a smart comeback. He knew it was the power of prayer at work.

"I hope for Michael's sake, you're right," Verona interjected. "Because we don't have a case. To be honest, it seems impossible to win."

"Thanks for the vote of confidence." Michael gave her a baleful eye. "How does it look if my own attorney doesn't believe in my innocence?"

"I didn't say you weren't innocent," Verona snapped. "I said it wasn't winnable. There's a difference."

Keith felt the heat rising between them and intervened. "God specializes in the impossible. I have no doubt everything will work out in the end. As He wills."

"Since God helps those who help themselves, can we go talk with Mindy?"

Verona's drawl depicted a significant lack of confidence in Keith's abilities, which irked him. He had been at the top of his game before he entered the ministry. Nevertheless, Keith did not allow her to bait him. When you have talent, you let it speak for itself.

"Good luck getting through the front door. I can't see Bill or his attorney agreeing to meet," Michael said.

"I can't see us not trying," Keith countered.

Since Michael couldn't accompany them, Keith and Verona took the short ride over to his nemesis, Bill Laurelton's, suite.

Chapter Fifteen

"They gave the rapist the headline!"

Mindy shivered from her father's huge bellow. They had been enjoying muffins for breakfast until he saw the headlines. His skin was beet red. His cheeks puffed with rage. "Calm down, Daddy," she wailed. "You're scaring me. It's a newspaper. It'll be lining tomorrow's garbage."

"You're an idiot if you believe that," Bill roared. He tore the paper into shreds. "Michael Ward rapes my daughter and instead of demanding the death penalty, they're bragging about a family reunion."

"I'm not even sure if New York supports the death penalty," Mindy said.

Bill slammed his hand on the table. "That's not the point. It's like you're not listening to me."

Mindy trembled. Her bottom lip quivered. "Daddy, please get a hold of yourself. I can't take it when you're angry and mad. I—"

She stopped as her voice broke. In a flash, her father enfolded her in his big, bear-like arms. Mindy released her fears in his arms.

"Do you need a sedative?" Bill asked her.

She shook her head, trying to remain in control. "No, I don't like what they do to me." She pulled out of his arms to look into his face. With tears streaming down her face, she begged, "Daddy, can't we drop the charges? I don't think I can do this."

His gentle demeanor vanished and Bill gripped her arm. With a slight shake, he said, "You can, and you will. Michael Ward will pay for this." He glared at her. "Don't tell me you feel sorry for him?"

"I think I love him," Mindy whispered. She held a finger over her mouth. But there was no way to retract that confession.

Her father slung her from him with disgust. "How can you love someone who would hurt you in such a vile manner?"

Mindy closed her eyes. She shook her head from side to side. "I can't . . . I can't . . ." Rocking her body, she repeated over and over. "I can't . . . Don't make me . . . Don't make me."

Grabbing her shoulders, Bill commanded, "Stop this, Mindy. Open your eyes."

She knew better than to disobey. It took every ounce of courage she possessed, but Mindy opened her eyes. Her father gave her a rewarding smile. She lifted her hand to touch his cheek. "Daddy," she sighed.

"My sweet little girl," Bill said. He rushed over to the cabinet and retrieved her prescription medicine. Next, he grabbed a bottle of water from the refrigerator. "You're falling apart. I've got to help you."

Mindy nodded as he approached her. She opened her mouth open to allow him to place the pill on her tongue. Ever so compliant, she waited as he unscrewed the cap, and then took a sip.

"There's my good girl," her father acknowledged. "Finish your muffin, then get dressed." Bill gave her an obligatory pat before leaving the room.

Mindy stayed where she was until she was sure her father was gone. Then she spat the pill out of her mouth. She ambled over to the garbage disposal, taking great pleasure in hearing it grind to pieces.

She didn't need the tiny tablet. Closing her eyes, she summoned assistance. "I need your help. Now."

"Now let me do all the talking," Keith advised Verona. They were in the elevator headed to Bill Laurelton's suite. He owned a home in Queens as well, not too far from where Keith lived. Bill had refused to meet at Verona's offices, or at Keith's church. The mogul had demanded they meet on his home turf.

She rolled her eyes. "Do you want us to hold hands Kumbaya style and pray?"

Keith was about to say he liked her idea when he saw Verona was joking. "Are you like this all the time?"

"Pretty much." She shrugged.

"Huh."

"What does 'huh' mean?" she asked, with attitude.

There's a boulder on her shoulders. Keith made a mental note to add Verona to his prayer list. He decided to change the subject. "Gina tells me you plan to attend Bible Study this Wednesday."

He saw her shift her heels, but she confirmed. "Yes, she warned me not to be late."

Keith laughed. "My wife is bossy."

He didn't miss Verona's first genuine smile. "I like her," she said.

"She's impossible to dislike. There's something about her that draws you in."

"Is that why both you and Michael, brothers, fell in love and married her?" she taunted.

A discreet tinkle signaled they had reached the desired floor. They exited the vestibule and Keith held her arm.

Verona knew the sordid tale of how he and Gina had cheated on Michael. She knew for years Michael thought he had fathered Gina's son. The enemy was using her to haunt him with his past. He needed to set things straight. "Think what you want, Verona Stachs, but Gina is the love of my life. All of that back-story is in my past and I'm not going to allow you to discredit our love. What we feel was bigger than the both of us. As far as I'm concerned, God brought us together, and only He can pull us apart." Keith's chest heaved when he was done.

A light blush tinted Verona's cheeks. "I'm sorry. I was way out of line. For what it's worth, I do understand loving someone so much that reason fails."

Keith discerned she referred to Michael and his anger cool. "I know I came off a little harsh a moment ago, but I don't take love lightly. True love is too rare, too precious, to treat with disrespect."

Tears spiked her lashes. "I won't discredit your relationship again."

They started walking down the hall toward Bill's suite number.

"You're in love with him, aren't you?" he asked.

Verona didn't even pretend she didn't understand what he was asking. She looked him square in the eyes. "Yes. I love Michael like I've never loved anyone before."

They were now by the door, but Keith felt compelled to add, "I should mind my business, but I think you need to forget those feelings you think you have for Michael."

"Why?" she sputtered.

"Because Michael loves Lauren and she's—" He stopped. Maybe he should leave well enough alone. If he opened his mouth, he would be breaking a confidence and violating a trust.

"What about Lauren?" Verona insisted.

"She's not dead. She's alive."

"I don't believe you." Her hazel eyes flashed red. Keith saw the "tiger" emerge.

"I can prove it."

Chapter Sixteen

"You've got to tell him."

Perched next to Nigel on one of the Chesterfield sofas in the lounge of the Raines Law Room, Verona nodded even as her heart protested.

Located between Fifth and Sixth Avenues on Seventeenth Street, the Raines Law Room boasted an unassuming door, which opened to a cozy nineteenth century–themed décor. With low music, it was the perfect place to relax and have a private conversation. Verona pressed the electric bell to summon the wait staff and ordered another Spyglass.

"You can't keep this from Michael." Nigel sipped his stronger drink aptly bestowed with the name Arsenic and Lace.

"Stop pestering me," she snapped. The waiter returned with her order and she took a huge gulp of the fancy cocktail. "I know what I have to do."

"I know you think you're in love with him and you're in a race against your woman clock to settle down. You'd better come clean. If the truth comes out—no, when it does—if Michael learned you knew and didn't tell him, you can kiss your love affair good-bye."

Woman clock? Verona winced. "I'm sorry I called you."

Nigel reached his hand to cover her own. "I'm not sorry you called. You're sorry I'm not telling you what you want to hear. And, since I'm spilling truths, you shouldn't have left Keith with Mindy. Your being there would've done more to help Michael's case than anything else."

Verona knew stalking off from Keith had been totally unprofessional, but he couldn't drop news like Lauren being alive on her right before they interrogated someone. She had done everything but faint at his feet. Then, she had run off, leaving Keith to meet with Bill on his own. Curious to hear Nigel's opinion, Verona gazed at him and asked why.

"Because Mindy needed a woman's presence. Her mother died when she was a young child. She would've let you in. Keith doesn't stand a chance and no amount of prayers will help."

Verona groaned. She hoped Nigel was wrong. As it turned out, the arrogant know-it-all was right. Nigel had just left the bar when she'd received Keith's phone call.

"Short of slamming the door in my face, Bill Laurelton was furious at my attempt to sabotage his daughter's case," Keith informed her. "His words, not mine."

"I'm sorry I bailed on you," she apologized.

"I know I caught you off guard." There was a pause on the line before Keith asked, "Are you going to tell Michael? I broke my word by telling you about Lauren."

Verona paid her tab and walked outside the pub. "How can I keep this from him?"

"My plan is to encourage Lauren to make contact. I hope you'll give me time to convince Lauren to reach out to Michael. I'm actually trying to garner her as a character witness."

"You can't be serious," Verona shot back, while flagging down a cab. She put Keith on hold while she gave the driver her address. Then she continued her call. "You're going to use the reporter and Michael's former lover who assisted him in blasting television's most beloved pastor as a character witness?"

"I'm not television's beloved pastor," he answered.

"What does Gina think of all this?" A thought occurred. "Does she know about Lauren?"

"Yes, she does, although I haven't told her about putting Lauren on the stand. But Gina will understand," Keith said, before ending the call.

Verona envisioned a much different response. "What I wouldn't give to be a fly on the wall," she mused. Since it was well into the evening, Verona made it home in no time. She paid and tipped the driver before rushing up to her suite. Her bladder protested from the three cocktails she'd had earlier that evening.

Verona had just exited her bathroom when her cell phone rang. She sent it to voicemail when she saw it was Michael calling yet again. She needed time to think before talking to him. If she told Michael about Lauren that would eliminate any chance she had with him. Verona needed Michael to be in love with her before she told the truth. However, as Nigel said, if Michael found out she had withheld such important information, he would never forgive her.

Love was too complicated. She moaned, meandering her way over to her sofa. How she wished she could've avoided this emotion. She was a reputable attorney before she had gone all mushy and falling for her boss. How predictable.

But, when Verona was in Michael's presence, she was anything but predictable. She was flustered, searching for words, and alive. More alive than she had been in years. No. She would wait. Goodness, she felt stuck in the middle of a romantic comedy. Except this was no laughing matter.

Verona didn't know how long she'd sat there until her mind registered someone was pounding on her door.

She looked through the peephole and sprung her door open when she saw Michael outside. "What are you doing here?"

Michael pushed his way inside her space. "Why aren't you answering my calls? I pay you good money to answer my calls."

Verona's emotions swirled out of control. "I'm sick and tired of you talking about how much you pay me. You don't own me, because I'm earning every dime; no, make that every penny."

"For what I'm paying you, I should own you." He gave a light chuckle.

She inhaled. Her fingers itched to connect with Michael's cheekbone at his insulting words. Suddenly, she wondered, *why am I taking this abuse? This isn't love.* "I quit," she said.

He cracked up. "Quit clowning around, Tiger. We make a great team."

Verona had shocked herself at her proclamation, but she straightened her spine. "I do. I quit." She had come too far to allow any man to make her into a mockery. She was not going to allow anyone to wipe the floor with her.

Michael clenched his jaw. They faced off like two bulls in a pen. Neither backing down.

Then he blinked.

She sighed. "Get out. I'm done."

He blinked, again.

"Are you hard of hearing?" she said. Verona swung away from him to grab her bag. She emptied the contents on the floor. Spotting his car keys, key card, and checkbook, she snatched the items before jumping to her feet. Then she swooped toward him and all but threw them at him.

Michael blinked. "Take that back."

She folded her arms. "I won't. I quit."

Two powerful arms snaked around her waist and pulled her so close her nose touched his chin. "Take that back," he demanded.

Verona rocked her neck and pushed against his arms. A futile attempt, of course. She raised her voice. "I quit! I quit! I—"

Emitting a guttural snarl, Michael grabbed her head and crushed his lips to hers.

Chapter Seventeen

Babies. Babies. Babies. They were everywhere. Out in droves. Or so it seemed at the Source Mall. Dr. Darryl Whitehead, Verona's gynecologist, had an office in Westbury, Long Island. After the news she had received, she sought retail therapy nearby in Neiman Marcus and Saks Fifth Avenue.

Verona had found the cutest outfit to wear to Bible Study on Wednesday. Several bags filled her hands. Her heart, however, remained void.

She could not have children.

Verona mulled over the news as she dragged her way to her car. "I can't believe it," she breathed. She pressed the key to open the trunk. Without care, she tossed the bags in.

Verona slid into her seat and put on her seatbelt. Then she sat there. Blinking. Thinking.

A mom pushed her stroller past her car. A couple walked by with their children. She sat trancelike. Blinking. Thinking.

Dr. Whitehead was certain of his diagnosis. But she knew he was wrong. It was not that she could not have children. Rather, she could not have any *more* children.

She had given birth before. Verona had a child. A son.

A son her parents made her give away. "Is that why you're doing this to me, Lord?" she fisted her hands. Tears dimmed her eyes. "Is this some sort of sick poetic justice?" Verona yelled. "I was young. I fought as hard as I could to keep him."

She gagged, feeling nauseous. Cupping her mouth, she opened her car door and heaved. Nothing came up.

Verona slammed her door and pulled down the visor. Her eyes widened at her tear-smudged face. She reached inside her purse and pulled out her makeup bag. She quickly repaired her face removing all sign of her turmoil.

She plumped her lips and gave herself the final once-over. It took effort, but she started her vehicle and began the trek to MJW Conglomerate. She had a board meeting. Leonard would present the specs on how the company was doing in light of Michael's resignation.

All the way there, Verona gripped the wheel. When she arrived, she shook her hair. "Show time." Gone was the dejected woman. In her place was a woman of confidence. Plastering a smile on her face, Verona entered the building. She made her way to the top floor.

Michael.

What is he doing here? Verona's first thought upon seeing her soon-to-be ex-boss. She patted her purse. She had her two weeks' notice typed and signed.

Her next thought was how Michael looked unaffected by the kiss they had shared two nights before. He had swept her away and her body sang. Then he had pulled away and faced her with a sardonic grin.

Verona sniffed. She hated how pliant she had been in his arms.

She made her way to her usual spot then changed her mind. She wrinkled her nose. It was odd not seeing Michael at the head. Leonard now occupied his chair. Michael crooked his head toward her in greeting.

Patti was droning on. He gestured the universal sign for yakking. She bent her head to hide her smile not wanting to give him the impression all was well between the two of them. Then she pulled up a chair and sat beside

Michael. No use letting others wonder if things had soured between them.

Suddenly, Michael straightened. Keen eyes zoomed in on her face before he stood and yanked her hand. Verona had no choice but to comply. It was either that or risk having her arm pulled out of its socket.

Once outside, Michael asked, "Why were you crying?"

She touched her cheeks. *So much for a good cover-up.* "I went to the doctor. Heard some difficult news. Female stuff." She hoped her short answers would shut him up.

No such luck. "What kind of female stuff?"

Verona gave him a look. *Do you really want to know?* her eyes said. He repeated the question.

"I may not be able to have children," she whispered, clutching her stomach protectively.

"Is that all?" Michael asked. "I was thinking it was ovarian cancer or something. That's nothing."

Nothing. He dared to dismiss her feelings as nothing!

Michael must have seen her face because he took a cautionary step back. "I know it's something but it's not life-threatening. When you decide you're ready to have children, I'll ensure you get the best fertility experts."

"I can't believe you're so calm. You of all people should know how I'm feeling." She referred to his infertility.

Michael squared his shoulders. "That's why I know what I'm talking about." He had a faraway look in his eyes. "Believe me, if you're meant to have children, you'll have them. I know that firsthand."

Verona nodded. She was too emotional to continue this debate. If she had her wits about her, she would have picked up on the way Michael had said "firsthand" and questioned him a little bit further.

Instead, she opened her purse, which she had grabbed to take with her, and pulled out the resignation letter. With a flourish, she handed it to him.

Michael tore open the sealed envelope. His eyes scanned the letter. Verona tilted her chin higher awaiting his response. Ever so calmly, he ripped the letter in half and placed the contents in her hands.

"You may be a pastor, but you're a cheat and a thief," Natalie accused. Her choice of words was harsh but true.

Bishop Combs hung his head. Keith stared at Natalie. "This is what you call going easy on him?" his eyes said.

His assistant shrugged. "What!" her eyes said.

"Bishop, before me and God, please confess," Keith urged.

The bishop's bottom lip trembled. He raised troubled eyes to Keith in the face. "I meant to return it. It was only a loan."

"Only a loan?" Natalie held out her hand. "Well, let's have it. I take check, money order, cash, or credit card."

The bishop sat ramrod straight. His chin lifted in the air. "I'm an elder. You have no right to speak to me with such impertinence."

Keith spoke up. "Let me speak with the bishop alone."

He had invited Natalie into the meeting for her to present the spreadsheets, which she had done. She outlined the discrepancies. Then she called the bishop a cheat and a thief.

Natalie opened her mouth to protest but Keith gave her a warning look. "Whatever you say, boss," she said, stuffing her belongings forcefully into her briefcase, slamming the books closed, and doing anything else to make her displeasure known.

"Deacon Broderson isn't known for discretion," she said. "He will tell his wife and she's a gossip. It's only a matter of—"

"Natalie?" Keith cut her off. He gestured toward the door.

"Make sure he signs those papers." She stomped out the room.

Natalie referenced the requisition papers Keith had prepared. In essence it was a legal payment plan.

Bishop Combs hunched over. "What am I going to do? When the board gets wind of this . . ."

"It's not the board you should be worried about," Keith admonished. "It's God. What does He think? It's the federal government. Trust me when I tell you, the truth comes out."

The bishop groaned. "I ran into trouble with the mortgage and some other business investments. Suzette needed things, a new car, new wardrobe. I planned on returning it," Bishop Combs mumbled. "I invested the money in the hopes of making a big return, but that flopped. I'm in over my head. I'm sorry. I'm sorry." He repeated his apology several times.

Keith tapped the papers. "This is an agreement stating you will repay the foundation in three installments."

The bishop nodded. His hands trembled as he signed the form. Shame-faced, he said to Keith, "Please don't hold this against me, or God."

"I don't see this as a reflection against God. Others might. They will add you to the list of hypocritical ministers out there. But not me. You helped counsel me but you're human. I didn't build my foundation on you. Whatever you've done won't shake my foundation or my faith."

"Good. Good."

"It will shake others, though," Keith said. "You did wrong. But, I'm glad you're making amends."

Chapter Eighteen

"Don't these people have jobs?" Michael asked.

Verona rolled her eyes. "I didn't invite you to come with me to Bible Study."

"I wasn't aware I needed a special invite to come into God's house. Doesn't He welcome everyone?"

"Apparently, fleas as well," she bit back. *Sorry, Lord, but he's trifling as ever.*

Michael creased his forehead. "What's wrong? We were talking just fine earlier at the board meeting. What could I have done to make you . . ." He stopped, and nodded with a slight grin. "Wait a minute. I know what this is about. It's about the kiss. I meant to shut down your foolish idea of quitting and it worked. It was just a kiss. Lighten up."

Michael's knowing chuckle made her grit her teeth. Even if it killed her, Verona would not respond. To him it was a mere kiss. To her it was everything. It took everything in her power not to give Michael's cheek a five-fingered salute at his blasé attitude.

Verona stormed down the aisle until she was at the third pew from the front. *Ugh.* He followed her. Gina had told her this small chapel, used for the midweek services, could accommodate about a hundred people. There were about thirty people in attendance.

"You can't ignore me, you know." Michael slid so close to her she felt every breath he took.

Verona's sanity was now in question. "I can ignore you, just as you ignored my resignation. How did you even know I was here?"

"I know you're not serious about leaving. That's why I ripped up that ridiculous letter," he said. "You really need to find another way to handle your frustrations. To answer your second question, you told me about Gina inviting you."

Oh, yes. She remembered bragging about it on their drive home from the foundation ball. She was surprised he had remembered as Michael had been frazzled after his run-in with Bill Laurelton.

Verona looked at Michael from underneath her lashes. "I meant it, Michael Ward. Find yourself another guinea pig, because I'm done."

His eyes raked her from head to toe, taking in her black Donna Karan jersey wraparound dress with matching Manolo Blahniks. With a salacious grin, Michael said, "You're no guinea pig. You're a tigress and one in need of taming."

Now, he chooses to flirt with me! Before Verona could respond, Gina entered the room. Dressed in a casual beige suit, Gina sauntered up to the podium. Verona elbowed Michael to move over, but the ignoramus refused to put distance between them. She scuttled her body away, but he stubbornly closed the gap each time.

With a grunt, she caved and remained where she was because Michael would just follow her.

Gina called the meeting to order. "Bishop Combs is unable to make it tonight. I'll be standing in for him. Please open your Bibles to James chapter one."

Verona grabbed one of the Bibles from the pew and located the passage. She recited the books in her head, until she located James. She saw Michael fiddling with his pages and sighed. Handing him her Bible, Verona took his and proceeded to locate the passage.

"Show off," he murmured.

Verona rolled her eyes, but said nothing.

"Verse 22 says we must be doers of the Word, and not just hearers. What does this mean?" Gina asked.

Verona knew the answer. Gina had a warm smile on her face as she scanned the crowd. Verona noted how Gina's smile froze once she noticed Michael in the midst. She knew Gina wasn't pleased to see him there.

After a moment, a couple of hands went up. Gina called on someone.

"It means we've got to follow God's Word if we want to get to heaven," the young lady said.

"That's true, Sister Althea, but there's more."

Verona felt a poke in her arm. "I know you know," Michael said. She gave him an intense glare daring him to say something. He saw her face and decided not to push her button. *That's what I thought.* Verona jutted her chin in the air. *Michael knows tonight is not the night to mess with me.*

Apparently Gina did not.

"We have a first-time visitor with us. Everyone, please say a hearty welcome to Verona Stachs. Verona, do you have any idea what the verse means?"

It took a moment for Verona to realize Gina had called her out in front of everyone. She wasn't sure if Gina had put her on blast with good intentions. Awkwardly, she stood to her feet. "I, ah . . ." She froze.

Michael chucked. She clenched her fists.

A sea of faces waited for her to say something. Suddenly, she was transported to another time in her life.

No, I'm not going back there. She was here, right now. With a firm voice, Verona explained, "To be a hearer of the Word means you know the Word and what it means but it hasn't impacted your life. On the other hand, to be a doer means you know the Word and you follow up by living the Word, by applying it in your everyday life."

Seeing Gina's nod of approval, Verona took her seat. Gina went on with the study.

"So which one are you?" Michael whispered. "A hearer? Or a doer?"

His question hit her core. Verona knew it was the Holy Spirit speaking through him to ask her the poignant question. She closed her eyes and turned away from Michael. She wasn't ready to go there with God just yet.

As soon as the service concluded, Verona gave Michael explicit orders to wait for her while she sought Gina out. She waited for the crowd to disperse so she could speak to Gina in private.

"Sorry to put you on the spot," Gina said as soon as they were alone.

"It's okay," she replied. "Well, it wasn't really okay, but I recovered."

Gina cocked her head. "I was being led by God to ask you to explain that verse. I never call out people like that. For some reason, God is pinpointing you."

Verona squirmed. Gina told the truth. "I'm not ready," she shakily admitted. "I've got some things I need to work out with God." Things like why He made her parents dirt poor. Why He made her have to give up her son. Why He had closed her womb.

"Don't keep Him waiting too long," Gina warned in a gentle tone. "When God wants you, there is no escaping Him. Where can you run?"

A verse came back to her. "If I make my bed in hell, He's there."

Gina arched an eyebrow at her. "Yes, you said it right." She tilted her head Michael's way. "I see you brought your shadow."

What a way to refer to her ex-husband. Verona wondered if Gina had ever been in love with Michael. Gina sounded like she was talking about a stranger and not someone she had pledged her life to before. Verona pursed her lips. It was time for Lady Ward to live what she preached. "Michael, come on over."

On stilted steps, he approached. "Hello, Gina. You were amazing tonight."

"I owe it to God," Gina deflected before asking him, "Why are you here?"

Verona admired her bluntness.

"I need you to stand up for me at the hearing," Michael returned with equal bluntness.

"Forget it." Gina stomped off without even a good-bye.

Verona watched her rapid departure. She faced Michael to offer some token word of sympathy. She saw him checking out his ex-wife and her stomach knotted from envy. "You'd better put out that spark before Keith finds out. I don't think he'd be as willing to help you if he sees you're still pining for his wife."

Michael's eyes widened. "Say what? Whatever I felt for Gina is long gone. I'm not checking her out. I'm contemplating. I know her. She'll testify. That's the person she is deep down. Her good nature will win no matter what she says."

Verona's stomach churned and it wasn't from indigestion. It was jealousy at Michael's faith in his ex-wife. She resisted the urge to roll her eyes. What she wouldn't give to hear him talking about her like that.

"By the way, I took a cab so I could ride back with you into the city," Michael said.

Verona slanted him a glance. "You took it for granted I'd . . ." She stopped. What was the point in arguing? She was going to end up taking him anyways. She motioned for him to come on.

She dropped Michael off before driving the short distance to her home. The doorman held opened the door and Verona strolled inside. She could not wait to soak her feet. Lavender Epsom salts.

Upon entering her penthouse, Verona threw off her shoes. On stocking clad feet, she started a bath, replete with candles and her bath pillow. Verona kicked herself for not coming clean about Lauren. She knew Keith said to give him time to speak to Lauren, but between Michael and God, she knew she was short on that.

The verse from James came back to her. *What a way to spend a Wednesday night.*

Chapter Nineteen

What a way to spend a Wednesday night, or, should she say, Thursday morning!

"It's been too long, Mousie!"

"Give us more! Mousie! Mousie!"

With a knowing smile at the men's pleas, Mousie pranced on the stage. She rocked her lower body. Her tail swished across the stage. The roars spurred her on.

With exaggerated movements, she strutted across the stage and executed a perfect split. Sweat poured down her body. Bills were tossed all over the stage. Finn's minions came and gathered all the cash.

She blew them a Marilyn Monroe–style kiss. As Mousie had directed, the stage effects kicked into gear. Smoke and huge fans blew her dress high above her legs.

More money!

As the lights dimmed, she clenched her fists and stormed off the stage. "I'm tired of this! Why are they cheering? I'm doing everything but selling my goods up there, and their tongues hang out with sick fascination!"

Finn helped her out of her costume without saying a word. Mousie knew he had long ago tuned her out. Taking deep breaths, she asked, "Did the cheese costume come in yet?"

"Yes, as you ordered, with studs galore."

Mousie slipped into a purple silk robe and turned to face him. "I know you think it's stupid, but they're going to love it. Mark my words."

"No doubt."

Mousie noted Finn's significant lack of enthusiasm. She knew she had made him close to $4,000. He had not even given her a high five or anything. "What's with you?" she asked.

Finn shrugged his massive shoulders. "I'm getting tired of your, for want of a better word, split personality. It's like you're bipolar or something. I don't force you to go onstage. You come here when the mood strikes, of your own free will, and you get on stage and do your thing. But once you're done, you're screaming and complaining at the catcalls." He shook his head. "I don't get it at all."

Mousie was at a loss for words. She shivered and looked around the dingy room. Chipped paint and sagging posters depicting women in suggestive poses lined the walls. In a childlike voice, she acknowledged, "You're right. I don't know what I'm doing here. Maybe I won't come back after tonight."

Finn held up his hands and stammered, "Whoa. Easy now. Don't get too hasty. I wasn't saying all that. You asked me a question and I was giving you an answer. That's all. I don't care about your rants, as long as you make me money. Please come back. You're my biggest draw."

Tears streamed down Mousie's face. "I've got to get out of here."

"I won't argue with you. There's no point." Finn walked up to her and touched her face with his large hands. "I wish you'd show me the real you. You undress and show your body, but you keep the real you on lockdown. You're untouchable. Mousie—I don't even know your real name—Mousie, let me in. I care about you." He placed a gentle kiss on the bridge of her nose.

Startled, Mousie jumped back. "We agreed! We agreed!" she screamed. "We agreed! No touching! No touching!"

"Mousie, cool down. I didn't touch you to harm you. You've got to relax. Breathe," Finn said.

It took some doing until Finn's words finally registered. Mousie nodded.

He turned toward the door, but swung back around to face her. "Why won't you let anyone close to you?"

"Because," Mousie answered, "no one touches me. I'll get hurt." The child within spoke those words. She had to protect herself. She could tell Finn thought she was cuckoo, but these were her terms for survival.

"Someone must have done a number on you. I've never met a woman so tightly wound. One of these days, you're going to bust and fall apart." He went to the door and opened it. "We all need someone, Mousie. Even you."

Once Finn had departed, Mousie stood frozen. "Someone did do a number on me, and he paid. You will too, if you come near me again." Her ominous words echoed off the walls. She grabbed her street clothes and got dressed. It was time to say good-bye to this place.

Finn ruined it for her when he talked about feelings. Mousie didn't feel anything for men, for no one. Her cell phone rang. Seeing the number, she scurried out the door. This was one person she would not dare keep waiting.

Chapter Twenty

Different doctor. Same verdict.

Verona left the Continuum Reproductive Center with her head hung low. Located on Fifty-ninth Street, the center boasted some of the country's leading fertility experts.

Her shop was closed. Unexplained infertility. What a cruel thing! The specialist had suggested all kinds of invasive procedures, but Verona closed her mind to it. Nope. She was not wasting her time. Not when she knew the truth. God had turned His back on her.

Verona tore up the paper with her results and tossed it in the nearest garbage can. Heedless of the nippy air, she walked the short distance to the parking garage with her coat in her hand. She paid and tipped the attendants for the hour.

Verona held the tears until she was inside her vehicle. Then she dropped her head onto the steering wheel and released them. Her shoulders shook. She could barely catch her breath.

"God, why?" she cried. "Why are you punishing me?" This was her second meltdown in her car and she hated it. It would be the last time.

Verona shook her head. She had the beauty, the body, and the brains. She had done it all right. She exercised and, for the most part, watched what she ate. *What did I do to deserve this? How can this be happening to me?*

Her cell phone jingled a reminder. Verona swiped away her tears. She was expected at Keith and Gina's in less than hour. Her eyes were reddened from crying. "Get it together, girl," she told her reflection.

Verona lowered the visor to look into the mirror. She pulled her compact out of her purse. She wiped away the dried mascara. Using bottled water, she washed her face. Then she fixed her face. If only it were so easy to repair the pain in her heart.

She experienced a moment of déjà vu.

"No more crying in your car, Verona," she scolded. She put her car in gear. With each mile, she added to her armor. She wouldn't let her internal pain distract her from the job she had to do. When all else failed, she had her career. Her job was her constant. She could rely on her skills. She knew better than to put her faith in God.

"It popped out," Keith explained. The couple had taken a stroll around the perimeter of the property when Keith broke the news. He bundled his jacket around him.

"It didn't just pop out. You forget I know you." Gina's teeth chattered. "Let's get inside." She picked up the pace. Keith had no problem keeping in step with her much smaller stride.

She continued, "You knew what you were doing when you told Verona about Lauren. You're hoping she'll tell Michael so you'll still be keeping your promise."

Gina opened the front door and Keith followed her inside. They went into his office to finish their conversation.

Keith shrugged. *She knows me too well. Might as well come clean.* "Technically, I promised Lauren not to tell Michael, which I didn't. I told you. I told Verona."

Gina shook her head. "You were wrong. You shouldn't have brought Lauren into this. She's a reporter. She's seen the headlines. If she wanted to help, she'd have come out of hiding and she'd be here. Bottom line, it wasn't your secret to tell."

Keith took her small shoulders in his hands. "Aren't you tired of secrets, Gina? Because I am. Don't you realize how keeping our love hidden destroyed other people's lives? Keeping secrets ruined my relationship with Michael." He held his head and confessed, "It's driving me nuts, the guilt of knowing where Lauren is and not telling Michael. You didn't see what I saw. Michael is falling for Verona because a part of him is beginning to let Lauren go."

"It's not your business, Keith," Gina countered. "You made a promise and there are innocent children to consider."

Keith groaned. "I am considering the children." He gave Gina a tortured look. She turned away from him when she saw his face.

He touched her arm and slid his hand under her chin. "Gina, I love you so much." His voice broke. "It pained me when I lost those years with Epiphany, years I can never get back. It did something to me as her father. I can't sit back and let Michael continue to face that agony."

Tears pooled her eyes. Gina clutched her fist to her chest. "And, what about my agony? My pain? Keith, do you know what it was like living with someone who didn't love me and who couldn't stand to look Epiphany in the eyes?"

Pain united them. Keith bit out, "I know what you feel. We're connected. I feel every ounce of your pain." He adjusted himself and pulled Gina to stand in front of him. He kissed her to dim the memories of pain, until passion arose. Once he felt her lips go supple, he released her. "God has forgiven us, Gina. We've got to let the past hurt go and lay it at His feet once and for all. We've got to step forward now. We can't stay here stuck between the past and the present."

She closed her eyes, pulling away from him. "Don't," Keith urged. "Michael's not here by accident. He's here by divine ordinance. We both are God's hands and His voice. God is depending on us to be examples. We can't fail Him."

Gina gave an imperceptible nod and Keith loosened his hold. Her arms circled his waist. "It's hard, honey. So hard to do," she said.

"I know, sweetheart. This road isn't easy," he soothed. "But the final destination makes it all worth it."

"I told her to give me time to speak to Lauren but tomorrow's the hearing. I have a feeling once the charges are brought, Verona's going to 'fess up."

Her little head nodded against him. "I'm not ready, Keith. However, I promise to pray about it and I'll . . . I'll speak on Michael's behalf if I absolutely have to. I hope I won't, though."

It was the first time Gina had mentioned Michael's name without rancor. *Thank you, Lord. Small steps.* "I won't call you unless Michael is convicted," Keith said. That was the closest he could promise. There was something about the case that bothered him. Something crucial he'd overlooked. Since he knew better than to question the feeling, Keith had invited Verona over to go through all the statements again.

"What time's Verona coming to work on the case?" Gina asked.

"You read my mind." Keith chuckled. "She'll be here in an hour. I invited her for dinner. Josie is setting an extra spot at the dinner table. Everything's handled."

Ever the dutiful housewife, Gina removed herself from his arms. "Still, I'd better go check for myself how dinner is coming along."

Within ten minutes of Gina leaving the room, Verona showed up.

Verona was a wonderful dinner guest. She particularly enjoyed Trey's and Epiphany's presence. After dinner, they had family prayer time. Before they prayed, they sang a verse of "Amazing Grace." Verona joined in. Her strong singing voice was a pleasant surprise. That and the fact she knew the words to the song. Normally, Keith would question her spiritual background, but they had Michael's case. He filed that away for a future conversation.

Once Gina went to settle the children into bed, Keith and Verona went to his office. For a half hour they poured through the documents in silence until Keith made an observation.

"Why didn't they take a sample?"

Verona did not follow his thought pattern. She gestured for him to explain.

"Standard procedure is for a rape sample to be taken, but it seems as if Mindy refused one. So, how could Michael be charged with rape? This is a big mess-up that might work in Michael's favor. We can make a motion to reduce to a lesser charge."

Verona took the pages and went through the files again. "I don't know how I could've missed this. I guess it's because I'm masquerading as a criminal attorney." She gave him a cheeky grin before returning to the case. "Bill's defense team must know it too. They've been giving us the runaround for weeks. They delivered the files a mere week ago. This explains why Bill doesn't want us near his daughter."

Keith nodded his assent. "However, her state of mind, whether she's been with a man before, the blood, all these things could factor into why a rape kit wasn't administered. Her words were compelling evidence and Michael's lack of words incriminated him." He flipped through the pictures several times.

Something was not right.

Keith leaned closer to investigate but he could not tell. "We've got to scan these and blow them up. I need to get a better look at them."

Verona quickly complied. Together they huddled over the computer screen. "It's as I thought. Some of her wounds look self-inflicted," Keith said.

"She could've done that while fighting her attacker," Verona countered.

"She could've done them to herself," Keith echoed. He studied the pictures at length.

"If she did, she'd have to be a sick woman."

"You'd be surprised at what I've seen." Keith scrunched his nose. He rubbed his eyes and glanced at the clock. It was close to midnight. "We have to get an expert to look at this. I'll contact Dr. Daniel Northman. He's credible and I've used him on countless cases in the past. My tired eyes can't see anymore."

"Aren't you forgetting there was a condom with semen found on the scene?"

He could see how much it cost Verona to bring that matter up. "No, I haven't forgotten. Though Michael protested, we need him to give a specimen. March may seem months away, but we've got to be prepared."

"He's refused. Michael's arrogant enough to believe he won't be indicted tomorrow. He doesn't think he needs to belittle himself with that indignity. His words, not mine. I think he's hoping for a miraculous confession before then."

Keith didn't reply because he knew Michael's real reason for noncompliance. Michael didn't produce a lot of semen and was deemed infertile. That compelling revelation led Michael to discover the truth about Trey not being his son. Keith and Gina had made sure to test Epiphany. She was 100 percent Keith's. All the more reason why Keith needed Michael to know his children—his own miracles from God. Chances were Michael would never have any more.

But, first things first. Keith needed Dr. Northman's expert eye to look over these crime scene photos. There were some midrange and close-up shots. The pictures held the truth.

Chapter Twenty-one

"Lauren's alive."

Seated at his dinner table, Michael almost choked on his spaghetti. He leaned forward, not sure he had heard Verona right. "Come again?"

"Lauren is alive. You were right and I was wrong."

Rocks lined his stomach and he pushed away the savory food. He shook his head. "How do you know?"

Verona bit into her meatball. Her appetite hadn't suffered any. "Your brother told me when we tried to talk to Mindy."

Michael scraped his chair and stood. "That was Wednesday. Today's Sunday." He had his arms akimbo with his legs spread apart. "Are you telling me you've been sitting on this news"—he counted on his fingers—"for four days and you're just now telling me? I don't believe you! We were at church yesterday, and you said nothing. Now today, you have the gall to come here cooking and eating with me like all is well. Now look at you, sitting there stuffing your face like it's a regular day."

Verona arched an eyebrow but kept on eating as if she hadn't flipped his world upside down. No, make that right side up. Lauren was alive. Michael banged his fist on the table to get her attention. She jumped from the impact.

She wiped her mouth. "I couldn't believe it when Keith told me. Honestly, I needed time to process before telling you."

114 Michelle Lindo-Rice

"You needed time to process?" he repeated, stunned at
her calm demeanor. It was like Verona was talking about
the weather or something insignificant. "Lauren's being
alive could change my life for the better and you made it
all about you." He got into her face. "I don't believe you
would hold this from me for so long. Where is she?"

"Back off, Michael," Verona warned. "I'm sorry I didn't
tell you sooner. Keith begged me to give him a few days to
talk with Lauren. He hoped she'd come to see you of her
own volition. But, I've been stewing on it, and I care about
you too much to hold this from you. If you want to know
more, you'll have to see Keith. Thanks for the meal. I'll see
you later." She left him without even a second glance.

Michael knew he should go after Verona but he had
bigger things to think about like Lauren being alive.

His chest heaved from the rage building within him at
Keith's deception. Why would his brother have kept this
from him? Payback? How could he forget how good Keith
was at keeping secrets?

Why wouldn't Keith tell him?

Questions swirled around his head. Michael grabbed his
coat. He needed answers. Before the night was through,
he'd know everything.

"Michael? I didn't know you were coming over? Keith
didn't say . . . Are you okay?" Gina asked.

He read the conflicting emotions on his ex-wife's face.
She cared. That was good to know. "I'm fine. I needed to
speak with Keith, if he's . . ." His eyes narrowed at the
little hand circling Gina's waist.

Gina pushed Epiphany behind her. Michael couldn't
fault her protective move. Gina wasn't likely to forget how
he'd tried to take her children from her. Michael smiled
and reassured her. "I don't want trouble. I need to see my
brother."

He watched her internal debate before she stepped aside to let him in. Michael tried to sneak a glance at Epiphany. He was curious to see if he would still feel apathy when he looked at her. Michael could not believe how much he had placed the demise of his marriage on Epiphany's little shoulders.

"I'll go find Keith," Gina said. She took her daughter's hand. Obviously, she did not feel safe leaving Epiphany in his presence.

Michael couldn't fault her, but it hurt. Epiphany turned to greet him with a shy smile. Michael took one look at her dimpled cheeks and fell in love. She was precious. With quick strides, he snatched her from Gina and gave her a whirl in the air. Epiphany squealed with glee.

"Michael, what're you doing?" Gina asked, tugging on his Armani suit jacket. "Put her down, please."

He complied. As soon as he put her down, Epiphany ran to parts unknown. Michael could not take his eyes off Gina. Her cheeks were reddened. He reached out to touch one of them. When she did not flinch, he allowed instinct to take over. In one fluid motion, he kissed her full on the lips.

A heartbeat later, he felt her push against him and stepped away. She swung her hand and he grabbed it before it connected with his face.

"Care to tell me why you're kissing on my wife?"

Michael lifted his head to see Keith standing behind him.

Gina's head snapped around and her eyes widened with horror. "Keith, this isn't what it looks like. I . . . I . . . " She pointed an accusatory finger toward Michael. "He kissed me."

When Keith said nothing, Gina stomped off mumbling under her breath. Keith was going to hear about it later for not coming to her defense. Michael looked at Keith expecting to see anger or jealousy. He saw neither and felt compelled to apologize.

"I'm sorry. I don't know why I kissed her. Please don't drop my case because of such a stupid action. I should never have disrespected you."

Keith leaned on the wall and closed his eyes. Michael wondered if Keith was praying but he didn't think so.

Then Keith whispered, "I know why you kissed my wife." He wandered off in the direction of his study.

Michael followed. Out of nowhere, he thought, *I miss Mom. I wish she were here.* Where were all these emotions coming from all of a sudden?

Michael plopped down in a chair across from Keith wondering why they weren't firing punches after the stunt he'd just pulled.

"You kissed her because you wanted her to remember what you once shared. Gina used to love you. You once had a life together."

That made sense. Michael supposed Keith was right. He shrugged. "It doesn't excuse my actions."

"You're right, brother. Consider that your one and only look into your past. If you touch my wife again . . ."

Michael nodded with understanding. "I need her to testify if I get a guilty verdict."

"Well, pressing your lips onto Gina's isn't the right way to go about it. Please don't tell me you came here with the intent of manhandling my wife."

"I came to ask about Lauren."

Keith settled further in his chair. "Verona told you."

The hurt surfaced. "Why didn't you tell me?"

"I made a promise and I wanted to keep my word."

Great. What a time for his heart to defrost. Michael was feeling things he had not felt in a long time. "But, we're brothers. Blood. When is that going to count for something?" He looked Keith in the eyes unashamed of what was written on his face. Michael took rapid breaths to hold it together.

"I'm sorry," Keith said.

Two simple words. No longwinded explanation. No defense. Just an apology. Michael gulped. He knew Keith was saying sorry for everything: all the pain, hurt, betrayal, and for ruining their relationship.

His heart cracked. He strove to utter the words but they would not come. Taking a deep breath, Michael stood, turning his back to Keith while he composed himself. "I miss Mom. I have no one. Maybe that's what kissing Gina was about. I needed to reconnect to feel something. I saw Epiphany and I saw a happy little girl; my niece. How could I have ill-treated her? She was an innocent child. No wonder Lauren left me just as Gina left me."

Michael flinched when he felt a hand on his shoulder but he was tired of running away. He faced Keith. "Am I so unlovable the women I love leave me?"

Keith looked Michael in the eyes. "You're not unlovable. Love isn't the only ingredient. You're loving but if someone crosses you, you can't forgive."

"That's because I love with everything I have. I gave Gina the best of me and look what she did. She slept with you and you fathered her two kids, right under my nose." Michael knew he sounded bitter but he had to release it. It had become a festered wound he had buried for too long. Now it was a hardened mass, like granite around his heart.

"Yes, Gina and I both betrayed you. It was wrong and it was low-down, but God has forgiven us. Until you can find it in your heart to forgive us, you won't be able to move on. Lauren told me how you pushed her out of your home and out of your life. The way she said it, it's like she was talking about a monster and not a human being."

"She's right. I don't know me anymore. I used to be trusting and fun-loving but I don't even know . . ." Words failed him. Michael was smelling himself, so to speak, and he stunk. But it was time to get clean. "I don't want to continue not caring, not allowing anyone to get close. I need to feel free so I can open my heart."

Keith dropped to his knees and held out a hand. "I can't free you but I know who can. God is a balm, the remedy for your anger, your pain. Pray with me."

Michael did not care about his thousand dollar custom-made suit. He wanted what Keith had. He wanted to love and be loved. He took his brother's hand and joined him on the floor. Keith's physical act chipped at Michael's heart. "I don't know what to say. When I came here, it was with the intent to curse you out."

Keith bent his head and closed his eyes. "Holy Father, I come to you on my brother's behalf asking for you to heal his heart. Lord, let him feel the power of your love. Father, I ask for your finger to touch Michael's heart and melt away all the past hurt and anger he's feeling. God, perform surgery on his hardened heart. Let your love pierce the fleshy tables of his heart. I pray this prayer, in your Son Jesus' name, knowing it is done and you will complete your good work in him. Amen."

When Michael opened his eyes, he was surprised to feel the tears. Slowly, methodically, he wiped them away with his hands. He looked at the crystal drops, feeling amazed. He had cried. These were real tears. He knew he looked crazy but Michael laughed. It felt good to cry, to feel again.

They chatted about sports, life, everything. Keith and Michael discussed the case. Keith told him about his suspicions with the photographs. He showed him the pictures and told him about hiring someone to evaluate them. He had contacted Dr. Northman but the doctor was in Argentina on vacation. Keith wanted to wait until he returned. Michael agreed. Three hours passed before their conversation slowed.

Keith captured Michael's attention with his next topic of conversation. "I know you said you feel alone because Mom's gone but, Michael, that isn't true. You have God and you have me in your corner. And, speaking of Mom . . ."

Michael knew what his brother wanted to ask. He squared his shoulders. "I wanted to be here. I wanted to be here for her. I called and I thought . . . I thought I had more time. I thought she'd bounce back and be her usual self, telling me off about something. I didn't know she would . . . die before I returned." He hung his head. "If I wasn't all about business and into myself, I'd have been here. I hate I can't undo it."

"Forgive yourself. Mom knew you loved her. She prayed for you all the time, even on her deathbed. I was angry when you didn't come to her bedside and when you skipped the funeral. Why?"

He had to face his ugly truth. "I didn't want to see you, Keith. I didn't want to see you with Gina. I cried for days, filled with grief. I didn't have the guts to say good-bye and I didn't want to see Mom lowered into the ground."

"Have you been to her gravesite?"

The gentle question was almost Michael's undoing. He would have understood if Keith had railed at him, but his brother sounded calm. There was a serenity that surrounded Keith that Michael found hard to comprehend. His brother was a changed man. Had salvation done that? Michael was beginning to see Keith as a man of God. Michael admitted, "I've visited her grave on many occasions but the guilt tears at me. The guilt of knowing I wasn't there when she needed me most."

"Let it go, Michael. I'm not going to sugarcoat things and say I totally understand. But I know this isn't God's plan. God doesn't want you carrying all that guilt. The devil has you all tied up and God wants you to be free. He's already forgiven you. All you have to do is accept His pardon. It's the only way you'll find peace and move on."

There was a knock at the door. Gina entered with two glasses of lemonade and a plate full of goodies.

Michael's tongue felt parched so he appreciated her thoughtfulness. He gave her a look of apology. "Thanks, Gina. I'm sorry for kissing you earlier."

She skirted her eyes away from him and wiped her hands on her jeans. She mumbled, "No problem. It's forgotten," but he could see her uneasiness.

Then the old Gina he knew surfaced. "Are you going to see Lauren?"

Lauren!

"I . . . We were praying and talking . . ." Michael was hesitant to say he'd broken down.

"Talking to Keith will do that; besides, you need to work on you, first. This whole thing with Lauren will work itself out." Gina patted him on the arm: her first voluntary physical contact.

Michael willed himself to act normal and not react. Her fleeting touch whipped at him. More than a message or any spoken word, Gina's touch did wonders. Like a television screen, he saw himself berating her and treating her like dirt. He remembered the pleasure he had felt in shaming Gina before millions when he had all but called her a whore and announced how Keith was the father of her children.

Michael was humbled. While he experienced those shattering memories, she vacated the room with a soft, "Welcome home."

What a night for emotions. Michael could not hold back the tears. He looked at Keith. "She touched me. She touched me." He paused. How could he put it into words?

"After all I've done, she touched me. Only it wasn't a human touch, it felt almost like . . ." He stopped, not wanting to sound stupid.

"We are God's voice and hands at times. God wants you, Michael. He has a whole party planned for your return."

Michael's mouth popped open at Keith's perceptiveness. It was all too much. He grabbed his coat, eager to meet the cold air. He needed to feel the brutality of the low temperatures. All that warmth was killing him. "I need some time to think. We'll talk about Lauren another time."

Michael was pushing his second hand in his coat when Keith grabbed his sleeve. "Don't run, Michael. Stay."

Chapter Twenty-two

"If you'd told me a week ago Michael would be spending the night in my house, I would've slapped you upside your head."

Keith grinned at her comment. Gina was bent over her nightstand rubbing Oil of Olay on her face with her cute little butt perched toward him. From his position at the head of the bed, Keith crossed his feet at the ankles, enjoying the sight.

"I couldn't have him drive home at this hour," Keith explained.

"Well you should've asked me." Gina turned to give him an evil eye.

Dressed in barely there silk shorts, he watched her shiver from the cold. "Gina, come over here so you can get warm. It's time for you to pay me some attention."

"If you think you're getting nooky while your brother sleeps under this roof, you'd better think again." Gina shut off the lights before scampering toward the bed.

As soon as she was under the sheets, he pulled her into his arms. "Your feet are cold," he growled. Keith felt her body trembling next to him. "Why are you wearing this skimpy outfit when you know you're going to freeze?" It didn't matter how warm the house was, Gina was always cold.

She pulled her feet under his thighs to warm them. He grunted and waited for what would come next. Sure enough, she started her wiggling. "Keep still," he warned, though it was pointless. She had restless legs, constantly moving her feet, which was why Keith insisted she keep up with her pedicures.

Gina snuggled even deeper into him. "You feel so warm."

Keith hugged her close.

"Did you tell Michael how to find Lauren?"

"No. We talked about Mom and we settled some things. Then, we prayed. We're going to talk about Lauren tomorrow."

"He looked pretty shaken up when I came in," she observed.

He yawned. "We'll talk in the morning," he directed. "Right now, sleep is calling."

She poked him in the ribs. "Michael had better be gone in the morning."

"I'll make sure of it," he assured her. *Lord, please soften Gina's heart. She's driving me crazy,* was Keith's prayer to God before sleep claimed him.

Michael was at the breakfast bar, still dressed in a borrowed pair of Keith's pajamas. They were loose and a smidgeon long, but they did the job.

"I see Josie hooked you up." Keith eyed the plate of fried dumplings and salt fish. His belly grumbled and his tongue watered. He loved how Josie made codfish, or salt fish, as Jamaicans coined it. She boiled it several times to get rid of the salt, before preparing it with light seasonings, onion, and olive oil. He rubbed his hands.

"Yup. This is delicious."

Josie dished Keith a plate. Keith said his grace and dug in, savoring the hint of pepper.

He and Michael made short work of their meal. Keith placed their plates in the dishwasher and crooked his head toward Michael.

"I should get going. I don't want to push my luck with Gina."

He could not argue with his brother's comment. She had ordered him to have Michael out of the house before she got back from her ministry work at the hospital.

Nevertheless, he found himself saying, "Kick back for a minute. We have plenty to discuss."

Keith held his breath. Michael grappled with conflicting emotions. Keith knew he was being pushy but he wanted his brother back. He had been praying for years and God was doing His thing.

"You sure you don't mind?" Michael asked. "I'd definitely rather be here than cooped up in the penthouse all day."

Keith released the breath he had been holding. He gestured to Michael and they headed into his study. "Now that's settled. Let's talk about Lauren; and Verona."

"Where is she? How long have you known? Where are my children?"

Keith was prepared for Michael's questions. "Lauren is safe. She came to me, pregnant and angry. It took a lot of persuasion for her to settle here in New York where Gina and I could keep an eye on her. Gina was there with her when she had your children."

Michael's face crumbled and his shoulders drooped. "I should've been there."

Keith empathized but had to tell the truth. "Lauren didn't want you there, Michael. I urged her on many occasions to reach out to you but she refused. She is one determined woman. Lauren said you kicked her out when she told you about her pregnancy. Is that true?"

"Yes, I did. I threw her out without a backward glance. I didn't want to stop my vendetta against you. I was so bent on revenge I wasn't thinking about the future. Plus, I couldn't believe she was pregnant. I mean the whole world heard me say I couldn't father children. I was too cynical to hear her out." Michael covered his face.

Keith wanted to hurl some "how could you?" type questions his brother's way, but knew it wouldn't do any good.

"I spoke to Mom about it," Michael confessed. "I wish I'd heeded her warnings. She died never seeing her grandchildren."

Keith swallowed, wondering if he should divulge the truth. *Might as well. The truth must come out sometime.*

"She did. Mom saw them," Keith said.

Michael's eyes bulged out their sockets. "Mom met John and Olivia?" he shook his head. "She never told me."

"Mom was sick. On her deathbed. I convinced Lauren to allow Mom to see them before she went on to paradise."

Instantly, Michael was on the alert. He looked around the room as if searching for answers. "Lauren must live close, then. Bro, you have to tell me where to find her. I'm in torment. I must set things right. Children need their father."

Keith changed the subject. "What's going on with you and Verona? You two seem chummy."

"Verona's the best," he said. "She's loyal and I trust her. We've always maintained a loose professional relationship until the other day when I kissed her."

He arched an eyebrow at Michael. "And?"

Michael waved him off. "It was nothing. I wanted to shut her up. Keep her from quitting. We're friends. Nothing more. Besides, with Lauren in the picture . . ."

Though Michael downplayed his relationship with Verona, Keith was not convinced. He had seen the electricity between them. He knew Verona was in love with Michael. Michael was besotted too, but he did not—or, rather, would not—acknowledge it. Michael did not step without asking Verona's opinion. His airy tone when he mentioned Verona's name was also a dead giveaway.

"I've set up a meeting with Lauren. Gina and I plan to see her today. As soon as she returns from her ministry at the hospital."

Though Michael nodded, Keith knew his brother was not going to sit idly by and simply wait. When they parted ways, all Keith could do was hope. Hope Michael would let him help him. Or, rather, let God.

Chapter Twenty-three

"I don't want to see him!" Lauren bellowed. She twisted her hands as she rocked back and forth.

Keith was glad Gina was with him. She went over to comfort Lauren.

"Shh. It's all right," she said. "You don't want to wake John and Olivia, do you?"

Lauren was too upset to lower her voice. "No, Michael's going to take my children away from me. I know it. Look at what he did to you and he was in love with you. What will he do to me? Michael made it clear what he thought about me." Her face was red and covered with tears. Keith could practically smell her fear. Her green eyes were filled with abject terror.

"He's changed," Keith said. He, too, went over to sit next to Lauren on the couch. Lauren was now sandwiched between him and Gina. Her body was curled over so far all he could see was red hair. Over her head, Keith gave Gina a pleading look. Only his wife would able to convince the distraught woman she had no need for concern.

Gina read his look and searched for words. Keith knew this wasn't easy for Gina to do. He reached over and took her hand and gave it a small, encouraging squeeze.

"Lauren, I wouldn't have come here with Keith if I didn't agree Michael is a different man. He's becoming the man I knew before all that madness went down between us." Gina stroked Lauren's hair. "Michael has been coming to church and Keith's been counseling him."

"Ha! I'm not buying it. I can't believe you of all people would fall for his act. I know how manipulative Michael can be. He's playing nice because he's in trouble. Once Michael gets himself out of this mess, he'll be back to his old conniving, underhanded ways."

Uh-oh. Keith saw Lauren's words take effect. Gina gave him a widened stare. She bit her lip. Doubt filled her face. Another minute and Gina would fold.

"I have the Spirit of God within me," Keith intervened. "He leads me and guides me. I can discern Michael's genuineness." He tucked Lauren gently under the chin. "Michael does play a good game, but he can't outplay God. I'm assuring you, with the authority of God on my side, God Himself placed Michael in this position to lead him home. I've been praying for Michael's salvation for years, and this is God at work."

His words took root. With trembling hands, Lauren scooped her hair out of her face and granted him her first shaky smile.

Gina stood. "Let me get you some water."

"I've never seen Michael at church." Lauren assessed him with a sharp gaze. The reporter was back. *Good,* Keith thought. He could talk to this Lauren better.

"He attended our Bible Study." He phrased his statement in a way to make it seem like Michael had been to a lot more church services. "Michael will be there again this Sabbath. I hope you'll meet with him before then."

"I knew this time would come," Lauren whispered. "But I was prepared to fight it tooth and nail." She shifted focus. "Keith, if it weren't for you and Gina, I don't know where I would've ended up. I was one of Michael's chief helpers in destroying your reputation. I couldn't believe how you both opened your doors and heart to my children and me. I'll forever be grateful."

Gina returned while Lauren was speaking. They had heard this thank-you speech countless times. "Lauren, as we've told you before, you don't have to thank me. You're family. It wasn't anything for me to lease you my home."

Lauren snorted. "One dollar a month. That's not rent, Keith. You could get at least three thousand a month for this."

Closer to five, but he would never tell Lauren that. Keith held up his hand. "Water under the bridge. I don't want to hear anything about this house."

"Imagine the irony that all the time Michael's been looking for me I've been here in your former home."

"I borrowed the idea from him," Keith said.

"I was out of my mind when he kidnapped Trey and Epiphany all those years ago," Gina said. Realizing the implications of her words, she stammered, "Kidnapped is a harsh word. I misspoke. This is different."

"I understand," Lauren said, addressing Gina. She then looked at Keith. "You don't know this but before I sought you out, I was holed up in this tiny apartment. I was heartbroken, lost, and confused. Then I started watching the tape of that awful show. I watched it over and over, replaying the part where you talked about your feelings for Gina. I thought to myself I want a man to love me like that."

He gave his wife a wink. She cut her eyes. She had not forgiven him for Michael's invasion into their home, into their life.

"Anyways, I started watching your show, *Second Chances,* and I fell in love with God."

Keith nodded. His mother had met the Lord through his show too. How he missed her! "I'm awed at how He chose to use me," Keith shared.

"If God can change me," Lauren said, "I believe Michael deserves the same chance to meet Him. I can't believe I'm

saying these words. Keith Ward, you have been gifted with the power of persuasion." She took a deep breath. "I'm ready. Tell him where I am. Tell him it's time he met his children."

Keith and Gina held hands and prayed with Lauren. By the time they left Lauren's home, the temperature had fallen well below thirty degrees. On the drive home, Gina rejoiced. "Hallelujah. God is amazing!"

"I was wondering how you held it for so long." Keith grinned. "I could see the praise bubbling up inside you."

"Lauren's right, you know. You do have a gifted tongue."

The man in him rose up. Keith's voice dropped. "I'll show you what I can do with it later," he promised, cracking up at her openmouthed expression.

"How can you switch from praising God so fast? One minute you're praising. The next you're saying kinky stuff." She squirmed.

"You like it when I do," he teased.

She folded her arms. "I'm still mad at you."

Keith drummed the steering wheel. He would let that comment slide. "I prayed for an hour this morning for God to soften Lauren's heart." Gina's too, but he kept that to himself. He lifted a hand off the wheel and pumped it in the air. "Lord, you're good! You're better than good!"

"Watch the road and don't go off speaking in tongues like you did before," Gina cautioned. She fiddled with her scarf. "Talking about Jesus take the wheel while I'm screaming for my life."

Keith cracked up. "I wasn't that far gone, Gina," he said, holding back his praise. "But wherever I am, I'm going to praise God when my spirit bids."

"Well let your spirit bid you when we're at home."

How he loved this woman! Keith reached over to kiss Gina on the cheek.

"Listen, will you keep your eye on the road?"

"Gina, who you fooling? You know you like it. I can't hold my praise. This is the modern-day version of the prodigal son returning home. But, unlike that older brother, I'm not jealous. I'm ready to throw a party." He gave a little dance by moving his shoulders up and down.

"Did you forget the court case? Hold on to your rejoicing for now."

He knew Gina was trying to keep him from getting his hopes up too high, but Keith was a preaching man and he was fired up. "You must not know my God like I do. Tell me, when did the Jericho wall come down?"

"You know when."

He slanted a quick glance her way. She rolled her eyes. Keith would not be deterred. "I'm going to start praising because the wall is coming down, Gina. Mark my words. It's coming down!"

Chapter Twenty-four

Three minutes passed.

Three whole minutes.

Michael stood transfixed in the doorway of Keith's former home in Jamaica Estates and, still, he could not get his fill.

He released short, staccato breaths. His heartbeat pounded in his ears. Yet, he stared. Lauren had addressed him at least four times, but he had not spoken a single word.

The tears rolling unheeded, streaking his face and chin, provided a clue as to the magnitude of emotions he felt. Then he cracked, bending slowly to his knees. With both hands to the floor, Michael lowered his head and uttered his first words: "Thank God."

Lauren zapped into motion and closed the front door. He registered the click of her heels and her rapid movement before she dangled tissues in his face.

"Thank you." He wiped his face.

"Can I get you a cup of coffee?" she offered.

Michael rubbed his hands. "Thank you. It's brick cold out there. With these temps, we might get snow before Thanksgiving. Coffee would warm me up."

Lauren went to fetch two steaming mugs of coffee. When she returned, Michael stood to relieve her of one.

"Come," she commanded and led him into Keith's—no, her—living area. Michael surveyed the room while he gathered his wits. She had changed it up a bit. He liked it.

He wiped his face and neck. Feeling warm from nervous sweat, he removed his jacket and slinked onto the couch. "I've waited for this day for years. I prayed, I hoped. But I never thought it would happen. I searched for you everywhere. Not once would I imagine you would be in Keith's old home."

"Seems fitting doesn't it?" Lauren returned testily. Though her voice held spirit, she did not stop moving her hands: a sure sign she was nervous.

Michael understood what Lauren meant by those words. He'd "hidden" Gina's children in their former home. What a payback. "Touché," he said, with a slight nod. While he spoke, he listened for the sound of little feet. He bit his tongue to keep from asking for the children.

Surely, she hadn't left two-year-olds unattended for this long? Michael's heart thumped with worry. He knew Lauren was prickly and didn't want to scare her off by demanding to see the twins. *Patience. Lord. I need it now.*

"I . . ." Lauren cleared her throat, and began again. "I know you want to see the children, but I want you to promise me you're not going to try to take them from me. I'm stepping out on faith here because after the way you threw me out—"

"I'm sorry," Michael interrupted. He read the pensive look on her face, and repeated, "I'm truly sorry."

Lauren's shoulders heaved with tears. "Good. Because I'm tired of running, of hiding, of wondering if today will be the day the monster takes my kids from me."

Monster? Michael's heart slammed into his chest. Who said words didn't hurt? "Monster?"

She quickly reframed her words. "Sorry, in my mind you were the Big Bad Wolf . . ." Lauren trailed off. She must have realized calling him a wolf didn't sound much better.

Michael grimaced. He deserved it. He had been a monster, a wolf seeking to devour any who stood in his path. "Lauren, you're right. A few months ago, I probably would've swooped in and who knows? I can't say for sure what I would've done, but I can speak for now. I'm a changed man. God is changing me." He looked at his watch. He did not want to make small talk. He did not want to drink coffee. He wanted to see his children.

"I want you in John's and Olivia's lives. I haven't told them you were coming. I figure you could meet them, and we'd play it by ear. I debated if I should tell them, but . . . this is new to me. I don't know the protocol of saying, 'kids, here's your daddy who's been missing for two years of your lives.' Luckily, they're too young to know any better." With a shaky breath, and a decisive pat on her flower-print skirt, Lauren jumped to her feet. "Come, meet your children."

Taking deep breaths, Michael struggled to walk slowly behind her. He wiped his sweaty palms on his pants, before allowing them to dangle by his side. His body shook. The walk up the flight of stairs and down the hall seemed infinite. With each step, doubt grew.

What if they didn't like him?

Once they were outside the door, Michael grabbed Lauren's hand. He could hear little voices. Happy voices. "Wait," he frantically whispered. "I . . ."

She looked at him with warmth in her eyes. "You'll be all right. They're children who want to be loved. Can you do that?"

Could he? Could he open his heart and love again? Let people inside knowing there was the possibility of feeling pain and rejection? He exhaled. "Yes, I can."

"Okay, then." After a firm nod, Lauren opened the door.

"Mommy!"

"Look, Mommy!"

Rooted by the entrance of their playroom, Michael froze. His body was statue still, but his eyes scanned the two children in their playpens. He saw two sets of watery mouths, gapped teeth, lopsided grins and fell in love. They were perfect—perfect miniatures of a blend of his and Lauren's best traits.

"Hey, babies! Let Mommy see what you're doing." Lauren rushed to take them out of confinement. She dropped to her knees and started playing with the children.

Lauren waved him over. Michael bent on all fours and crawled on the toy-filled floor, trying to remember when he used to play with Trey. So far, he was drawing a blank. As he drew closer into their space, the twins took notice of him and huddled into their mother. He saw Olivia's chin quiver and John's eyes widen. Within seconds, both of them were pointing and wailing.

Michael stopped moving. Unsure. He had commandeered million dollar deals with finesse but here he was out of his element. In that moment, he felt what Keith must have gone through with Epiphany. He had kept her from Keith on purpose. Lauren was right. He was a monster. Crushing thoughts whirled around his head. He might be the worst thing to happen to these children.

"Hush, now," Lauren cooed. She kissed them both on their cheeks and tickled their tummies. Grabbing a toy, she distracted them by pulling it so the music could play. Then, in an excited voice, she said, "John, Olivia, I'd like you to meet your daddy. Daddy's here. Daddy's going to read you your favorite story."

"Daddy." John tilted his head to look at Michael. John's facial expression mirrored his. It caught Michael off guard.

"Yes, that's Daddy." Lauren crooked her finger at him. Michael followed her cue to join his family.

"Daddy?" Olivia said, batting long lashes at him. She was going to be a heartbreaker. Fatherly pride rose within him.

"Get the *I'll Love You, Forever* book off the rocking chair," Lauren said.

Michael quickly complied. It took him a minute to realize she intended for him to read the story. He drew a breath and opened the book. He had just finished reading the first line when he felt a thump on his leg.

Olivia and John sat on his leg with expectant grins. He scooped them into his lap and waited. No cries. He relaxed. *Thank you, Lord.*

Lauren shuffled closer like a mother hen guarding her chicks. Even though he wanted to howl with joy, Michael began to read. He read the story three times. By the end of the story, he had cramped legs, slobber on his cheek, and several popped buttons; but he was in heaven.

He had a slight kink in his neck and his back protested from his crouched position, but Michael had no complaints. He had loved spending this time with his children. An hour had passed. On leaden feet, he trudged down the stairs. He had helped Lauren get the twins settled into bed and now faced the dreaded moment.

"I wish I didn't have to go," he said.

Lauren nodded, but didn't say anything.

"If the court agrees, may I move in here?"

Lauren stepped back. "Move in? Michael, that's crazy and too fast. You need to slow down."

Slow down? Slow down? After all these years, he had plenty of time he needed to make up for. Michael asked God for patience, again. "It was a stupid question. I don't know if you're even seeing anyone or anything. I shouldn't have asked," he conceded, already counting the hours until he could return.

"I'll see you at Thanksgiving," Lauren said. "We'll work something out."

Next Thursday. Thanksgiving was next Thursday. She was talking about waiting a whole week. Michael sighed. What choice did he have? "All right. How about I come for an hour tomorrow?" he asked. It was worth a try. He missed John and Olivia already. A vision of two little bottoms perched in the air had been impressed upon his heart.

"One hour."

"Do you need help feeding them breakfast?"

"No, I've been managing fine on my own all this time. I think I'll be just fine." Lauren came to him. "Michael, your children will be here. You'll be in their lives forever, but you have a serious court case and I still want to protect them as much as I can. If it were to get out you had children, reporters would be camped outside my door. I don't want Olivia's and John's faces plastered all over national television. The press would eat this up and sensationalize it. As a former reporter, I know, because I would do the same thing."

"You're right." Michael bunched his fists. This case was ruining his life. He wondered if it was time he took matters into his own hands. "I didn't do it, Lauren. I didn't hurt Mindy."

She tossed her hair back. "I know. If I thought you were a rapist, you wouldn't be anywhere near my children."

"Our children," he corrected.

"Right. One hour. Eleven good?"

She had gone all businesslike on him. Michael wondered if Lauren harbored any feelings for him or if he had crushed them to pieces. He knew though, this was not the time to ask. *Small steps,* he told himself as he departed.

But, as he drove away from his family, he vowed to do all he could to get this thing with Mindy handled. Michael pressed the Bluetooth to activate his cell phone. It was time to give Frank a call.

Chapter Twenty-five

"She cuts herself."

"On a scale of one to ten, Daniel, how certain are you about the pictures?"

"In my professional opinion? Eleven," Dr. Daniel Northman replied. "I'm certain." He flipped through several frames where he'd zoned in on cut marks on Mindy's inner thighs.

"I knew it." Keith pumped his fists. This was his first break in Michael's case. It was worth leaving his house during the first snowfall of the year. Mindy was unstable and, from the look of things, she was one unhappy girl. "Can I get a forensics psychologist to speak to her and gauge her mental state?" Keith asked.

"I imagine her father will fight, but even he can't override a subpoena. She's most likely seeing someone already. Start there. I'll be happy to see her myself."

Keith gathered his files and shook Daniel's hand. "I appreciate your offer. How was Argentina?"

"Beautiful. The country and the women," Daniel answered with a smile.

Keith gave a noncommittal reply. He knew the doctor considered himself a ladies' man. From the pictures on Daniel's desk, Keith guessed the women agreed. He did not care about the doctor's personal life. His professional reputation as an expert was unparalleled. Daniel's exorbitant fee was well worth his testimony. Dr. Northman never swayed in a cross-examination.

"I'll be in touch," Keith said. He dug into his briefcase and retrieved a small card. He slid it across Daniel's desk. "That's the address to my church again. In case you've lost the other one. You're welcome anytime."

"One of these days."

Keith nodded. He had heard that one too many times to count. He left the office and entered his car. He called Gina to let her know she had the evening off. He was going to pick Trey and Epiphany up from their respective schools and take them to play laser tag. He had been promising to take them. Well, today was the day.

But, first, he would pop over to see Bishop Combs. His former mentor had been avoiding him. Bishop Combs had not delivered the first payment. Natalie threatened to alert the board. Keith held her off. He wanted the chance to confront Combs. No time like the present.

Keith didn't bother to call ahead. He drove to Hamlet Estates in St. James. He pressed the codes that would let him into the gated community. Within minutes, he pulled to a stop outside the bishop's five-bedroom home. He didn't see any cars parked outside.

Keith's shoes crunched in the snow. He walked up to the front door and rang the doorbell. No one answered. That was odd. He knew Suzette did not work.

Keith called Natalie. He could see his breath in the cold air. "Natalie, where is the Bishop's spare? I know the alarm code."

"He ran!" Natalie shrieked once she had told him where to locate the key. "I can't believe he would take off!"

"Let's not make any rash proclamations," Keith said. "I'll call you back." He opened the door. The alarm chirped and Keith entered the code. Then he looked around. At first glance, everything looked in its place. But, it felt empty.

He walked toward the winding staircase. "Bishop!" he called.

Keith made his way up the winding staircase. As he did, he remembered the housewarming party. Members invited had been impressed. Some whispered in wonderment. They wondered how Bishop Combs had afforded this $2 million home.

Keith gulped. He knew.

He called the bishop's phone again. No answer. He left an urgent message.

He knew what he would find but ventured into the master bedroom anyway. The entire room was in disarray. He pictured frantic packing. Clothes and shoes were tossed without regard. Keith's head hung in disappointment.

There was no disputing the fact that Bishop and Suzette had run. There was no avoiding the aftermath of their decision.

His cell phone vibrated. He knew it was Natalie.

He heard the pain in his own voice. "He's not here."

Natalie's huge sigh came through the line. "I'll call the board. We'll meet after Thanksgiving. You tell your wife."

Dread filled him. Keith did not relish that upcoming conversation. Things between him and Gina were already tense because of Michael's case. This would further exacerbate things. But there was no avoiding it.

He would wait until after the holidays. Then he would tell her.

Chapter Twenty-six

"Trey, stop making both twins and your sister run up and down the stairs! This isn't a playground."

The clamor of feet continued despite Gina's call.

"I've got them," Keith said, eyeing her haggard expression. There were enough children in their home to fill a classroom: Colleen's twin daughters, Kim and Kaye, Michael's children, and their own made for a lively group of kids. All were there to join in the scrumptious Thanksgiving feast Josie had prepared before leaving for Jamaica to spend time with her family. Keith, however, had overseen the turkey preparation himself.

"You think Trey would be the example; instead he's the ring leader." Gina shook her head and called out again. "Trey!"

Her strong voice rang in his ears. He knew he had to intervene. "I'll take them outside." He bent to give Gina a kiss on the cheek.

"Listen, don't go starting something you can't finish." Gina shook her finger at him. Before heading into the kitchen, she said, "Have fun. I'm going to hang with the grownups."

"Go, I'll have more fun with the children," Keith returned. He stood by the stairs. "I'm going outside, who's coming?" he yelled.

Sure enough, he heard their "Yay's!" and the dash to find shoes, socks, and winter gear.

As they were going through the door, Michael approached.

"You're right on time," Keith said. "Help me herd the kids to the backyard."

"What are they cattle?" Michael asked.

Keith arched an eyebrow. "You don't want me to answer that."

Keith's backyard consisted of a pond and a huge play area decked out with every sort of amusement. It boasted a tree house, jungle gym, seesaw, and a safety mat. It was a kid-friendly hazard-free zone.

Keith noticed Michael's eyes were pinned to Olivia and John. "I'm glad you're going to be in their lives."

Michael breathed, "There's no feeling like this. I'm not sure I can even put it into words."

"I know. I felt that way the moment I knew I was Trey's father. It took every ounce of willpower I had within me to walk away and leave him with you." Keith swallowed at the memories, but shoved them into the past. There was too much love in the world. He refused to harbor bitterness. He continued, "Then when I saw Epiphany, my heart literally expanded in my chest. I was afraid it was going to burst from pride. How did I bring such a precious little girl into the world?"

Keith turned slightly to face Michael, surprised to see small water pools forming in his brother's eyes.

"I'm sorry."

Keith tried to shrug it off. "It's in the past," he assured Michael.

"No, I need to acknowledge my dirt. I loved Trey because I thought he was my son and I had loved him from birth, but Epiphany . . ." Michael lowered his head with shame. "I barely acknowledged her presence. Even if they weren't my children, they were still my blood. No matter what, they were family. Innocent. I shouldn't have involved them."

Keith listened to Michael's impassioned speech. "I accept your apology because I love you. I forgave you years ago, but it feels good to hear you say the words and own up to your wrongs. I respect that." He shifted the conversation. "Since we're going down memory lane, I want to take this moment to say I'm sorry for breaking the man code; no, make that the brother code. I betrayed you by sleeping with Gina. It was wrong to do. I won't try to make any excuses. The only explanation I can give is I was bound by a love bigger than me. I loved her almost from the moment I saw her."

Michael nodded. "Yes, Gina is a special woman. It took me years to accept and admit you two were meant for each other. When I found out about the affair, I was hurt. I wondered what I could've done to make her love me. But now that I think about it, most of my hurt stemmed from the fact our bond as brothers had been damaged."

Keith gulped. "That guilt rode me for years, but it led me on the path to salvation. If I hadn't been such a lost soul, I wouldn't have met Christ. I prayed for years for God to open up a way to heal the past and repair our relationship. Today is answered prayer." He patted Michael on the back. "God's going to see you through this court case and He'll raise you higher than you were before. His Word says if we wait on the Lord, He'll renew our strength and we'll mount up on wings like eagles. Michael, you're low now, but you're going to soar. You're going to be back on top again, even higher than before."

"Funny you should say that . . ."

Before he could continue, Gina, Colleen, and Lauren walked up. "We're here to relieve you," Gina said. "Terence is inside waiting on you guys to start up the Monopoly game."

Keith nudged Michael on the arm. "He doesn't know who he's up against. Right, Mike?"

Michael laughed and cracked his fingers in anticipation. "It's been awhile." The brothers began the small trek back to the house.

As soon as they were out of earshot from the women, Keith returned to the subject at hand. "What were you saying?"

"I was going to say your comment, about my going to be back on top again one day, reminded me of when you brought up Joseph from the Bible. I remember Verona said Joseph went from prison to second-in-command over the entire land of Egypt."

The brothers dusted off their shoes by the back door and entered the kitchen.

"Hearing Joseph's story gives me hope," Michael said.

"The Bible says without hope, we'd be men most miserable."

Michael studied him. "You're always preaching."

"It's not a button I can turn off," he defended. Was he always preaching?

"I'm glad," his brother said. "I like the new, inspiring you and your messages are on point. I never imagined when we were growing up this was where you'd be. But, if ministry is a suit, it fits you well."

Keith was moved by the compliment. "Thank you. Coming to God was like coming home."

"About time you both got here," Terence Hayworth interjected. "I'm ready to show you who's boss." He cracked his knuckles as a means of playful intimidation.

Keith grinned at Michael's fierce expression. His brother's competitive nature had led to many overturned boards and scattered game pieces. Terence had met his match. Within minutes, all three men were embroiled in the game.

On Keith's third trip to baste the turkey, Terence and Michael eliminated him from the game. Keith shrugged.

He prepared both the adults' and children's tables with festive trimmings. If asked, he would not be able to put into words the fullness of his heart seeing everyone gathered together. His family.

When it was dinnertime, Keith had everyone hold hands as he led them in grace. "Father, we thank you for friends and family. We ask you to bless the food spread before us and we remember those who are alone and in need. Bless them as well today, as we partake with grateful hearts. Amen."

Chapter Twenty-seven

"You've been dumped. Admit it."

Verona toyed with her fancy takeout. It was an upscale spin on the traditional Thanksgiving meal. She hissed her teeth at Nigel. "Shut up. I agreed to share a meal but I won't be put through an inquisition."

"It's not easy getting tossed like a rotten tomato," Nigel teased.

She dropped her fork. "Why don't we address the fact that you're scared to face your family with the truth about your sexuality?"

Nigel glared. "Why do you always do that? Why do you always fight back with a taunt about something I've tried to fight all my life? You think it's easy for me to spend Thanksgiving away from my family because I don't want to fence questions about why I don't have children, why I'm not married?"

Seeing his hurt, Verona felt a little ashamed. "Then why don't you tell the truth? It sets you free."

"How can I tell the truth when I myself am living in denial? I keep thinking I'm going to shuck this feeling and get back to what I've been taught all my life."

Why was he looking at her as if he thought she could provide guidance? Verona broke eye contact by reaching for a sip of water. "This is getting too serious for me."

Nigel leaned over and touched her knee. "No, we're not going to avoid this anymore. Verona, I know you've been angry with me for years. Heck, I was just as angry at you, and it's time we dealt with it."

She squirmed under the heat of Nigel's gaze and his firm tone. She did not want to go there, but she was curious about something. "Come to think of it, I do want to know why you've been mad at me. I know my reason for being mad at you, but you had no right to . . ."

"Be furious?" he filled in.

Verona nodded her head. Her heartbeat accelerated. She took another sip of water.

Nigel slammed his fist on the table. "I was mad at you because you were supposed to fix me, to change me. I mean look at you," he said, waving his hands at her. "You're a beautiful, desirable woman. There isn't a male alive who wouldn't want you."

There are two, she thought. Him and Michael. Why was it that the ones she wanted were not available? Was she doing that on purpose?

"I did want you, Tiger," he confessed, using her pet name. "I wanted you; but, I was overcome with a temptation bigger than me. I look at Donnie McClurkin's testimony and I have hope. Frankly, I thought you were my cure. I was mad when you weren't."

Her eyebrows shot up to her forehead. "That's where you went wrong. I can't be your cure. The only One who can cure you, so to speak, is God."

Nigel's sardonic grin returned. "I think God and I have reached an understanding. I'm prepared to meet my judgment."

The air tightened. Verona chose the easy way out. She stuffed her mouth with food to keep from talking. Nigel took that as a sign to return to his meal. The scraping sounds of metal hitting crockery made her grit her teeth. She should say something. As the silence grew, Verona grappled with her conflicting emotions.

In the end, she decided to speak what she knew. "Nigel, I care about you. We're friends, I think. I won't lie and say

I agree or understand your choice but you know the Bible. It's up to you to search the scriptures for the truth."

He gave her a piercing look. Verona read the yearning in his eyes. He whispered, "Let me try. Give me a chance." He reached for a tendril of her hair and rolled it around his index finger. His hypnotic voice urged her, "In many ways, I'm your equal. We had something once. We can have it again. You get the husband and children you want, and I'll get a respectable wife to take home."

Nigel was persuasive. Verona would give him that. But she was neither crazy nor desperate. "Aren't you forgetting about your partner? What would you tell him?" she asked.

His eyes slinked away from hers.

"That's what I thought," she said. "Case closed."

Nigel sneered, "Well, it's a more lucrative option than you pining for a man who doesn't know you exist."

Verona jumped to her feet. "Better that than to be used as a substitute."

"Why are you just telling me about Bishop Combs? He could be in Timbuktu by now," Gina fumed.

"I didn't want to ruin the holidays. All this drama with Michael kind of took preeminence."

"We have to alert the board." She glared at him. "You need to set your priorities right. I know Michael needs you but so does the foundation. A foundation we set up in Trey's name."

"I already called a meeting. We have to notify the federal investigators. It's going to hit the news."

Gina's body slumped. "The foundation might not recover."

He did not like how dejected she sounded. Quick to reassure her, Keith said, "It'll work out somehow. We will get through this. Together. I know Michael's case is time consuming, but my priorities are still in order."

"They'd better be. The foundation needs you. I need you. Your children need you." She lowered her voice. "If it came down to it, I need to know you'd choose us."

"Over my brother?"

Her neck rolled. Gina dared him. "If need be."

"It won't come to that," Keith said. Once he had uttered the words though, he faced doubts. Fortunately, he was a praying man. Keith slid to his knees. If there was ever a time he needed God, this was it.

Chapter Twenty-eight

"I'm seeing someone."

Lauren's bombshell punched him in the stomach. Michael twisted his cap in his hands. Then a thought struck. "Has he been around my children?"

With wide eyes, Lauren answered, "No, he hasn't. It's too soon." She clutched her chest into a protective gesture like she was hugging John or Olivia. The twins were spending the night with Keith and Gina. Michael had jumped at the chance of accompanying her home. Well, he had followed her.

Michael nodded in agreement. He stood outside her front door, ignoring his red-tinged ears, which stung from the cold and wind. Lauren shivered and stepped back, before inviting him inside. He closed the door behind him with a thud. Sort of the way his dreams of a reunion with Lauren were ending. But, Michael had never been a man to give up easy.

"You loved me once. You can do it again. I'm ready."

Her green eyes flashed. "Where do you get off thinking all you have to do is to come back into my life, wave your hands, give me an okay sign, and I'd fall back into your arms?"

When she put it like that . . . "I never imagined you'd have moved on," Michael said. "Not once, not even when you faked your death. Good one, by the way, but I didn't buy it. Not even when you skirted all my attempts to make reparation for my rotten behavior, I didn't consider you wouldn't be waiting for me, waiting for me to get my act together." It took a lot for Michael to admit that. However, his words were not leading to the desired effect.

"Is this the part where I swoon and confess my undying love for you? As if!" Lauren swiveled and stormed into the direction of the dining area. Her heels click-clacked on the shiny wooden floor as she walked away from him.

Michael tossed off his jacket as the heat crept under his cashmere sweater. Feeling like a chump, he said, "I didn't expect you to be . . . Well, I hoped . . ." He stopped, clearing his throat. Maybe it was time he shut up.

"I've got to get out of these shoes," Lauren said, and headed up the stairs, presumably to change.

At least she hadn't kicked him out, yet. Michael sank into one of the chairs and rested his head in his hands. He had sacrificed a lot to have everything life had to offer at his fingertips. Now, he was losing it all. He wished it hadn't taken such drastic circumstances for him to see what truly mattered: family and the love of a good woman. Michael had one out of two, but he wanted more. Seeing Keith with Gina and Terence with Colleen had created a hunger for him to have a woman by his side.

Lauren would be perfect since she already had his children.

"I thought you'd left."

Michael looked at his watch. He had been sitting there for twenty minutes. He sprang to his feet. "I didn't realize . . ."

"His name is Martin. Martin Weston. He's a wonderful uncomplicated guy and he's financially stable," Lauren offered.

Michael yawned. He wasn't impressed. Hope flared. He'd be able to swat this guy out of her life. "He sounds safe and boring."

Michael made a mental note. He was going to get Frank running that name as soon as he left. Michael would find out everything he needed to know about this Martin Weston: his competition and potential daddy replacement.

Lauren's sharp intake of breath was followed with, "Martin's what I need. I'm a mother and a Christian. I don't have time to run after self-absorbed millionaires."

Okay, he deserved that. Michael strutted close into Lauren's space. Her eyes widened with apprehension. Good; he liked that reaction. She was not as unaware or unmoved by him as she projected. Michael's confidence rose and he reached over to curl a strand of her red hair around his index finger with slow, practiced precision.

"Say what you will, Lauren Goodman, but I know you. You could never settle for safe or boring. You need more." With a quick move, he snaked his arm around her small waist and dragged her against his chest. Lauren let out a startled sigh that did things to his insides. He kept his gaze pinned to hers as he kissed the lock of hair still wrapped around his finger. Desire sprung to life in her eyes.

Her eyes said one thing, but her mouth opened and said another. "I won't try to deny I'm still attracted to you. That may never change, but my response is something I can control. I'm not going down that road with you, Michael Ward. Not now, not ever." She patted his cheek before pushing herself out of his arms. "Besides, you can't expect me to believe you've been living like a monk, pining away for me these past few years. Please."

Her words taunted him. An image of Verona flashed across his mind. Michael had had brief affairs, but they had been inconsequential. He had kissed Verona, but it was a little kiss. No harm done. Nevertheless, Michael knew it was time to stand down. For now. Tomorrow was another day. He bid Lauren good night and strode toward the door.

Her voice stopped him. "I'll testify for you!"

He executed a slow about turn.

Lauren sauntered over to him. "You're the father of my children and, for them, I'll do what I can to help."

Michael had a quick flash of years ago. He had grabbed Lauren so hard he bruised her. If anything, she would make a good witness for the defense. Michael was surprised she would be willing to take the stand for him. Michael shook his head. "I don't get you, Lauren. In one breath, you reject me and in the next, you want to help me. I can't figure you out."

"Then, don't try to," she said. "All you need to know is I'll do what I can to help you. I've been reading my Bible and praying and I'm at a good place. I'm happy and I want the same for you. It just won't be with me."

"I'll respect your wishes." Michael's lie rolled off his tongue with ease. He had no intention of letting Lauren slip through his fingers. He did not want another man raising his children. He would have it all. But, first he had to take care of his tarnished name and rebuild his torn reputation.

Michael turned on the car and rubbed his hands to warm up. He stopped at looked at both of his hands. It was time he took matters in his own hands. It was time for this rape charge to go away.

Chapter Twenty-nine

I'm going nuts. Verona paced her apartment. She was seeing Michael everywhere. It was her living space but she could not be in a room without having a flashback of his being there.

She opened the freezer and eyed the container of ice cream. *Nope, not doing it.* With a bang, Verona closed the door. She returned to thinking about Michael. She had waited too long to tell him about Lauren.

She groaned. Michael was with Lauren now.

Verona stomped into her bedroom, the only place Michael had not been, and plunked onto her bed. She was dressed in her nightclothes. It was the day after Thanksgiving. Six long days had passed and not a word. Before that, every day Michael called or texted almost on the hour. She pulled out her phone from her pajama pants.

It's charged. She tested the volume. It was turned up.

She threw the phone on the pillow and turned on the television. Verona hated how she was driving herself stir crazy but her insides were all mushy, bumbling, and confusing. She had called. She had texted. But no response.

In a weak moment, Verona dialed Keith but he wasn't of any use. He'd only said they would meet the Monday after Thanksgiving to continue their work on the case.

Normally, she would have stormed Michael's penthouse but she was afraid. Afraid to see him and Lauren all googly-eyed and lovey-dovey while she was in torment. She swung her arms in the air and shouted, "I hate love!"

Verona sniffed. She needed a shower, pronto.

She stripped and entered her walk-in shower. Welcoming the force of the heated water beating on her skin, Verona decompressed. It was not long before the tears came. The longer the water flowed, the more she cried.

Spent, Verona hunched over in the shower stall. She had not cried like this since her parents' betrayal. She squelched those thoughts. She was not about to take that trip.

Verona stepped out of the stall and wrapped herself in a huge robe. An engraved robe Michael had bought her during their business trip to Florida. He had been searching out property for his resort and she complained the towels in the hotel room felt like sandpaper. *Ugh!*

She donned her pink silk pajamas and dived under her sheets. Within seconds, she was toasty warm. Like an addict, Verona checked her phone. No message. She resisted the urge to squeeze her fists and kick her feet. Tantrums were for girls not grown women. "You know what, I'm done with that jerk. Michael Ward can go sit down somewhere with his oversized ego and his bald head." Well, she liked his bald head, his smile, his body . . .

Whatever! She was through. No more mooning over a man who did not even care enough to return her calls. Here she was home on a Friday night when she could have been out at the club meeting some hot guy with a hot car and a hot place. Wait, she should rephrase. She sounded too much like a teenager. She could be at a ritzy spa wrapped up with a successful businessman who had surprised her with a trip to Milan or Brazil.

Caught up in her dream, Verona snuggled deeper under the covers. With a yawn, she vowed, *come morning, Michael will be out of my system.*

Sunlight came and found herself dressed and on her way to Keith's church. As she put the finishing touches on her makeup and dabbed her lips with lip gloss, Verona told herself she was going to hear the Word. It had nothing to do with Michael.

She made it in time for praise and worship. Verona lifted her hands and clapped along with the rest of the congregation. Some of the songs came back to her and she didn't need to use the overhead, which tracked the words. If Michael invaded her thoughts, she sang him out.

Her soprano caught the attention of a few people in the pews. They started egging her on: "Sing it, sister," "All right now," and "Give God your praise," which made her sing even louder. Verona had forgotten how much joy singing had been. It had also been a part of one of the saddest times in her life, but she would not dwell on that. She kept on singing as they transitioned into a worship song.

With her eyes on the screen, Verona sang along to *"I give myself away."* The words pierced her heart and she looked up toward heaven as she talked to God through song. The lyrics seemed written for her. She closed her eyes allowing them to sink into her being. Verona didn't care about the tears streaming down her cheeks, wetting her silk blouse. She needed to give herself away to God. She'd been gone too long. Someone pushed a tissue in her hand. She nodded but she kept her eyes closed. She stayed like that until she heard Keith's voice.

Verona wiped her face and slinked into her seat, feeling a little self-conscious, but she was not sorry.

"We all know the story of Esther very well," Keith began.

Several heads nodded in agreement. While familiar with Esther's story, Verona needed a refresher course.

Verona scanned Keith's black suit, burgundy shirt, and coordinated tie. Keith Ward was well put together.

Though she had promised herself not to, Verona roamed the aisles in search of Michael. She spotted him in the third row with a notebook on his lap and pen in hand. Dressed in a charcoal gray suit with a yellow shirt, he looked good. *Real good.*

It took some effort, but Verona brought her mind back to Keith's words.

"The book of Esther is the only book in the Bible that doesn't actually mention the name of God. However, Esther represents a type of Christ. She was willing to sacrifice herself for her people. She risked her life to save theirs."

Verona's spine straightened. She liked the sound of a woman willing to take matters into her own hands.

Keith continued. "There are times when we need someone to stand in the gap for us. Helpless, the Jews needed someone to stand up for them and Esther became that person. My question today is, are you willing to stand in the gap for someone?"

She looked around, amazed at the hands that shot up. She could not resist the unladylike snort. *Yeah, right. Easier said than done.* Memories of her parents rose. She had not seen them in thirteen years. Not since they had turned their backs on her when she needed them most. Bitterness filled her being. She swallowed in an attempt to still the past. But, it would not be held back.

"I see all those hands, and I'm impressed." Keith moved away from the podium and ventured close to the edge of the stage. "I wonder how many hands would stay up if I were to put you to the test right now. The Apostle Peter was confident in his ability. He swore to Jesus he would stand by Him. But when it came down to it, Peter faltered and denied he even knew Christ. He was more concerned with what people thought than with what Jesus would do."

Verona stifled her chuckle when she noticed the slight
bending of the elbows. A few lowered their heads in
shame. *Preach!* she screamed on the inside, knowing
from experience the truth he spoke. *If only the good Pastor and First Lady Stachs were here to hear this Word.*
Verona scrunched her nose. She hadn't thought about
them in ages. Why were they now invading her thoughts?

Oh, she was going to pretend not to see him. Michael
touched his chin. He supposed he deserved it after ignoring her calls all week. He studied Verona from under
hooded lashes, taking in the frilly white shirt tucked into
her thin pencil skirt, revealing a tiny waist. *Those red
pumps should be filed under "too hot for church."*

Keith had made an altar call and Verona had taken
the trek with about twenty others to the altar. Michael,
however, had remained rooted in his seat. His bottom
burned as he fought the pull to follow them, drop on his
knees, and confess all.

He adjusted his tie. He was not ready for the public
display. He would speak to God another time. Besides,
he needed to stay under God's radar for the moment, he
thought, remembering the directions he had given Frank.

Once the benediction was pronounced, Michael jumped
to his feet, intent on finding Verona. He saw her making
her way toward the rear and pressed forward. "Verona!" he
finally called out to snag her attention.

Her barely restrained curls swung across her face as
she whipped around to see who had called her name.
When Verona's eyes met his, Michael registered her stiff
spine and the renewed determination to exit the building.
Michael spurred into action.

She was by her car when he caught up to her. He
grasped her arm. "Why didn't you answer me?"

Verona tucked her chin and gave him the evil eye. "Why do you think?"

"All right, Tiger. No need to snap off at me."

"All week I wait to hear from you and you shrug me off without a word. I drop the news of Lauren being alive and suddenly I'm persona non grata." She pummeled him with her bag before slinking against her car.

Michael eyed her poked-out lips. His Tiger was in a funk. Well, she wasn't his Tiger, per se. Crooking a finger under her chin, Michael moved into her personal space. "Verona, this week wasn't about you. It was about me reconnecting with family. I spent these past few days getting reacquainted with my brother and Gina." The tears spiking her lashes caught him off guard.

Verona voice trembled. "Oh, I thought you were with Lauren, or something. I didn't know what to think."

Michael noticed the lot had cleared out considerably. He needed to move this conversation elsewhere. "Feel like driving me home?" he asked. "I came to church with Keith and Gina this morning. I'll leave my car at their house and take a cab over to get it at some point." Michael was unconcerned about his ride. He had several vehicles at his disposal. Right now, he wanted to mend fences with Verona. Her quick nod of the head was all the encouragement he needed.

Michael had not even tightened his seat belt before she sped off. His body hit the door. Grabbing the dashboard, he said, "Take it easy; we're not in the jungle running away from predators."

Verona did not respond but he noticed she decelerated. *Thank God.* He sent Keith a quick text letting him know he had left with Verona and would retrieve his car later. Within minutes, Verona was on the highway zipping through cars, a testament of her agitation. Once she entered the strip leading to the Triborough Bridge, Michael broke his silence. "Pull over!"

Her hands gripped the steering wheel and she faced him. Then she accelerated. Michael commanded, "Verona, pull over here. Right now!"

"Did you forget we're on a bridge? Are you crazy? I'm not pulling over."

"Do it! Do it, now!"

With skill and deft maneuvering, she complied. Michael exited the car and flung open the driver side. Heedless to the traffic zooming by, he pulled her out of the car.

"I wasn't driving reckless," Verona said, while he dragged her to the rail. Her head bobbed as she matched his longer strides with her ridiculously high heels. Michael did not care.

"You do realize we're on a bridge and it's almost December?" She shivered and rubbed her hands. "I left my gloves in the car."

Michael was not bothered by the cold. He pointed across the bridge to the other side. "There. Look right there." He glanced at Verona. She was looking at him as if he were a madman. He drew in a deep breath. "I almost lost my life right there at that spot, years ago. I wanted you to see it. I could've died, but God spared me. For some reason unknown to me at times, He thinks I'm worth living."

Her body went limp and her mouth hung open. "I . . . I had no idea."

"I was in a coma for a few days. I don't know maybe God was trying to knock some sense into me," he joked. His joke fell flat.

Verona had tears in her eyes. She appeared to grapple with some emotion before reaching over to hug him tight. As her body molded to his, he felt . . . loved. His heart stopped for a second.

He had no idea how long they maintained that position but Michael had to break contact. He was feeling things he was not ready to feel. Suddenly, he recalled they were illegally pulled over on a windy bridge. They had to leave. Or, maybe, he needed the escape.

Verona's teeth chattered so Michael held Verona close to him to share body heat. Together, they walked toward her car and went inside. Once it was safe, she eased on to the highway. He had not expected her to be shaken. He certainly had not expected his heart to trip at her hug.

Michael tugged his chin, missing his goatee. He thought he wanted Lauren, but he couldn't help but wonder, was Verona the one? Confused, he shook his head. No, Lauren was. His thoughts swung between the two women like a pendulum. Michael acknowledged he did not have a clue.

Once Verona swooped to the curb in front of his building, Michael exited the SUV, gave her a little wave, and departed. She did not seem to be in the mood for conversation either. He entered his penthouse suite and dropped his body onto the couch to think.

When Lauren was around, he was positive. She was the mother of his children and they had history. But, so did he and Verona. Verona was . . . He smiled. Verona. As unique as her name.

A new thought interrupted his musings. A much more pressing matter. For the first time, he questioned his actions, especially with Keith preaching on depending on God. He dug for his cell phone and called Frank.

"Voicemail. Oh, no." Michael hunched over. It might be too late. He had been quite ruthless about what he wanted done. He tried again. Still no answer. This time he left a message: "Frank, if you get this message, give me a call." Not wanting to say too much, he said, "I want to make a U-turn," knowing Frank would know what that meant, if he heard the message. Within him he felt he was too late. He repeated, "Frank, a U-turn."

Once he had ended the call. Michael fell to his knees. "Lord, forgive me. What have I done?"

Chapter Thirty

"Tell me I didn't just hear that. Turn up the television!" Keith boomed. *Josie must be in the bathroom.* He'd been in the kitchen when he heard the morning news from the television in the next room. Maybe he had heard wrong. He propelled himself as fast as he could into the family room.

"Mindy Laurelton, daughter of building tycoon Bill Laurelton, and key witness in the alleged rape case against Michael Jason Ward, has been found badly beaten. She's been hospitalized at Mount Cedars hospital where she's under heavy guard. No other information has been provided, but stay tuned as we bring you up-to-date information," Roslyn Barnum, the anchor, stated.

Hunger forgotten, Keith bounded up the stairs. "Gina, you've got to listen to this," he said, turning on the bedroom light. Gina sat up in bed, blinking rapidly and wiping her eyes. He surfed to find a station featuring the news.

He watched Gina's face snap to attention. She shook her head. "Michael didn't do this. He couldn't."

Keith's shoulders sagged with relief at the surety of her words. She had voiced his fears aloud. "I hoped . . . I didn't think so, but hearing you say that . . ." Keith shifted gears and reached for his cell phone.

"I didn't do it," were Michael's first words. "I didn't hurt Mindy."

"I know. I believe you. Get Verona on the phone and the both of you get over here." Keith disconnected the call.

He noticed Gina's head bent in prayer. Keith fell to his knees and began to pray as well. He knew if he thought Michael was the perpetrator, so would Bill, the press, and everyone else. The world would think Michael was involved in Mindy's demise.

When Keith opened his eyes, he saw Gina's gaze pinned to his face. He returned her look, stare for stare. She bit her lip and broke eye contact. "What is it?" he asked.

"Nothing." Gina slid off the bed. She moved toward the bathroom to take care of her morning rituals.

Keith remained pensive until she returned. "Gina, what's on your mind?"

"I think I might know something to help your case," she said. "Or rather, I think Colleen does."

He frowned. "Colleen?"

"Yes, she told me something when we met for dinner a few weeks back. At the time, I was mad at Michael and . . ." She stopped and picked up her cell phone. Keith listened in as Gina placed a call. "Colleen, I think you need to stop over. It's about Michael's case."

Gina ended the call and looked at Keith. "She'll be here in about a half hour. She's dropping Kim and Kaye off at school."

For some reason he could not fathom, his wife looked guilty. "You wouldn't be holding out on information that could free my brother, would you?" he asked with a halfhearted grin, expecting her to laugh at his jest.

With a furtive glance his way, Gina mumbled, "You'll have to decide once Colleen gets here. I've got to take Epiphany to school. And, Trey's due for his blood work."

As a cancer survivor, Trey had to keep up with his screenings to make sure he was still in remission. Keith knew his son had been healed, but did not discourage the practical steps toward maintaining good health.

Great. She was leaving him in suspense. Before she left, Keith said, "I have to talk to you about something else later."

His wife nodded. She breezed through the door. While he waited, Keith tried the bishop's phone. This time the number was disconnected. *Bishop Combs, why?*

Keith heard the doorbell and pushed the matter from his mind. Right before Colleen's arrival, Michael and Verona barged in, bickering about something or another. Keith was too preoccupied to pay them any mind.

Colleen Hayworth settled herself onto the couch. "Mindy Laurelton has—or rather, had—a brother, Carl. He was a student of mine at the high school."

"Mindy has a brother? That's the first I'm hearing of this," Michael voiced. "Wait, what do you mean, had?"

"If you'd give her a chance to talk, maybe we'll know," Verona sniped.

What's going on with those two? Keith wondered.

Colleen turned toward Michael to answer his question. "Yes, she did. Carl was one of the most brilliant minds I've ever encountered. That's why I remember him. He was profoundly gifted. He scored a perfect score on the SAT and he was only in tenth grade."

"Wow, that's impressive," Keith said.

Colleen smiled. "Yes, tell me about it. We were all impressed, but Carl wasn't. Despite being smart and popular, Carl didn't like himself. He was depressed; and I'm no psychiatrist," she said, holding up a hand in the air, "but, I feared he was mentally ill."

"What made you think that?" Verona asked.

"I can't put it into words, but it was the look he'd get on his face at times. It gave me an eerie feeling." Colleen shuddered. "And, sometimes his papers were a bit morbid.

Carl was an amazing writer, but never pleased with his work."

"Did you ever talk with his father about your concerns?" Keith asked.

"I spoke with his mother. She was battling cancer and his father never seemed to be home." Colleen shrugged. "For a couple months after I spoke with Mrs. Laurelton, I saw a change. Carl was brighter, more upbeat. I thought I was wrong. Then, out of the blue, he committed suicide. He . . . he hung himself."

"Where was Mindy when all this was happening?" Keith probed.

"Mindy was a little girl. I remember seeing her long ponytails and her sad, round face when I went to the funeral," Colleen reminisced. "It wasn't until later I learned Mindy had been present when this happened. She was the one who found her brother hanging from the ceiling. Imagine what that would've done to a child. One who, from her mother's account, had idolized her brother."

Verona inhaled sharply.

Michael's eyes bulged. "She found him? Where was her mother?"

"Sick on the bathroom floor. Bill Laurelton was out of town."

Keith rubbed his chin. "I don't remember hearing about this at all."

"Bill Laurelton is a powerful man," Verona said. She jumped to her feet, pacing while she voiced her thoughts. "He could've kept this hush-hush."

Colleen agreed. "I only heard about it because Mrs. Laurelton blurted it out to me. She was consumed with grief at the time. I was her sounding board. She died within months of losing her son."

"But, he must've gotten Mindy help," Michael said.

Keith snapped his fingers. "I agree. Mindy must have seen a professional. She definitely would've needed help."

Michael snorted. "I bet she still does."

Keith zoned in. "Why do you say that?"

"Mindy always seemed fragile and a little unbalanced. I really hope she's okay," Michael said.

"Mental illness can be hereditary," Verona chimed in. She raced for her cell phone. "I know just the person to call. If Mindy sneezed wrong, Frank will find out. I'll go call him."

"Use the library," Keith offered.

"Michael, I heard about Mindy getting beaten. You're suspect number one," Colleen stated.

"I didn't," he ground out, with clenched fists.

Keith studied Michael's face, taking in the jutted jaw and his rapidly blinking eyes. "Well, you're the obvious culprit, since you'd have benefited the most from her . . ." He didn't want to say "death." "Demise."

"I didn't hurt her in the first place," Michael pointed out. "Regardless of anything, I wouldn't want Mindy dead."

Colleen patted Michael's arm. In a tone laced with sympathy, she took his hand in hers. "Let's pray."

Michael lowered his head and closed his eyes. Keith bowed his head as well. Colleen's soothing tone echoed throughout the room.

"Father, we know the enemy desires to trap us and to keep us bound. Lord, you have not given us a spirit of fear, but of power, love, and a sound mind. We ask for your healing power to stretch toward Mindy in that hospital bed. We ask for your help in capturing her assailant. Lord, I put Michael before you. Give him the strength to face this trial and give him peace. In Jesus' name, we pray. Amen."

"Peace be still," Keith said, with uplifted hands.

Coming out of Keith's office Verona heard the collective "amen's." She knew she should join them, but her prayers would not pass the roof. Verona made her way into the kitchen to get a glass of water. She needed a moment to compose herself.

Verona slipped onto one of the stools by the breakfast counter. While she sipped her water, she mulled over her fight with Michael during the drive to Keith's house. Michael had gotten under her skin in the worst way. She could not understand him. A young woman was laid up in a hospital, badly beaten. He was the chief suspect. What did he want to do? Go see her.

"See how she's doing," he said.

"Are you out of your mind?" Verona roared back. Michael obviously didn't understand the seriousness of his situation. "You'd better not step within two hundred feet of that hospital or you're going down."

"I'm not guilty. I cared for her. Before all of this, she was the daughter of a man I did business with for years."

Verona gave him a look. "Yes, a very dangerous man who wants you dead."

"I'm human," Michael countered. "I have feelings. I want to know she's okay."

"Why? Is this guilt talking? Or, do you intend to finish what you started?"

He inhaled. In a swoosh of breath, he gritted out, "You think I could do this?"

Verona rolled her eyes at him. She pinned them on the road. She wasn't going to dignify that question with an answer. Of course she knew he didn't do it. She couldn't handle the jealousy swirling in the pit of her belly. He sounded worried about Mindy; like a man in love? She wasn't sure. She didn't like it.

One strong hand gripped her chin and tilted her head. "Well?" came the imperial tone.

*She said, "I'm not going to Long Island Jewish. We're
going to Keith's as planned."*
"That wasn't my question."
*Verona ignored him. She was chicken to admit her
true feelings. Their funk took them all the way to Keith's
house. Their argument continued from the car into
Keith's home.*

Verona heard the back door open, bringing her mind
back to the present. She rested her glass on the counter as
Gina sailed in. "Whew, it's cold out there."

"How's Trey?" Verona asked. Keith had told them
about his appointment.

"He's fine. Thank God." Gina shrugged out of her bulky
coat. "I dropped him off at school, which he wasn't happy
about at all."

Verona chuckled. "I have to agree. Getting an all clear
from the big cancer should constitute a free pass to stay
home."

Gina looked around. "Where's everyone?"

Verona crooked her head toward the living area. "In
there. Colleen told us about Carl." She scraped the stool
as she stood, and ambled over to Gina. "How long did you
know?"

Gina avoided eye contact. "Colleen told me about it but . . ."

Seeing her chagrin, Verona patted the shorter woman
on the shoulder. "I'm having my contact investigate all he
can. I should hear back from Frank in a couple of days at
most."

After a slight nod of the head, Gina moved to join the
others. Verona took a deep breath and straggled in after
her. By the time she had entered the room, Gina had si-
dled up to Keith. Seeing Keith's arms draped over Gina's
with such ease gave Verona a jolt. She wanted to feel the
assurance of someone's love. She gazed at Michael with
longing, but he was chatting it up with Colleen.

Verona moseyed over to their direction in time to hear Michael ask Colleen, "Do you think you would be able to pay the family a visit? I need to know she's okay."

When Verona heard Michael's words, she clenched her fists. "Why are you concerned about someone who wants you behind bars? What are you, a masochist?" she screamed. Whipping her head to face Colleen, Verona heaved. "Don't go within ten feet of that hospital, Colleen. Don't listen to this lunatic who doesn't even care about his own life."

Wide-eyed, Colleen shook her head. "No, I couldn't go anyways. It's been years since I've been in touch with the family. I wouldn't think of imposing on them."

Verona struggled to remain calm. She knew her face was red from her exertion. "I'm sorry. I didn't mean to yell."

"Yet you seem to enjoy it," Michael drawled.

Verona spun her head *Exorcist* style and wailed on him. "It's you. You're making me crazy!" She felt all eyes on her. Verona knew she was in over her head. She saw the compassion in Gina's eyes and backed up. "I can't be here. I need a moment."

Ignoring Gina's calls, Verona grabbed her jacket and briefcase and left. She knew what she had to do. With a swipe, she placed a dreaded call.

"I need you to take over Michael's case." She blinked back tears. "I'm too emotionally involved. I can't be what he needs right now." She held her breath waiting for the mockery.

"What happened?" Nigel asked, with surprising gentleness.

Tears rolled down her face. *Ugh!* Verona pulled over to the curb. "It's almost lunchtime. Do you have plans?"

"I'll clear my schedule. See you at our usual spot."

They had a usual spot? Verona swung her car into traffic with the skills of a NASCAR race driver. She noticed her phone was vibrating. She pressed the phone button on her steering wheel. She preferred the Bluetooth but had forgotten to connect the earpiece.

"I'm checking on you," Gina's voice echoed through the car.

Verona smiled at her thoughtfulness. "I'm sorry. I had to bounce before I hit Michael senseless."

She heard a low chuckle. "Be patient with him. I know from experience Michael doesn't always think things through. Keith axed his idea of going to the hospital. There are no worries there. You be safe. I'll see you Wednesday night. Why don't you come early? We can have dinner together first."

Verona tapped the wheel as she considered Gina's offer. She knew the dinner invitation was a disguise for something else. She was not sure which conversation: Michael or her past church history.

"Hello? Did we get disconnected?"

Verona rushed to answer. "No, I'm here. I was thinking. I'll see you about five-thirty."

"Looking forward to it, friend."

Her dashboard read, call ended, but Verona was caught up on Gina's last word. Friend. Friend. Gina Ward. Michael's ex considered her a friend. If that did not beat all.

"He's a dead man!" the voice roared.

"No," Mindy groaned, failing in her attempt to shake her head. It was like moving lead. "No, don't hurt him," she whispered. Her father was talking to someone. Her throat felt dry and achy from her screams. She forced her eyes open. They closed of their own volition. She must be drugged up. *Ugh!* She needed to move. Her body refused to obey.

"Water," she croaked, trying to make her eyes stay open. She needed toothpicks because they were refusing to cooperate.

In slow motion, Mindy lifted a hand to her face. "Owww," she moaned with a stronger voice. She felt bandages on her right cheek and forehead.

"Mindy?" She heard her father's gruff voice and strove to reply. His hand touched her hand. "Don't try to move," Bill cautioned.

"I'll do whatever I need to do to make sure he pays for this," another voice belonging to a younger man threatened. Mindy shivered at his menacing tone.

I know that voice! She fought with her eyes until she won the battle. It took effort but she focused. Slowly her vision, cleared. "F . . ." She stopped. "Water. I need water."

In an instant, Mindy felt the cool liquid pressed against her lips. She guzzled it down in seconds. Her father pressed the button to raise the bed. Mindy's head throbbed but she did not care. Her eyes remained glued to the man standing in front of her. Her father performed the introductions.

The other man did not let on this was not the first time he had seen her. She would be eternally grateful for that.

Bill's cell phone buzzed and he left the room.

"Finn! How do you know my father? What are you doing here?"

In two steps, Finn was by her side. Gently, he kissed her forehead. "Thank God, you're awake. Mousie, why didn't you tell me who you were? I had no idea you were Bill Laurelton's daughter. I almost choked on my breakfast when I saw your face on TV and heard Bill was your father."

At the mention of her stage name, Mousie emerged. "Don't touch me," she snarled with contempt. "You know I hate when you touch me."

Finn lowered his voice. "Cool down, princess. Now you know I won't hurt you. You must know how I care for you. You have me feeling some kind of way. I can't even explain."

Bill Laurelton reentered the room. He signaled to Finn. They huddled in the corner of her room. Mindy strained to hear their hushed voices but it was of no use. She did not even know when she closed her eyes. Somewhere in her subconscious she knew Michael Ward would be a dead man by the time she awakened.

Do something! the voice belonging to Baby screamed. She almost never spoke. Mindy was surprised to hear from her.

Baby, what can I do? Mindy asked. *You know Daddy's stubborn.*

Well, if you ask me, Michael Ward deserves what he gets. He had it coming, Mousie voiced. *He rejected us.*

You've got to help him, Mindy, Baby pleaded with a cry. Her shoulders shook. *You can't let him die like Carl. You can't.*

Quit your wailing, Baby, Mousie snapped.

I'll help him, Baby, Mindy decided. She hated when Baby cried. *As soon as I get up from my nap. You and me, we'll think of something.*

Chapter Thirty-one

"I need you to take over Michael's case." Verona took a bite of her market salad with organic chicken from JoJo's enjoying the taste of feta cheese.

"Tell me why," Nigel said.

"I'm too emotionally invested in this case, or, rather, Michael. I'm in love with him. It makes me irrational and that's dangerous. He needs clearheaded objectivity. Not a simpering fool," Verona said.

"Simpering fool?"

She rolled her eyes. "Nigel, be serious, will you? I'm here baring my soul to you and that's what you focus on? You know what I mean."

He snagged a grape tomato from her salad. "Yes, I do. If you need my assistance, I'll do it. I hope you know I don't come cheap."

"Don't worry, you'll be paid triple whatever you're imagining."

His eyes rounded like dollar coins. "Triple? I'm in. What do you need?"

Verona wiped her hands on the linen napkin draped across her pants. She retrieved her phone. "I'm expecting to hear from Frank with some information. If you come over later this evening, I'll bring you up to speed."

Nigel sank his teeth into his JoJo's burger and crunched the onions. "You're forgetting one thing." He chewed. "Michael hasn't agreed to my representation. Keith may also object."

"I'll handle them," she said with confidence. "I'm sure Michael will agree once I explain my position."

How wrong she was. When Verona met up with Michael at his place later that day, he was not pleased.

"Too bad. He'll be here in an hour, along with Keith," Verona said. She had arranged the meeting at seven p.m. so Nigel could be debriefed.

Nigel had predicted this would happen, but Verona was not prepared for Michael's vehement reaction.

"You're not quitting on me, and you're not quitting this case!" Michael railed.

"She does make a good point. You need someone who is not so invested in the case," Keith interrupted.

Nigel had his head buried in the court documents. He did not flinch at Michael's outburst.

"I'm not quitting on you, you imbecile! I'm helping you win the case. Nigel is the man for the job." Verona didn't miss Nigel's sideways glance at her compliment. She was surely going to catch heat later. But, she only told the truth.

"I can vouch for that as well," Keith said.

Michael snatched her by the arm and led her into his study. Verona felt charred from the heated darts aimed her way. "Are you finished with your temper tantrum?" she taunted.

He glided right into her space. His powerful arms flanked her sides, effectively holding her prisoner. "I'm fighting for my life and you're making this about you. It's childish and amateurish. I insist you get your act together."

Who was he calling childish? She would show him childish. Verona stuck her tongue out at him. Before she could return her tongue to its warm cave, Michael held it with two of his fingers.

Michael tugged her tongue to bring her closer to him. He stroked her appendage and she tasted the saltiness of his fingers. Verona squirmed, hating how her heartbeat increased. She jerked her head for Michael to release her.

"My own personal tiger," he drawled, playing with her loose ringlets. "This hairstyle suits you well."

So he noticed she had been to the hairdresser to have it cut and layered. "Let me go," Verona whispered, pushing against steel.

"No." He lowered his head. "I've discovered the best way to tame you."

Her mind registered Michael's intentions. She pushed harder against him. "Quit playing games this—"

His mouth crushed hers. Verona heard a moan. Startled, she barely recognized her own voice. Sensations rocked her being. She had forgotten the thrill of being thoroughly kissed by a man who knew what he was doing. Oh, yeah. Michael definitely knew what he was doing.

Who knows how long they were caught up in the love play? Michael ended the kiss. He gloated. "I think we have to answer that."

"What?" she asked in a daze.

"Keith's been calling our names and knocking on the door. We'd better go see what he wants."

Heat seared her cheeks. Verona covered her face with her hands. Keith and Nigel had to know what they had been doing in here. How embarrassing! Oh, Lord, Keith was a minister. He was bound to reprove them with a Biblical tongue-lashing.

Michael remained unfazed. He adjusted his clothes and glided through the door with a puffed chest. She, however, needed a moment to gather her wits. Verona rushed to the nearest bathroom and splashed her face with cold water. Examining herself in the mirror, Verona concluded there was no way she'd be able to hide the fact she had been kissed. Her lips sparkled with a rosy hue.

"Come on, Tiger, you can't hide out in here. You're made of tougher stuff than this." Holding her chin high, Verona ventured out in the living room and stopped short at the woman grasping Michael's shirt.

"What the—"

"I think we should get married," Lauren suggested, clinging on to Michael's shirt. Her demeanor bore the remnants of a desperate woman. That was the only explanation Michael could think of for why Lauren would announce that in front of everybody.

Talk about awkward.

"Married?" Verona sputtered.

Michael glanced at Verona. Her face testified of what had been going down in his study. However, he was preoccupied with the woman grabbing on to him. He wiped the sweat beads lining his head. Self-conscious, Michael eyed the occupants in the room praying for a rescue.

He watched Verona edging closer. How was he going to extricate himself from this without bloodshed? Both women were feisty and were likely to think fist first. Keith signaled to Nigel. They left the room. Verona remained rooted. Michael knew better than to ask her for privacy.

"This must be the infamous Lauren," Verona said.

He stammered, "Lauren, you told me you were dating someone. What's his name again?"

Lauren addressed Verona. "Yes, I'm Lauren, Michael's girlfriend." Then she looked his way. "I've changed my mind. I want us to be a family." She twisted her hands.

"Are you offering marriage because you think it'll help Michael's case?" Verona asked.

Michael held up his hand to ward her off. "Let me handle this," he cautioned before turning back to Lauren.

Lauren's eyes widened. Her gaze swung between the two of them. "Are you and she . . . Are you? I can't even say the words."

Michael shook his head. "No, you're wrong."

"No? Tell that to my lips," Verona yelled.

Lord, if you could intervene right about now, I'd be at your mercy forever. Michael tried to decipher the expression on Lauren's face. She was . . . disappointed?

Then Lauren squared her shoulders. "Did he tell you he wanted to be with me and our children?"

Verona's eyes bulged. She pierced Michael with a look able to freeze Hades. "Children? You have children?" Verona held her stomach as if she'd been sucker-punched.

Michael had not told anyone about John and Olivia. No one knew about them except for Keith, Gina, and his mother, who was resting in her grave. "Yes, I have twins. John and Olivia."

"Why am I just hearing this?" Verona hurled.

"Michael does know how to keep a secret. Believe me. I know," Lauren said with a contemptuous curl of her peach-colored lips.

"Who keeps their own children a secret? What kind of father does that? What kind of man are you, Michael Ward?" Verona asked.

"Verona, calm down and let me explain—"

"Don't tell me to calm down! Answer the question, Michael. Did you know about your children?"

"Yes, I—"

Verona cut him off. "How could you neglect to mention you had two children when you had your tongue stuck down my throat not even five minutes ago?"

"Ah, I—"

"Answer me!" she bellowed. Her eyes flashed red.

Michael scratched his head. "Yes, but let me—"

"I don't want to hear another word from your lying, deceitful mouth." Verona grabbed her belongings. "I'm out of here. I never want to see your sorry face again!"

"Verona, wait!" Michael rushed after her.

She ignored him and rushed out of the door and possibly out of his life for good.

Michael trudged back to where Lauren stood waiting. She played with her nails with the smuggest expression written on her face. *Lauren is enjoying this.*

Lauren eased off the wall and clapped her hands with slow deliberation. "I deserve an Academy Award. Your girlfriend bought that act, hook, line, and sinker." Lauren pumped her hands in the air.

Was she high? That would explain Lauren's erratic behavior. "Why did you come here?" Michael demanded. *Besides to ruin my relationship with Verona.*

She smiled. "The reason no longer exists. I had hopes for us, but I'd be blind not to see how you feel about her. May I use your restroom?"

Michael had whiplash from her conversation switch. Confused, he pointed toward the bathroom. Imagine his gratitude when Keith walked into the room.

"So you and Verona?" he asked.

"Are over," Michael said. "Lauren made sure of that. I'm not even sure why. She's using the bathroom." *Wait a minute, where were his children?* Michael asked her as soon as she returned.

"They're safe. Speaking of children, I'm going home to them." Lauren opened the door.

Keith's cell phone rang. Michael had been about to go after Lauren when he heard, "How is that possible?" Keith raged to the caller. "He's right here. I'll have to ask him."

Michael dismissed Lauren from his mind. He had too much going on. It would take him the rest of his life to figure out the enigma known as woman.

Seeing the dread on Keith's face, Michael's heart thumped. "Ask me what?" He mentally prepared himself, but Michael wasn't ready for Keith's revelation.

"The semen found in the condom on the scene is yours."

Chapter Thirty-two

"He swears it's not his. When Michael heard about the semen, he sank to the floor," Keith informed Gina. Snuggled under their thousand-thread count sheets, he wrapped Gina close to him welcoming her comfort. Her presence soothed him. He had been stewing on the devastating news for hours.

Gina cupped his face with her hands. A tear slid down Keith's cheek. "I don't know what to believe. DNA doesn't lie. There's no doubt it's Michael's. He says he didn't touch Mindy."

"Shh." She pressed her mouth onto his.

"I can't lose him, Gina," Keith whispered. "I just got him back. I'll love him no matter what he's done but"—he gulped—"this would be a bitter pill to swallow. The thought of Michael doing harm to that girl . . ." Keith shook his head.

"Are you listening to yourself right now?" Gina asked. "Where's your faith? Did it evaporate under some DNA? What about God? You said He brought Michael home. I admit I fought your decision to defend him. But, I've seen the old Michael, the one I married. I'm telling you there has to be an explanation."

"Well, look at how the tables have turned," Keith said.

Gina averted her eyes. "Yes, I can't believe the words coming out of my mouth either. But, I know God's leading me to encourage you. Michael needs you. He needs you to fight for him. I've always felt guilty I came between the two of you. I destroyed your bond. Now I'm seeing the rebuilding and I know this is God's doing. All praise belongs to God. If this isn't the modern-day prodigal story, I don't know what is." She gripped his arm. "I have faith in you, Keith. You're walking in your calling. If you remember, getting there wasn't easy. Now Michael is at that fork in the road. I know it's only the beginning. The road isn't easy. But, it's better if you're walking it with others."

"You're right. When did you get smart?" Keith squeezed her with affection.

"I was born smart," she quipped.

"I'm sorry I even doubted him for a minute. I left Michael at his lowest point. Even if he's guilty as ever, I should be by his side."

"Don't be sorry or too hard on yourself. You wouldn't be human if you didn't have doubts. Counteract every single doubt by finding the truth."

Keith felt love swell in his heart at Gina's encouragement. He whispered, "I don't know what I'd do without you in my life. You complete me. I love you."

Gina's eyes filled with tenderness. "Oh, honey, I love you too." She touched his cheek. "Michael loves you. He needs you. He needs his big brother to be his champion. I'm going out on a limb here, but what if both stories are true?"

He shifted. "What do you mean?"

Gina sprinkled his bare chest with kisses. "I mean what if both Michael and Mindy's version of the events that night are correct? What if the truth is a puzzle? Put all the pieces together. What if someone is setting him up?"

A bolt flashed through him. Keith sat up. "My Lord, I never thought of that angle! Gina, you may be on to something." Vestiges of Michael's and Mindy's statements sprang to his mind. Since Mindy had refused a rape kit, there was no way of knowing if she had actually been penetrated. What if the assumption was made because of her incoherent words and the blood on the scene? He rubbed his chin. Something was not adding up. There was an element missing. He needed to figure it out.

Keith slid his body to the edge of the bed and jammed his feet into his slippers. He had to get to his study.

"Don't I get a reward?"

Hearing Gina's suggestive tone, Keith senses went on full alert. He made an about turn and lost his breath. She had removed the covers and had fashioned herself into the most intriguing pose. Keith rejoined her on the bed. "You most certainly deserve to be awarded for your insight." He splattered kisses across her neck. "Your brilliance," he continued, moving to her bared shoulder. "Your unequaled intelligence." He dipped lower.

With bated breath, she egged him on: "Yes. What about my, ah, my . . ."

"Superior reasoning?" Keith finished, working his magic with his hands and lips.

"Hmmm hmmm. That and my . . . my . . ."

"Logic?"

"Yes, ah, oh, logic," Gina added.

Keith searched for another word. By this time his brain was on lockdown. He spoke to her in a more intimate way. She screamed. He smiled.

When he went to sleep, Keith was optimistic all would be well.

When he woke up the next morning, things fell apart.

Natalie called. "Bishop Combs tried to kill himself," she said.

Keith's heart hammered in his chest. "What? When? How?" His voice rose with each question.

"Gunshot wound to the head. He was found inside his vehicle. He left a note confessing to everything. He didn't die, though. The news reporter said he's unrecognizable," Natalie said.

Gina stirred and questioned him with her eyes. Keith covered the phone to fill her in. Her eyes widened and she shot out the bed. "I'm going over to the foundation. We have to prepare a press release." She raced into the shower.

"If he was going to off himself, he could've at least left a check," Natalie bemoaned through the line.

"Somebody almost died."

"Yes, a coward. I know. But the foundation is going to face the brunt of the public's disapproval. Please tell me he signed the requisition?" She phrased the statement as a question.

"Yes, he did. I'll write the check to cover the funds. I know the government will dig but we have nothing to hide."

"Keep your money. We'll go after Suzette. The police are looking for her. Massive manhunt in progress."

Keith hated how cold that sounded.

His other line beeped. It was Deacon Broderson. His house phone rang. It was not even nine a.m. Keith massaged his temples and turned on the news.

Bishop Combs's face was plastered all over the screen.

Chapter Thirty-three

"It's three o'clock in the morning! For the fifth time, go home!" Michael yelled, suppressing a yawn. He had spent a harrowing day helping Keith sort out the mess with Bishop Combs. His brother had then asked him to find Suzette Combs.

Michael had also poured more money through Tiger Trust into the foundation. He was sure they would rebound. His case was another matter. Michael tossed and turned for most of the night dwelling on it. Just when he had fallen asleep, crazy showed up at his door.

"I'll kill myself!" the woman screamed through the door. "Did you hear me? I'll kill myself."

Michael thought of the bishop. *Is suicide in style?*

Michael paused. What if she made good on her threat? He could not take that chance. Against his better judgment, Michael opened the door. He pulled the bedraggled visitor into his penthouse.

When the door slammed shut, an eerie sensation filled him. He should have stayed in the hallway. After all, it was his accuser who stood before him.

"Mindy, you shouldn't be here," he warned.

The raging woman now had a childlike voice. "I had to come. I had to warn you." Nervousness apparent, she contorted her hands like a pretzel.

Michael touched her arm. She flinched.

"Listen, big boy, we're here to help not to be manhandled."

He backed off. "I'm sorry." *Did she say we?* Now Mindy sounded like a jaded ingénue. What was going on? He eyed her with careful precision before realization hit. This girl was mentally ill. As ill as her brother Carl must have been. Her hair was uncombed. Her hospital gown stuffed into a pair of jeans. Mindy's face bore the bruises from her brutal beating.

Michael felt compassion but he had to ask the question that had his head throbbing all night. "Mindy, how did my semen end up in the Ritz?"

She blushed and covered her cheeks. "You said semen." Her girlish giggle made Michael's head spin.

"Mindy?"

She straightened. "I don't know how it got there. I think Mousie's friend, Elle G, put it there." Her eyes glazed. "Things are kind of murky in my mind." She nodded. "Yep. I think it's her."

Michael could not follow this conversation. It was like he was in an episode of that old-time television show, *Herman's Head.* "Who's Elle G?"

Mindy placed a finger over her mouth. "Shh. She made me promise not to tell. She's my secret friend."

Now Mindy sounded like a five-year-old. Michael lost patience. Mindy must be high on prescription drugs. She was not making an ounce of sense. And, who had an imaginary friend at her age?

Michael wondered what was in his body scent to make him attract psychos. He needed to get Mindy out of his place before she brought even more trouble on his head.

In a gentle but patronizing tone, he said, "Mindy, I'm going to have to ask you to leave. How did you get here?"

She shrugged.

Michael strode to get his phone he'd left on his kitchen counter. "I'll call you a cab."

"No! I have to warn you. My dad told Finn he wanted you dead!" Mindy said.

Michael stopped. He did not doubt her sanity this time. He knew Mindy told the truth. Bill Laurelton would seek revenge for her attack. What he had envisioned, however, was a brutal takeover of his dwindling assets. He had not expected such a lethal reaction. Then Michael thought of his children. If it were Olivia . . .

Michael rushed over to where Mindy stood. "What else did you hear?

"I was drugged up. I could barely keep my eyes open, but Finn is a dangerous man. I know him because I worked . . . I know him." She leaned forward. "You don't have to call a cab. I have one holding downstairs."

Michael was already running names through his head of people he could call. He needed someone with stealth and experience to handle Bill. He did not think to call God, did not know that line was never busy, did not know God was the answer.

"Michael, can I use your bathroom?"

Mindy! He had forgotten about her while plotting his next move. "Sure! It's down the hall on the right."

"Thanks."

Think, Michael, think. He had to keep a low profile. He had not been in touch with men of certain ilk in months. But, how else was he going to deal with Bill?

Trust me.

Goose bumps rose on Michael's flesh. The Holy Spirit had spoken. Michael took a step back from the powerful impact. *How? How do I trust you, Lord?* He looked heavenward as if the answer were imprinted on the ceiling.

Let go.

He did not know how. "I can't," he whispered. Michael's faith failed him. He bunched his fists relishing the feel of his fingers against his palm. Yes, this was real to him. He understood fighting for himself. That he could do. "Let me do this first, Lord," he beckoned.

"Who are you talking to?"

Michael jumped, not realizing he had dropped his cell phone near the couch. "Ah, no one. Just thinking out loud. I'd better see you downstairs." Once again, he had forgotten Mindy. Gently, he guided her into the elevator and then outside the building to the waiting Yellow Cab. In an instant, lights flashed at him from all directions. Michael held his hands across his face from the blinding glare. Why was the media camped outside his building?

Realization hit. Mindy had set him up.

"I'm sorry. I had to keep you safe," she said.

Michael nodded. What else could he do in that moment? He held out his hands to the two uniformed men. Metal cuffs met his wrists.

"Michael Ward, you're under arrest for violating the conditions of your parole. We're remanding you into custody."

He was shoved into the back of the patrol car. He sat there for hours. Michael spotted Bill's arms around Mindy. She had set him up but every eye in the nation would see her as a helpless innocent.

Michael bent his head. *I'm done. I'm going down.*

He's going to be mad! Baby wailed.

We saved his sorry butt from death! Mousie protested.

But, he's back in jail, Mindy reasoned. *Neither Daddy nor Finn can hurt him now.*

He didn't do anything and you know it, Baby protested.

Well, somebody's got to pay for all you've gone through and it might as well be him!

Shut up, Mousie, I can't think. Mindy's heart refused to quit its thumping. She wiped her palms on her pants. When Mindy turned her head, she noticed her father eyeing her. There was no way Bill was going to let her out of his sight.

What do you mean? Do what you always do! Mousie commanded.

You mean what you do, Mindy amended. She bit her lip. She hated feeding her father one of her sleeping pills. It worked like a charm whenever she needed to escape his clutches. Since her brother and mother died, her father suffocated her. She knew he was afraid to lose her. He said it all the time. However, he could not keep her under lock and key, like a caged bird.

She did not have friends. No one to talk to about Carl and how he died. No one to cry with when Mama released her final breath. Mindy only had herself. So she invented her friends. People she could talk with about anything. They knew her well.

There was nothing wrong with that. The doctor did not agree though. Dr. Forrester slapped her with the title dissociative identity disorder and pumped her with pills. Pills Mindy no longer took because her brain felt mushy. She liked her reality.

Mousie was the part of her who refused to take any mess. Mindy chuckled at how often she had to keep that rebellious nature under wraps. However, there were times when Mousie wanted to play. She had let her too because Mousie had made a friend, Finn, and she liked him.

Actually, she had made two friends. She was not allowed to talk about the other one. That was Mousie's other friend, Elle G. Elle G wanted to remain anonymous. Mindy understood, but she had a big dilemma.

Elle G knew the truth. Her testimony could set Michael Ward free.

Too bad, so sad!

Mousie, that's childish. I need to tell the truth. Besides, Michael is my friend. I love him.

Puleeze. I don't see what you see in him. Finn's fine.

Then why don't you let him touch you? Mindy taunted. *No! Baby roared. Don't let him!*

A strong hand grabbed her arm and twisted it, catching her off guard. "Ouch!" Mindy swung her head to meet a set of baleful eyes.

"Are you talking to yourself, again, Mindy? I don't understand you. I invest all my money into curing you. Yet, you still persist with this behavior. Why can't you be normal like everyone else?" Bill turned back to the road.

She forgot her father had been watching her. "This is my normal and I like it." She silenced him with an icy stare. She knew from Bill's wary look he did not know who was talking. Bill slid his eyes away from her but he was not done fussing.

"You waited until I left, then checked yourself out of the hospital to go see him. Since you can't stay away from Michael Ward, I'm taking you to our home in Westbury. I need to put some distance between the both of you."

"Yes, I went to see Michael. And I'll do it again! Distance won't stop me," she yelled at the top of her lungs.

Mousie! Stop it! He thinks I'm crazy.

You're mentally ill. There's a difference. I'm tired of his putting you down. Since you won't say anything, I did it for both of us. I'm telling you, one of these days, I'll silence him for good.

Don't you dare! Mindy revolted. Mousie wisely backed off. Mindy closed her eyes, needing to rest from her never-ending thoughts. Maybe she had been too hasty when she stopped taking her meds. Maybe she needed to pull that bottle from under her mattress. She needed a clear head.

You don't want to talk to me anymore? Baby asked.

Go ahead. Punk out and go back to being a pill pusher, Mousie snarled.

Her father's words echoed in her head. *"Why can't you be normal?"* Mindy blinked back tears and gulped. He could not know how much she prayed for that. God did not like her ugly. Bill did not believe in praying and "all that mumbo jumbo." However, she did. Mindy had heard one preacher on television say He could walk on water and do all kinds of magical things. If He could do that, then He could heal her pain and make her whole. But, until then, she would take a round tablet.

Yep, she was going to do it that very night. As soon as Bill pulled into the driveway, Mindy jumped out the car. She rushed into the house and entered her room. She sank to her knees and reached far under her mattress until she felt the small bottle. Mindy knew it was there because that was where she kept her pills in all her rooms.

Aren't you forgetting something? Mousie taunted. *Only I know the truth. That's why you stopped taking the pills. I'm the one you need to help clear Michael's name.*

Oh yeah. Mindy slumped. She'd forgotten about that. Hopeless, she released the bottle and it rolled under the bed. She didn't care.

Elle G was there too, Baby said.

Mindy straightened. "She was? I knew it! I had my suspicions. I'm glad you told me."

She made me promise not to tell.

"Baby, you've got to tell me!" Mindy slung her head onto her mattress. Why couldn't she remember everything without them? She gritted her teeth. *Think! Think! You've got to put it all together in your mind.*

Nothing.

She would have to call Dr. Forrester, whose offices were in Garden City, Long Island. Only she could help. Her father used the doctor as a drug pusher. He no longer agreed to ongoing therapy sessions. "No 'wet behind the ears' doctor is going to tell me what to do," he had ranted. And why? Because Dr. Forrester invited him into their sessions. He was not having any part of that.

She lifted a hand to heaven. "God, if you do exist, please hear me. Help me figure this out."

Chapter Thirty-four

"Go away, Nigel!"

"Can't. Your man's been holed up in jail for the past two days. We have to go see a judge. They waited this long before the paperwork went through."

Michael's in jail? Verona's heart hammered. *Whatever.* She did not care. "Let him rot for all I care. He's not my man!" She looked heavenward. "And, why won't anyone listen to me when I say I'm off this case?" Verona said through the locked door.

"Open the door," Nigel pleaded. "I've got to see for myself you're all right."

Hearing genuine concern, Verona acquiesced. She winced at his stunned expression. Her eyes were swollen from crying. Her hair stood on its ends like fiery darts. She lowered her eyes. "Come in."

"As the saying goes, you look a hot mess." Nigel plugged his nose. "Go freshen up. We need to have a good friend-to-friend chat." He wandered through her living space and picked up the blanket she had slept on.

Verona had indulged in her own pity party. She could not have children. Michael had children. She could not have children. Michael had children. And, so it went.

Self-conscious, Verona hurried to take a shower. She washed her hair twice. Ten minutes later, she donned a pair of slacks and a sweater. Then she rejoined Nigel.

Nigel nodded. "Glad you tamed the animal. I need to speak to a human being."

Verona threw a pillow at him. Nigel grabbed the small square before diving into the conversation. "Quitting is not the answer, and you know it. You've come too far to turn back now."

Nigel was right. She had a reputation to maintain and should not have allowed her personal feelings to carry over into her professional relationship. However, when it came to Michael, the tiger became a simpering kitten. Truth be told, Verona was tired of hearing herself talk about quitting. She was vested in the man and the case. She could not back down.

"Okay, no more talk of quitting from me," Verona said.

"Great! Now let's deal with the big elephant in the room. I'd have to be blind not to see how you feel."

She nodded. "I broke the cardinal rule. I fell in love with Michael. Everyone can see it but him."

"Maybe he does know but isn't ready to acknowledge it. Tiger, the man is fighting for his life. He has a baby mama coming out of the woodwork with two children in tow. He has a lot going on. Now is not the time to bail. You can't say you love someone and leave him high and dry in his greatest moment of need."

"But, the feeling is all one-sided," she argued.

"I don't think so. Right now, this isn't about how Michael feels. It's about you and how you feel. Do you only love those who love you back? I don't think God would approve of that kind of thinking."

"You're right, Nigel. I didn't see things that way," she admitted. God loved her and did for her every day whether she returned the love or not.

"Say that again?" he teased.

Verona knew what he wanted to hear but deflected. "Fill me in on the latest with the case."

"You haven't watched the news?" Nigel's eyes bulged. "Your beloved Michael was arrested for violating probation. He had Mindy in his suite."

She sprung forward. "What!" First Lauren, then Mindy. Verona could not keep up with the number of women waiting in line. She should rejoice she had escaped being a proverbial notch on Michael's belt.

"I don't know what Mindy was doing there. The cops must have been keeping him under surveillance. As soon as Michael and Mindy exited his building the police had handcuffs waiting. There was a throng of media present to capture his being rearrested."

"How convenient."

"Much too convenient for my liking. Did you ever hear from Frank?"

Verona tilted her chin toward the manila envelope on her end table. She had lacked the drive to open it. Selfish, she knew, but she was not thinking straight.

Nigel's long fingers curled around the envelope. He gently slid his index finger under the flap. "Still sealed." He ripped it open. "Verona, this man has you off your game. There was a time when nothing messed with your job."

Verona did not grace him with a comeback. Nigel spoke the truth. She was off-kilter. She could not get her groove back for nothing. Love had her all in limbo and she hated it. "What does it say?" she asked, as his eyes skimmed the documents.

"Frank confirms Colleen's story. However, the real jackpot is right here," Nigel said, lifting the business card stapled to one of the pages. "This is Dr. Forrester's information: Mindy's psychiatrist."

Anticipation crept up her spine. "We need to know what Mindy's on. We could prove her an unreliable witness, or unstable. It all depends on how many prescribed medicines she's been taking and for how long."

"Get dressed. We're meeting with Keith within the hour at Michael's place."

"Why there?"

"The police obtained a search warrant. They feel they have a right since Mindy went there from the hospital."

"Give me five minutes."

It was actually ten minutes before Verona was composed and able to slip her feet into her Manolo Blahniks.

"I think Michael was set up. In fact, I know it. The question is who and how?" Keith stated as soon as they'd arrived. He touched his chin. "Mindy has been seeing Dr. Forrester on and off for the past eight years. If anybody can give us the who, and the what, she can."

"And the why," Verona chimed in. The bustle around her was impossible to ignore. How what seemed like twenty cops fit into the room was beyond her.

Nigel was not able to see past the commotion. His head was turning left and right. "They're tearing this place up. Michael is going to go ballistic when he sees his rug."

Verona followed Nigel's gaze. She pointed to the circular stain spreading across the white Persian rug. One of the officers had spilled coffee. He had not seemed too sorry about it, either.

"I'll hire a cleaning service once they're gone. It'll be as good as new," Keith offered.

Verona shook her head. "That rug will never be the same. I'll look it up and order a replacement. How is Michael doing?"

"Not good," Keith said. "I was only able to see him for a few minutes, when I filed the release papers. I'm hoping they'll release him into my care."

"That's highly unlikely. He might be stuck in there until the trial," Nigel said.

Keith lifted his chin. Verona knew he was about to preach. "I'm trusting God to do the impossible. I know Michael's innocent. I'm searching for evidence from that angle." He patted his pants pocket. "At least I managed to swipe Michael's cell phone before they could. Someone's been blowing up his phone for the past hour. I'm curious to know who's been calling."

Verona was not in the mood to hear about Lauren's calls. She knew it had to be her. Who else could it be? Rolling her eyes, Verona changed the subject. "Speaking of God, isn't tonight Bible Study?" she asked, glancing at her watch.

Keith followed suit and checked the time. "I've already called Gina to let her know my change of plans. She's more than capable, as you've seen. Are you going?"

"Yes, I had planned on it, but I think Michael's situation takes precedence."

He bent over to address her. "Verona, I'm a pastor first. I'm concerned about your soul. Gina's been looking forward to seeing you. So, go. Nigel and I have this covered."

When she opened her mouth to argue, he emphasized, "Go."

Verona picked up her purse to leave.

However, an announcement captured the attention of all three occupants: "We've found something!"

The officer held in her gloved hands a round latex object. "We will get this over to the lab immediately," she said.

Verona's eyes widened and she dropped her purse.

"Mindy was here," she whispered. "You don't think Michael . . ."

"He wouldn't be so stupid," Nigel said. Verona felt he was all bluff.

She shook her head. Michael had done the unthinkable. He had slept with Mindy. *The idiot.* He had just blown his case. Everything he had fought for was in the tank. In a daze, Verona grabbed her purse and exited. She had no idea where she was going. She knew one thing. She had to get out of there.

Glad she had not driven, Verona hailed a cab and settled into the seat. For the millionth time in her life, Verona wished she had never laid eyes on Michael Ward. Never fallen in love. Her heart splintered into a million pieces. She released a sob. The cabbie gave her a worried glance, but she waved him off.

"Where to, miss?"

As tears streamed down her face, Verona contemplated. She had no one. She was alone, all by herself.

No. You're not alone. You do have people who love you, were the immediate counteracting thoughts.

"Miss?" She heard the cabbie's questioning tone. Nevertheless, her thoughts reigned.

That's right. She wasn't alone. Suddenly, Verona knew where to go. She took a brave gulp and said, "Take me to the airport. I'm going home."

Chapter Thirty-five

He was alone.

All alone.

Michael shivered in his cell, still dressed in his pajamas. At least he had been placed in a holding area by himself.

I'm here.

"Oh, God." Michael acknowledged His presence. "I've messed up big time."

Remember Joseph.

Michael looked over at the Bible, which Keith had dropped off for him. He had asked Keith where he could find the story of Joseph. He picked it up and opened the Bible to Genesis. Once he located it, Michael began to read.

Michael read and read. He paused after Genesis 37 to ponder on the Word.

So, Joseph's brothers sold him out? Michael visualized Joseph being betrayed by his brothers. Brothers who were supposed to love him, but instead were jealous of what he had. Goose bumps rose on his flesh. "Huh, I can relate." His voice echoed.

Keith had his share of women, but he had wanted Gina, and he had gotten her, too.

Michael opened his eyes and waited for the bitterness to rise. To his surprise, he felt nothing but sadness. He went back to the scripture, curious to see how the story would unfold. At the third verse in chapter thirty-nine, he paused. A line struck him. He read the words, "the Lord was with him." Michael voiced the words aloud.

God was with Joseph all the way.

Then why didn't He rescue Joseph? Why did God allow Joseph to go through all of that pain?

Michael felt a light breeze, a shiver, a sigh, before a thought tickled his ear. *If God's present, you don't need anything else, especially not rescuing.*

"I can't argue with that logic," Michael said, not realizing the Holy Spirit guided him.

He kept reading. The more he read, the more he admired Joseph: the dreamer, the visionary. Michael saw vestiges of himself. He sped through the chapters with a hunger that surprised him. He was stunned at Joseph's willingness to forgive his brothers. Tears streamed down his face at the family reunion that ensued.

That story was there for you.

"What a lofty thought," Michael said. "But, somehow it's comforting." For the first time in his life, Michael felt surrounded by a powerful presence. He was not alone. He acknowledged a higher power greater than himself. The fact that Joseph had been accused of rape, a crime he did not commit, was too much to ignore.

Michael reopened the Bible and flipped through the pages to chapter thirty-nine. There was another voice that had stood out. It was the latter part of verse nine. "'How then can I do this great wickedness, and sin against God?'" Joseph's question was achingly similar. Although this had nothing to do with God, Michael could not have betrayed Bill by sleeping with Mindy. His honor was rewarded with a false rape accusation.

However, Joseph had not dwelled on the past. He did not worry about what he could not change. Instead, Joseph prospered. Whether it was in the dungeon or in the presence of Pharaoh, Joseph stood apart.

Michael took a deep breath. Closing his eyes, he uttered, "God, I need you with me like how you were with Joseph.

Amen." Those few heartfelt words did him good. When Michael opened his eyes, he knew no matter what happened, he would be all right.

He banished thoughts of bedbugs and critters and went to lie on the small cot in the corner. He rested his head on his hands. There was no way he would put his face on that pillow.

"Are you a modern-day Joseph?" a voice boomed behind him.

Michael jumped awake. He looked at Terence Hayworth as if he were an extraterrestrial being. *For a man of six four, how does he move so quietly?* Michael raised his eyebrows. "How did you get in?"

"I'm clergy, remember? I've counseled many wayward youths."

"What about grown men who know better?"

Terence approached and sat behind the middle school–sized desk. His large Bible took up most of the small square.

Michael was still ruminating how Terence had brought up the very person in the Bible he had been reading about earlier. "What made you mention Joseph?"

"Seeing you here alone in your cell," Terence answered. "Joseph had many high moments only to be struck low again. It was usually because of something he didn't do."

Michael clenched his fists. "I didn't do it, Terence. I didn't touch Mindy and I didn't invite her over to my place. I didn't do any of it. I don't know why this is happening to me."

"I do."

Michael narrowed his eyes. "Did God tell you? Is that why you're here? To offer an explanation for why my success is now flushed down the toilet?"

Terence shook his head. "I don't know why all this is happening but God has a way of revealing things in His time. I will share some things about Joseph, though," Terence said. "Joseph was betrayed by someone he least expected. Then he was thrown into a dungeon because he decided to maintain his integrity. Joseph more than anyone could've have tossed his beliefs aside. Instead, he chose to cleave to God and trust Him." He zoned in on Michael. "That's what you need to do. Place your heart and your life in God's hands. Trust Him."

"But, that's just it," Michael pleaded. "I've forgotten how to trust. I want to trust God," he said, pointing to his head, then his heart. "But, in here, I'm still trying to do things my way."

"How's that working for you?"

Michael looked around his cell and humped over. "Not too good."

The conversation halted when they heard a noise from behind. *What now?* Michael heaved a sigh of relief when Keith came into view.

Keith dragged a desk next to Terence. "I didn't know you'd be here."

"I had to come by to offer a word of encouragement. We were talking about the story of Joseph," Terence said.

Keith nodded but didn't say anything. Michael supposed it was because Keith didn't want to be compared with the brothers who had betrayed their own flesh and blood. Instead he said, "Nigel sends his regards."

Michael asked, "What about Verona? I thought she would be here." He strove to project an "I don't care" attitude. But, he did care. A lot.

"Verona left."

Why wasn't he surprised? Michael gave Keith a look urging him to elaborate.

"She ran off when the cops searching your apartment found a used condom in your bathroom."

Whoa! Say what? Michael stood and walked over to the edge of the cell. Gripping the bars, he spat, "It's not mine. I haven't had any in a long time." A thought caused him to rock back on his heels. He shook the bars. "Get me out of here! Mindy set me up. She came over and asked to use the bathroom. That's when she must've dumped it. I don't believe this is happening," he railed.

"Michael, keep calm. God is on your side," Terence advised.

He did not want to keep calm. He wanted to holler and scream with frustration. Michael reined in his emotions and bid Keith to continue.

"Honestly, brother, it doesn't look good. I believe you. However, the evidence condemns you," Keith said.

"I don't give a row of pins what the evidence says. You know me, Keith. I didn't do this. I didn't touch that girl," Michael shouted.

"Then why did you let her in?"

Michael slinked against the bars. He rested his head on the metal rail. He felt the beginnings of a major headache. His stomach growled. After several seconds, he faced Keith and Terence. "I admit as soon as I shut the door behind Mindy, I realized it wasn't my smartest move. It was three o'clock in the morning and I was concerned about her. She threatened to kill herself."

"How did she even get access to your penthouse?" Keith asked. "She needs a special card or your permission."

Why did Keith sound suspicious? Michael spoke through clenched teeth. "I worked with her father. Bill and I were good friends. They used to come over for dinner and business. With all the upheaval going on, I didn't think to change my visitor list."

"I'm asking what everybody will be thinking and asking," Keith said. "Your answers are good."

"That's because they're true," Michael countered. He strained to keep the sarcasm out of his tone.

"They've sent the sample to the lab. I'm sure they'll find someone else's DNA. In the meantime, get comfortable. It looks as if you won't be getting out anytime soon."

Unbelievable! Fury straightened Michael's spine. He knew exactly where to lay the blame. "All this wouldn't be happening if Tiger had done her job and cleaned up my visitor list. She should be here working her magic to get me out of here. I can't believe she's deserted me."

"Blaming Verona doesn't make any sense," Terence interrupted. He opened his Bible and turned the pages, searching for a verse.

I don't need a verse right now. I need to get out of here.

"Terence is right, Michael. I've tried. There isn't a judge who's ready to release you until the DNA results are in. I've pulled some strings to expedite the process, but it's a waiting game," Keith said.

Terence located his scripture and said, "I'd like to share Romans 8 verse 28. It says, 'And we know all things work together for good to them that love God.' Michael, I know I'm not in your shoes. I'm not sitting where you are but I would want someone to tell me God will work it out somehow. That's the word I'll leave with you. You're going through a storm right now. But at any moment, God can calm the waves with a single word."

Michael nodded. He heard what Terence was saying but his faith was limited. "Thank you," he politely responded. Terence prayed and said his good-byes. As soon as he was gone, Michael asked Keith, "Did you manage to grab my phone. Or, did the cops nab it in their raid?"

"I have it," Keith confirmed.

"Thank God." Michael lifted his hands. "At least God has my back with something."

Keith squinted his eyes. "Why? What's going on?"

"Besides finding Suzette Combs, I gave Frank another special assignment. One I fear is going to bite me in the behind."

"Oh, yes. Speaking of Suzette Combs, you've been locked up so there was no way for you to know the cops found her. A lucky tip led them to her hideout. Suzette was holed up in some rat-infested motel in Las Vegas. You know that money is gone, right?"

Michael laughed. "I'm sure Frank hated tracking her to a dump. He'll probably bill me extra."

"That Frank is one good investigator. I'm guessing you didn't use him to find Lauren," Keith said.

Michael shook his head. "No, he wasn't available at the time."

"What did you have him do? I'll fix it."

"I hired Frank to find Martin Weston. The punk Lauren's dating."

Keith came to stand toe to toe with Michael. He whispered, "I don't believe you had your goon go after Martin. He's a good man."

Michael could not help it. He cracked up. "He doesn't exist." Michael took pleasure in seeing genuine shock reflected across his brother's face. There was not much that surprised Keith.

"I don't understand. Lauren said . . ."

"Lauren has been feeding us lies."

Keith shook his head. "I don't understand why she would."

"Simple. She knew it was only a matter of time before I reentered the picture. She wanted to cover her bases. For some reason, she wanted us all to think she was dating someone. When I called Frank to tell him to abort the mission, he texted me to say there wasn't a mission for a man who didn't exist."

"But if the cops see your texts . . ." Keith's eyes shone with understanding.

"Exactly. They'll tie this in to Mindy or who knows what else. At this rate, I won't be surprised if they blame me for any and everything." He knew he was having a pity party but Michael felt he deserved one.

Keith did not. "No need to become a martyr. I'm sorry this is happening to you. But, I'm not sorry it has united us. If it weren't for this case, you and I would still be at odds with each other. You wouldn't be back in my life. So there are positives."

Michael gestured with his hands. "I don't think I needed all this for it to happen."

"You were so high. God had to bring you low. If he hadn't . . ." Keith said, "But I prayed for you. I prayed God would lead you home. Soften your heart."

Michael mulled over Keith's words. How could he regret what God was doing to his heart? His humor kicked in. "Please rethink setting God on me next time. I can't take His lessons."

Keith chuckled. "God has your back. He won't leave you. When we walk through valleys, He's there."

"Save the message for the pulpit, brother. Put your lawyer hat on and get me out of here."

Chapter Thirty-six

"Verona? Verona!" Louisa Stachs eyes were as large as saucers.

Standing by the front door, Verona acknowledged she didn't know why she was at her parent's doorsteps. When she'd left thirteen years ago, she vowed never to return.

Her mother's green eyes took in her unkempt appearance. Verona wiped her puffy face. The waterworks had been in full effect all the way to the airport, through the flight, and in the cab until she had rung the doorbell.

Louisa stepped aside and motioned for her to enter. As if years hadn't passed, Verona walked into her childhood home. Louisa hugged her.

Verona welcomed the feel and smell of the slighter woman. In her mother's arms, Verona released her pain. She felt a large palm settle on her back. Pulling away, she turned to face her father, Pastor Noel Stachs. After a slight hesitation, she plunged into his chest. More tears flowed.

"I can't believe you are here, standing in front of me." Louisa gazed at Verona as if she were seeing a ghost.

Noel reached to touch her arm. "Welcome home, daughter."

"I needed to return home." She hiccupped, unable to expound on her thinking. When she had left her penthouse this morning, Verona had no idea she would end up here. The California sun was a direct contrast to the wet and cold of New York. She had to stop and buy sunglasses.

Within minutes, Verona was settled between her parents, reminiscent of old times.

"I've been following the case on television," Noel stated. "Mainly to get a glimpse of you." He turned to face her. "You're a beautiful and gifted attorney."

"We're proud of you, honey," Louisa chimed in before standing to get them tissues.

Verona squirmed under such praise. It did her heart good to hear those words, but she was not about to stray from her main reason for coming. "I'm in love with him. I fell in love with my client, who appears to be as guilty as sin," she said.

"This is not like the last time. We will be here by your side," Noel said.

His firm sentiment washed over Verona's heart. Years of resentment, though, weren't easily buried. "Why now?" she asked. "Why didn't you believe and support me then when I was helpless, and . . . and . . ." She could not continue.

"We were younger, dumber, and less faithful. Your father and I had both lost our jobs. We were living on government assistance. Your child would've been one more mouth to feed," her mother confessed. "I've been praying to God for your return, for a second chance." Louisa took her hand in hers. "I'm sorry, Verona. I've waited thirteen years to look you in your face and apologize. I'm sorry for not being there when you needed me most."

Verona's shoulders hunched over. From the corner of her eye, she saw Noel slash a tear from the corner of his eye.

He cleared his throat. "Your mother's telling the truth," he said. "We've been praying nonstop for this day. I hope you'll hear me out."

Overcome, all Verona could do was nod. She wiped her nose surprised she had ducts left to manufacture more tears. It was time. Time to talk about Damien Foster, and Elijah.

"I'm sorry I threw Damien in jail." Noel hung his head. "I overreacted. I shouldn't have handled things the way I did, but he was six years older than you, an adult. I didn't know Damien would get four years."

Verona took deep breaths. Maybe she was not ready to revisit the past. "Dad, I don't think—"

He held up a hand. "No, please let me do this. I've practiced this speech for . . ."

Verona covered her face with her hands before choking out, "Damien was the reason I went into criminal law." Once in prison, Damien's original sentence had been lengthened after a fight with an inmate. The inmate succumbed to his wounds. "I was devastated when his sentence had been extended to ten years. I felt it was my fault. I practiced for a year before I tried to reopen his case. That's when I learned Damien had died in prison. Payback." She shuddered. Learning of Damien's death had crushed her.

But it was another male who tore at her heart. She continued, "I try not to think of him. I try not to think of Elijah. But, not a day goes by I don't wonder what he looks like and if . . . if he hates me for giving him up." A sob broke loose. "My son. My son."

Verona felt her mother's touch. She flung her mother's hand away. "You allowed them to take my child from me. I didn't even get to kiss him good-bye. You stood by and watched your only grandchild hoisted off into another couple's hands. How could you?" she raged. "I know I was young but to give him to Minister Smith and his wife was cruel. I had to see them every week in church and I couldn't . . ." Oh, God, this was too much. Tears smudged her face. Pain sliced through her body down to her very soul.

Verona clenched her fists. She looked up to heaven and released her anger toward God. "Where were you! Where were you?" Silence greeted her. "Answer me! Answer me!"

She zoned in on Louisa who fidgeted with her hands. "I blame you the most!" she screamed. "You went along with it. You're a mother! What kind of mother were you?"

Louisa cupped her mouth with her fist. With a cry, she ran from the room.

"That's enough!" Noel yelled. "We're sorry, but you're not going to disrespect us. You're still our child. You will speak to us in a civil manner."

"No, I'll speak however I please!" Verona's chest heaved. She stomped over to her father until she was in his face. "There is no going back for me. Do you get that?"

Noel squinted his eyes. "What do you mean there's no going back for you? Is this about Michael?"

Verona exhaled and willed herself to calm down. Louisa reentered the room. Verona held out her hand and mouthed, "I'm sorry." Her mother took timid, tentative steps until their hands were joined.

"Answer me. What do you mean there's no going back?" her father asked.

"I . . ." The words felt stuck in her throat but she gathered her courage and verbalized her deepest pain. "I might not be able to have any more children. Elijah might be it for me, and I gave him up."

Her father rebuked her. "We taught you better. Whether you have a child or not is up to God. He ultimately holds life in His hands. He decides."

Verona sought refuge in her childhood room after her talk with her parents. She used to spend countless hours in here worshipping and talking to God. Verona loved praise and worship. All through her pregnancy she begged God to change her parents' minds. When she had been forced to give her son up to "people who will love and care for him" she still kept her faith. However, when she heard her two-year-old son call Sister Smith "Mommy," she had run away. Verona vowed never to return to her parents' California home.

Now, look at her.

Verona heard a knock on her door. Glancing at the clock, she saw it was close to midnight. At her signal, Louisa entered, holding an ice cream sundae treat.

Her mouth watered. Verona held out her hands.

"Tell me more about Michael," Louisa said.

Snuggled under the warm blankets, Verona devoured her chocolate chip ice cream. *Mmm.* She loved whipped cream. "You still make the best sundaes."

"Thanks." Louisa lifted the blanket and got under the covers. She reiterated, "Tell me about Michael."

"Michael is handsome, rich, arrogant, insufferable, demanding, and totally wonderful."

"Your eyes are shining. He sounds positively dreamy." Her mother sighed. "That's how it was when I met your father. Noel was all that and more. I still get the jitters when I see him."

Verona touched her cheeks. "TMI. TMI." The two women shared a laugh.

"Does he feel the same way about you?"

"I think so," Verona hedged. "Michael kissed me. I know he cares but he's been harping over his ex, Lauren, for years. I just found out she has his children. I can't compete." She took another scoop to finish off her sundae. Then, she divulged her real fear. "Michael's a father to twins. A boy and a girl. That's when I ran. I'm not fit to be anybody's parent. Not after what I did to my own."

"Oh." Louisa drew her close. "Your father and I didn't believe you when you told us you would be a mother. You said we would find a way to make ends meet. We shouldn't have forced you to give up your child. Experience has a way of making fools of decisions we thought were wise."

"A part of me knew you meant well." Verona inhaled and then smiled. "You still smell like Johnson's Baby Powder, even after all these years."

"I know I said this earlier, but I'm glad you're home. Your father and I hope you'll stick around for a while. There are a lot of people at Mount Moriah who'd love to see your face."

She stilled. Elijah was there. "I don't know if I can face him, Mom. I'll think about it." Which meant no. Verona had broken her rule and was back at home. But she was not stepping foot back in Mount Moriah. They would want her to sing and carry on the pretense. Like they all did not know Elijah was hers.

Her mom left shortly after that. Try as she might, Verona could not fall sleep. She dragged her feet down the stairs to get a glass of water. She knew her father was up. Verona debated for a moment before rapping on his study door. Hearing his permission, she entered.

"I've been waiting for you to show up." Noel said once Verona was fully inside the room. She ran her hand across the furnishings as she walked around the small space. It looked the same to her. They had had many good talks in here. She inhaled, loving the scent of vanilla musk.

Eventually, Verona made her way to sit in the armchair across from Noel. She wiggled her foot out of her slippers and snuggled deep into the worn leather. She gave her dad a warm smile. He opened the tiny drawer on his desk and pulled out some pictures. "I want you to see something."

As he walked around his desk, for some reason, her heart rate escalated. With shaky hands, Verona grasped the pictures he held. She looked at the person featured knowing she was looking at her son. With rapid-fire speed, she tore through the pictures. She could not get enough: Elijah at the park. Elijah at the zoo. Elijah in church. Tears rolled down her cheeks. She sniffed several times.

Verona croaked a single word. "Elijah."

"When you left, we asked the Smiths to consider an open adoption. They agreed."

Did that mean what she thought it meant? Her heart thumped inside her chest.

"He spends the night with us, his Pop and Nana," Noel informed her with a gravelly voice.

Choked, she asked, "Does he know me? Does he know who I am?"

"He knows he's adopted. He has a picture of you by his bedside. Ronald and Edith made sure of that."

She studied his most recent picture. Elijah looked like a happy and contented fifteen-year-old. He was dressed in a baseball suit. He held the bat with a confidence she did not remember having at his age. Her heart expanded. Her chest felt like it was on fire.

Verona gripped Noel's hands. Never in her life did she think she would be given the opportunity to say her next words. Verona let out a heartfelt request. "I'd like to meet him. I'd like to meet my son."

Chapter Thirty-seven

"How long will he be here?" Gina asked Keith, her impatience already evident.

"Not long. I hope. The judge released him in my care. He warned it's my career if Michael doesn't comply. Thank you for agreeing to let him stay here," Keith said.

"Thank God. It was His doing." Gina gazed at him with troubled eyes. "I'm anxious that Michael could be living here for months. We were planning to take the kids to Florida, remember? Now, we'll have to change our plans because of your brother."

"I understand your frustration, honey. We can always go to Disney and Universal. Michael needs us. He's fighting for his freedom."

Like a runaway train, Gina was on to something new. "Verona didn't show up." She pulled her gloves from her hands with agitation. "We were supposed to have dinner before Bible Study. She stood me up."

Keith creased his forehead. "She had every intention of coming. That was until the officer showed up with a prophylactic saying it was found in Michael's garbage bin."

Gina's mouth popped open. "What? Who was he with?"

"According to him, no one. He says he hasn't been sleeping with anyone."

She gave him a "what you talking 'bout" look then said, "You seriously expect me to believe that? Michael and monogamy only have one thing in common: the letter M.

Did you forget about Karen?" she asked. When Gina and Michael dated, he had slept with his crazy ex-girlfriend, Karen Newton.

"Did you forget he's been pining over Lauren?"

"Lauren? I thought Michael was trying to get with Verona," was the cheeky comeback.

Keith caved. "I see your point. My brother doesn't have a good track record when it comes to women." Keith did not care for the "I told you so" look Gina had written all over her face. He changed gears. "I think his being here with us is a good thing. We'll use his time here to help him build a relationship with Christ and family."`

"I agree. God needs to work on Michael real fast," Gina said. "I'm going to give Verona a call."

"You like her," Keith observed.

"She's all right."

"Admit it. You're the ex-wife who likes the next wife." He chuckled at his spin on words.

Gina swatted his arm. "You think that's funny?"

Keith grabbed her hands and pulled her into his chest. Her little head barely rose above his midriff. In a deft move, he lifted her so she straddled his waist.

"Why do you always seek to distract me with your fine body? I want to argue."

"And I want to . . ." He whispered a suggestion in her ear. When he pulled away, Gina's cheeks were beet red. She could not even look him in the eyes.

"We're having a movie night, remember? Your idea will have to wait. I have to go oversee the popcorn or the alarm might go off again. I don't know how Trey messes up microwave popcorn."

"Let me get the blankets. Whose turn is it to pick the film?"

"Epiphany's."

He groaned. *Ella Enchanted.* That's what they were watching. Good thing he knew how to keep himself occupied.

Gina was a mind reader. "Michael's here. You're not sitting next to me to feel me up under the covers."

Keith should have known she would be a prude. "But . . ."

"I'm cuddling with E.J."

Great. I'll bring my Bible with me.

Gina read his thoughts again. "And, no scriptures during the movie. God rested. So can you."

He lifted his hands in the air. "You hear that, God?"

Michael felt a pang of envy watching Keith and his family all wrapped together. He stretched his legs in front of him. E.J. had her head on a pillow in his lap. He patted her little head. Michael never knew he would see this day. He had treated Epiphany like crap when she was younger. Now here she was, trusting him. Michael closed his eyes. This was the epitome of the fruit borne by forgiveness.

Michael pictured John and Olivia watching the movie with him. He and Lauren would be wrapped under the blankets. Or, maybe it would be he and Verona under blankets? Michael was not sure. But whoever it was, he knew he would be doing some naughty things. Unlike Keith and Gina, who sat apart from each other. Michael figured it was since Keith was now a preacher and all that. Maybe he and Gina saved all the affection for behind closed doors.

Well, he for one knew he could not be a stuffy Christian. Being married and saved meant he could get legitimate nooky with a high five from God.

As soon as the movie ended, Michael excused himself. He wanted to visit his children, but he could not leave Keith's home. That was the condition of his release. He was to remain in confinement at Keith's residence. The only other places Michael was allowed to go were the church and court. But Lauren could bring the kids over. It was only nine p.m. He would give her a call. Michael would love to see John and Olivia even if it were for five minutes.

"I can't."

Michael wanted to scream. "Why? Do you have a date with Martin?"

"Yes, I do."

Liar. "Lauren, I know you don't have a date with Martin because he doesn't exist. You made him up."

"What if I did?"

Michael had not expected that sharp comeback. He counted to five. He changed the topic. "Did you mean what you said the other day?"

He knew his conversation shift had thrown Lauren. "What did I say?" she asked.

He smiled at her confusion.

"You thought we should get married. Now that I know there's no Martin, I'm asking you."

"This is how you propose to me? Don't I deserve a better proposal than this? What about that funny-eyed lawyer you're seeing?"

Michael lowered his voice. "Verona won't be a problem. I assure you. You deserve the world for what you've given me. You've given me two gifts no amount of money could buy. I'm asking for your hand in marriage. I promise to cherish you, provide for you, and give you the best of what I have left."

He heard the sharp intake of breath and waited.

He waited.

And waited.

As Michael was about to ask Lauren if she was still on the line, he heard, "Yes, I'll marry you. I'd be honored.

You'd better straighten things out with Verona. I'm not about to tolerate any drama."

Thank God. "I'll make you the happiest mother in the world. Thank you," he said.

Michael swiped the end button. His first thought was, *I'm engaged.* His second was he could not believe he had proposed to a woman over the phone. It was borderline ghetto. However, due to his present circumstances, it could not be helped.

His last thought before he hit the pillow was, *how do I tell Tiger?*

Chapter Thirty-eight

Verona entered Mount Moriah Baptist Church with her head held high. There was a hush before recognition rippled through the crowd. She ignored the whispering and talking behind the hands and even the not-so-subtle finger pointing. As she walked to the front pew, she reminded herself she had a higher purpose for being there.

Each time she clapped and said amen to her dad's message, her eyes had roamed the crowds searching for Elijah. Verona spotted a blue-haired, lanky teen with double pierced ears. Her mother whispered, "That's him."

What happened to the clean-cut kid in the pictures she'd studied all night? She wondered about the Smiths' parenting skills. But, of course, Verona was in no position to say anything. She was the runaway parent, the absentee mom. She had no rights.

She barely made it through the service before dragging her mom in tow.

"Oh, I forgot to tell you he goes by Jah," Louisa said.

"Jah?" Verona enunciated the word like she was speaking Chinese.

"Yes, he prefers to be addressed that way now." Her mother pulled her forward. On wobbly legs, Verona made her way over to where Elijah stood. He had his hands shoved into his pockets and stood with his chest puffed out.

"Hello, Mother," Elijah said, and stuck out his hand.

Verona froze when she saw something on the back of his hand. A tattoo. She did not relish the idea of a fifteen-year-old sporting a tat. Nevertheless, she took Elijah's hand in hers and made her first contact with her son.

Her heart leapt and her mouth formed a perfect O. Wonderment filled her being. Verona was holding her son's hand.

With her free hand, Verona touched her chest. "My son," she whispered. Tears filled her eyes.

He gave a gawky grin. "Elijah," she said, testing his name out on her lips.

"Jah," her mother corrected.

Verona released short raspy breaths. "Jah," she said.

A crowd was forming behind them. Verona did not care. Self-conscious, Elijah pulled his hand away. She quickly released her death grip.

"I'm sorry. I'm just . . ." Verona trailed off. "I don't know what to say. You're much taller than I remembered."

He chuckled. "Yes. Grandpa said I'd probably be taller than he is, soon."

Her Cheshire cat grin was a bit off-putting. Verona knew that. But she could not stop her cheeks from spreading. "I dreamt of this day!" she exclaimed. She placed a hand on his cheek. Grazing her hand down Elijah's face, she felt signs of stubble. "You shave?"

He bent his head, his embarrassment evident by his slight blush. "Yes, I had to grow up sometime."

Verona's brain had frozen a different picture. This was not the two-year-old running through the choir stands she had left thirteen years ago. Elijah was almost a man. Fully grown.

"I think we should go," Louisa said. "Your father's waiting. We're going to Golden Corral for lunch."

Verona nodded. They walked toward her father's car. She took Elijah's hand. Savoring the feel of holding her son's hand. "Are you coming with us?"

Elijah froze midstride. "No, I'm meeting up with friends. My mom said I could. I didn't know . . ." Verona didn't miss he was looking at his grandmother. He was still very shy to address her. She understood. Even if her heart ached because of it.

"It's okay, Jah. We'll see you later."

"I'll see you later. Uhm, yes, Mother. I'll call you or something." He said "Mother" as "Moth-er." The endearment was stuck in his throat. Verona made a move to follow him. Her father held her arm.

"He'll come over to the house this evening," Noel said. "Remember yourself at that age?"

She nodded. She watched Elijah sprint across the parking lot. Verona pined for him already. "I wish he were coming with us. This is a special day for me. Why did the Smiths say he could go out with friends? Maybe they don't want him around me. Maybe he really doesn't want me popping up in his life now." Doubts filled her mind. Verona swayed into her father's chest.

Noel peered into her face. "It's a special day for him too, honey. He needs time to process. The Smiths will drop Elijah off later. This isn't good-bye. Don't get dramatic about it."

Verona stood, watching. Elijah went over to a group of kids. He piled into a car along with them. He had dismissed her already. She exhaled. As the car drove by, Elijah pinned her with a gaze. Then he lifted his hand in a small wave. He turned his head to watch her until the car was no longer in view.

Verona's heart lifted. This was not the end. This was just the beginning.

Chapter Thirty-nine

Keith bolted awake. He shook Gina from her slumber. "Three days and three nights," he voiced in the dark of the night.

"Who are you? Jonah the Prophet? Go back to sleep," she grumbled.

He shook her again. One evil eye popped open to zoom in on him. "God wants us to fast and pray for three days and three nights, beginning tomorrow," he told her.

Gina yawned. "For who? And, how is it 'us'? Why isn't it ever just you? How do I end up in the mix?"

He squeezed her thigh. "We're a team, baby. Mindy needs us."

"Mindy?" Gina propped up her body with her hands. Then glared at him. "You mean to tell me God wants us to do three days of praying and fasting for the girl who put your brother in jail? You sure you got that right?"

"Yup."

Gina rolled her eyes.

"Don't hate the messenger."

She smirked. "For the life of me, I don't understand why God can't talk to you at a decent hour."

"It's near the breaking of the day. Don't you know this is when God does His best work? Remember when Jacob wrestled with the angel? When do you think he received his blessing?" He tilted her body back and forth with his hand to tease her. Gina was cute when rattled.

"Listen, save the Bible trivia for someone who cares, vampire preacher," she protested and burrowed deeper into the covers.

Keith chuckled. He knew despite her protests, Gina would join him. She was a prayer warrior when she was awake. Right now, she was most concerned with getting back to sleep.

All that squirming took Keith's thoughts in a different direction. "Babe, are you asleep?"

"Yes."

"Now you know you couldn't answer me if you were sleeping."

"You asked me a stupid question, you get a wise answer. How am I supposed to fall asleep that fast?"

In a swift move, Keith moved Gina's body beneath his and rocked his hips.

"Was this a part of God's message too?" she asked, fully alert.

He could not help the deep rumble in his chest as he tried not to laugh. "It's been awhile."

She pushed against his chest. He barely felt her tiny hands but complied. "It's a hard road to travel," he sang loud enough for her to hear.

Gina's body shook with laughter. "I'll make it up to you. I promise. Trey and E.J. both have dental appointments at eight a.m. tomorrow."

"I know you're hands-on. So am I, but this is God's business. Josie can sit with them and drop them off at school when they're done." Keith poked her on the nose. "You're on the spiritual clock tomorrow. We'll go to the church and break our fast in the evening. I'll invite Michael. This will be a spiritual boot camp experience for him."

"Don't expect too much."

"I'm not wet behind the ears, lady. Of course, I know that. Michael can do what he can, but what better way to learn how to move God's hand? We need God to fight this battle or Michael's going down."

"I wish I'd known." Gina yawned.

"Known what?"

"That I'd be fasting tomorrow. I would have eaten those shortbread cookies and had my pistachio ice cream earlier tonight."

"Well, you're always saying you need to lose weight."

He was granted a hefty punch to the stomach.

"Are you calling me fat?"

Lord, couldn't you have bridled my tongue? There was only one way out of this pickle. Diversion. "Of course not. I know how you could burn a good five hundred or so calories."

That got her attention. "How?"

"I can show you," Keith suggested with a wiggle of his brows.

She gave him a playful slap. "Game on."

He did not need any further encouragement.

Now that what he wanted for the past three years was within reach, he was not sure.

In Keith's home gym, Michael started a slow jog on the treadmill intending to hit the five-mile point.

He was engaged to Lauren.

This meant she would need a very large token on her left hand. He increased the pace. Problem was he was confined here. He went a little faster. He could not ask Verona to use his funds to purchase a ring. He pushed it until sweat dripped from his body.

Grabbing a towel, Michael hit the stop button. Keith had entered the room just as he finished his pushups. Keith headed straight for the weights. Michael spotted for him.

"I don't know about you, but I've worked up quite the appetite from this workout. What's Josie cooking for breakfast?"

Keith had a sheepish expression on his face. "I should've mentioned this earlier. Josie is out of commission for the next three days. Gina and I will be fasting. The kids will eat cereal or something."

Michael's stomach chose that precise moment to signal its distress. He banished the visions of Josie's pancakes floating around his head. "I'll help myself to cereal as well. No problem."

"Well, Gina and I hoped you'd take up fasting and prayer with us. Fasting and prayer are the keys to communicate with God."

No food. Michael wasn't feeling that idea. He loved his meals and snacks. "I don't think I can go without food for three days."

"We break in the evenings," Keith pointed out.

"I suppose," Michael agreed. "What would we be doing exactly?"

"We read the scriptures. Share on the Word. We pray. We're seeking God's face on Mindy's behalf."

"Mindy?" That was his way out right there. There was no way Michael was going to give up his favorites for the girl responsible his getting tossed in jail not once, but twice.

"This is not about Mindy alone. Giving up your food shows God you're willing to make a sacrifice as He did for us."

Michael nodded, though he did not fully comprehend.

Keith added, "I know some of what I'm saying will go right over your head, but God directed me to go into prayer for Mindy. I want this case over and done with so you can begin a new path with God. "

"I want that too," Michael said as they left the room.

"You don't have to go all day. Do what you can. God is pleased with any genuine sacrifice you make for Him."

"As it happens, my schedule is clear," Michael said, attempting humor. He gave Keith a small pat on the back. "Speaking of new paths, I think this is the best time to tell you I asked Lauren to marry me last night."

Chapter Forty

"I'm not punching you in the face again. Don't bother to ask."

Mindy pushed at the door but Finn was using his foot as a doorstop. She had taken a cab into the city specifically to see him and she was not leaving until she did. Her father had kept her under tight security for the past month. Today was her first opportunity to get away. "Let me in. That's not why I'm here."

She felt the door give way and strutted into Finn's apartment. He lived above his nightclub. This was the first time Mindy had entered his space.

"Consider that the first and last time I put my hands on a woman. I may be many things but a woman beater isn't one of them."

"Finn, quit the nonsense. The couple punches you gave me didn't put me in the hospital. Obviously, I had help from another friend," was her blithe reply before she mumbled, "Not that it did any good. They thought Michael did it."

Finn must have heard her. He gave Mindy an odd look. "Why would you want to hurt yourself? Why would you want to mar your lovely face? I don't get you, Mousie . . . er, Mindy."

"If it's any consolation, I don't get me either." Mindy plopped her foot on his couch. "I have a problem. One I can't explain right now. But, I've taken care of my dad." She stopped, wondering if she had said too much.

Finn must have decided he did not want to know because he let her cryptic comment slide. "Fair enough. Why are you here?" he asked.

"I need to know what you plan to do to Michael."

He turned away from her. "That's none of your concern. You messed up the plan anyways. Your father wanted his head on a platter. Now Michael is staying with his brother so plans are on hold. Bill doesn't want to mess with a preacher."

Mindy smiled. "I'm glad I was able to help thwart the plan. I know Michael doesn't see it that way, but I saved his life."

Then, Mindy did something she had never done. She initiated contact. She walked behind Finn and circled his waist. With her head rested on his back, she said, "I don't want you involved. It would hurt me if you were arrested or took the fall doing my father's dirty work."

Finn faced her with wide eyes. "Are you saying you care about what happens to me? In all my twenty-seven years, I haven't had anyone care about me."

It took every ounce of will she possessed, but Mindy knew she could do it. She could reach out and love and be loved. "Yes, I care."

"May I touch you?"

Her heart thumped. *Don't back out now.* She nodded. As Finn's head lowered, Mindy held her breath. Tentative, he placed his lips on hers.

Mindy blinked. Nothing happened. Had she been worried for nothing?

After several seconds, Finn lifted his head. "Are you okay?"

Breathe, girl. "Yes." Mindy turned so Finn would not disappointment plastered on her face. She swiped at a tear forming under her eyelids. She was unlovable.

Suddenly, two strong hands clenched her arms and

twisted her around. Finn lifted her chin. He made her look at him. "Not what you expected?"

She shook her head.

"Was that your first kiss?"

She nodded.

"Well, the second will be better. I promise." This time Finn kissed her so good Mindy's toes curled. She groaned when he pulled away.

He laughed. "Better?"

She nodded. "More."

"Tell me what's wrong with you first."

Mindy took a deep breath. *Here goes nothing.* She needed to say the words. Even if it meant he freaked out. Even if it meant threw her out. Mindy needed to tell another human being. Her father refused to entertain the discussion.

"I have suffered from dissociative identity disorder since I was a young child," she said.

Finn took one step back. "What kind of disorder?"

"I have multiple personalities. I've been taking my medications. I've been good the past couple of days."

He eyed her like she was the girl from *The Exorcist.* Mindy took a step toward him. He took two steps back. *No, please don't reject me.* She felt her helpers waiting to take over. No, she needed to stand.

"I'm not contagious, Finn. Please don't run from me," Mindy pleaded. Every ache she felt at feeling alone in the world resounded in her words.

"What do you want from me?" Finn asked. He put more distance between them. "I thought you were crazy. I didn't know you were crazy crazy."

Mindy's shoulders slumped. *Let me have at him,* Mousie demanded.

Mindy closed her eyes. *No.* Overcome with pain, she whispered, "I am flawed. I might be crazy. But, I'm a human and I deserve to be loved." She walked up to Finn. "I want you to love me. Love me."

She saw fear in Finn's eyes. She lifted a hand and he flinched. Still, she pressed on. "I need to know someone in my existence loves me."

"I don't know if I can," he confessed. "Who am I, God?"

Mindy shook her head. Whatever she was looking for was not here. Gathering her belongings, Mindy left Finn's apartment.

The temptation to cut herself was strong, but she resisted. Mindy wandered the streets going over her conversation with Finn. Was there a better way she could have told him? *Naw.* There was no easy way to tell someone you have a mental illness. You had to come out and say it.

Mindy leaned up against a parked vehicle to rub her aching feet. *"Who am I? God?"* She kept hearing that question. She repeated the question aloud many times.

Then in a split second, it clicked. Mindy stilled all movement. She tuned out the honking horns, the cars whizzing by, the child wailing for his mother to pick him up, the couple chattering, and the street drummer.

The stillness surrounded her.

I am God.

Goosebumps rose and it was not because of the cold December air. God. God. He was who she needed. God was her last chance. Mindy held back her cackle. Finn had helped her. With a snap of her fingers, Mindy hailed a cab. She was going to see the only man of God she knew.

Chapter Forty-one

Keith left Dr. Nancy Forrester's office unsuccessful in his mission. The doctor had refused to break confidentiality as he figured. But still he had to try.

He then tried to reach Verona. It went to voicemail. *That girl sure loved to run.*

"God, you need to bind her feet," he uttered. With a nickname like Tiger, he had expected a little more spunk. However, it appeared her predator skills were limited to the courtroom and not to her personal life.

On impulse, Keith decided to stop by his church office. He felt an inexplicable urge to head to Zion's Hill. He did not know why. Maybe he would spend some quiet time with God. Finish up the Book of Zechariah. That was one of the books Gina, Michael, and he had read while they were in fasting and prayer. Keith wanted to zone in on Zechariah 4:6 in particular. "'Not by might, nor by power, but by my spirit, saith the Lord of hosts,'" he recited. That verse had a message in it for him and everyone else.

Michael had done quite a bit of praying as well. The first day, he had said two lines. But by the end of the third day, Michael was praying like he had been doing it for years. The fasting would take him some time to get used to.

Keith cracked up remembering how Michael had convinced his secretary, Dianne, to order pizza. He and Gina had opened their eyes after praying to find Michael missing in action. They searched and searched for him; worried he had broken the judge's orders. Keith would never forget the look on Gina's face when they discovered Michael in Keith's private bathroom wolfing down his fourth slice.

Keith parked in his designated space. A Yellow Cab pulled into the space next to him. Who could be coming to the church today? Curious, he waited inside his car to see who would be exiting the vehicle.

It was Mindy.

What's she doing here? he wondered before the thought hit. *Answered prayer.*

Mindy wrapped her coat about her, strutted over to his vehicle, and tapped on his window. Keith rolled down the power window.

"Perfect timing." She grinned and held out a hand. "I need cab fare."

Keith settled her tab and tipped the driver. He hurried them into the building. It was about thirty-six degrees, which for mid-December was high temperatures. He nodded at Dianne and left the door open. Once Mindy was seated across from him in his study, he asked, "How did you know I'd be here?"

"I didn't," Mindy answered. "I was worrying, too. Especially once I realized I didn't have enough cab fare."

"Why didn't you use one of your father's vehicles?"

She broke eye contact. "He doesn't want me driving. He's afraid to let me behind the wheel though I'm a very good driver. For the most part, I don't mind using cabs because it's easier. Sometimes, Elle G shuttles me around, if she can."

"Who's Elle G?" he asked. Distracted because he was sending a text to Gina, Keith did not hear her response. When he looked up, he saw Mindy eyeing him. "Sorry. I was sending my wife info about my whereabouts."

"I'm good," she assured him.

Gina responded: OK. Thx. Michael is working out.

Keith hit the silent button and placed his cell phone face down on the table. He opened his mouth to share that he had been expecting her. The Spirit urged him not to speak.

Listen.

Obedient, Keith said, "Why don't you tell me why you're here?"

Mindy straightened her spine as if she was gathering her courage. Then in a tiny voice, she said, "There are three people inside me."

Keith's ears pricked. He had been expecting a confession, not a revelation. "What do you mean?"

"I have multiple personalities," she explained. "I was diagnosed when I was a child."

Lord, I invite your presence and your power. Though he knew the answer, Keith asked, "Are you seeing someone?" The lawyer in him wanted to hit the record button on his phone, but this conversation wouldn't be admitted in court.

"I've been seeing a psychiatrist, Dr. Forrester, but my father made me stop going. He doesn't believe in it, calls it psychobabble." She gave Keith a sly look. "He doesn't believe much in God or church either."

"Yet, you're here," he noted.

"I am. I watch your shows. You talk about how God is a healer. I want healing. I want to be normal like everyone else."

Keith took in Mindy's expectant face. For a moment, he felt out of his league.

She wrapped her arms about her. "You think I'm weird. Are you going to be scared and treat me like a pariah like everyone else?"

Lord, help me. He opened his mouth and spouted a Bible verse: "'For God has not given us the spirit of fear, but of power, and of love and of a sound mind.'" *Thank you, Holy Ghost!*

"A sound mind. A sound mind," Mindy repeated. Her body straightened. "For a second there, I thought you'd be like everyone else. Is that in the Bible? Where can I find it?"

"It's here in Second Timothy 1 verse 7." Keith walked over to the large oak chest in the corner of his office and pulled it open. Taking out one of the wrapped giveaway Bibles, he tore off the plastic coating. Within seconds, he located the passage before handing it to her. This time he sat in the chair next to her.

Mindy read the verse with the enthusiasm of a thirsty wanderer who had found water. She repeated the verse at least three times. Then she pierced him with an enraptured gaze. "I want this. I want it. How can I get it?"

"You have to seek the One who gives it," Keith explained. God was filling his mouth with words. Mindy's facial expression was akin to an eager baby bird waiting for the worm. God used that moment to teach Keith a lesson. People were still hungry for the Word and he had to be ready to share it whenever, wherever.

He shared, "Mindy, I'm not like most preachers. I'm not going to anoint you and pray over you for hours."

She squinted her eyes. "You're not?"

Keith chuckled. "No, I don't have a magic wand to wave away your problems. Do you know what Jesus did with hungry people?"

"What?" Her eyes were round and eager.

"He fed them. He took care of the physical body first. That's where we'll start."

She drooped. Keith actually felt her disappointment.

"When Jesus heals, He makes you completely whole. This is the first step," he said.

Keith was about to go in preaching mode when Mindy changed lanes.

"There's another reason I'm here. I've been taking my medication. It dulls my thoughts. Taking pills is not the answer. Dr. Forrester told me I needed to confront my past. Even though it's painful," she said, gripping his arm.

Like an experienced car driver, Keith followed Mindy's conversation shift. "Did you ever take Dr. Forrester's advice and talk about it?"

She shook her head. "No. Dr. Forrester felt my father should be there with me. He refused. He called her a quack and banned me from going. But I'm nineteen now. I can go without his permission."

Keith nodded but did not egg her on. Whatever move Mindy made had to come from her.

"I want to see Dr. Forrester. But, I don't want to go alone. I . . . I want to help Michael. I want to remember what happened that night. But, I need Mousie and Baby to tell me."

Keith gestured for her to elaborate.

"They are my alters or, as I call them, my only friends." Mindy closed her eyes and hugged herself.

Keith experienced a wake-up call. He realized how scary mental illness was for the person living with it. He reached over and nudged Mindy on the shoulder. She stood. Her chest heaved. With timid eyes, she met his gaze. Keith inhaled from the pain, the torture, the loneliness he saw there. *Oh, Lord, thank you for opening my eyes*. Mindy was visibly suffering, filled with brokenness. Moved with compassion, he enfolded her in his arms and said. "God loves you."

Her body shook. She pushed against him for him to release her.

But, God spoke through him. "I'm not letting you go."

"No one wants me," she sobbed, "not even my own father."

He gave Mindy a fatherly pat. "God wants you." Now he understood the impact Michael's words from his e-mails would have had on her heart.

Finally, they broke apart.

Mindy lifted her eyes to his. Through the Spirit, Keith saw *them*.

She said, "Dr. Forrester can help us figure this out. Will you come with us?"

Chapter Forty-two

Brown or black?

Verona eyed the text message and the two pictures of the suits he had attached.
Michael.
Imagine the nerve of him! Days and days had passed with no communication, yet he could not even greet her with a proper hello. Verona had been watching television in the living room when the text came in. She had rushed upstairs to her room before she answered.

Black.

Seconds after Verona hit the send button her phone rang. "Took you long enough," she said.
"I can't believe you ran off," Michael shot back.
Not for a minute would she admit how much she had missed him. How glad she was to hear his voice. How her heart thumped against her chest like bongo drums. Instead Verona asked, "How is it at Keith and Gina's?"
"I'm out of that cell. As far as I'm concerned, I'm in heaven." Michael addressed the reason he had called. "When are you coming back? I have a court date a month from now. I need you here."'
"I'll be back this week. I came to see my family." She waited for that revelation to sink in.

"You went home? Who died?" Michael knew she did not have contact with her family, though she had never explained in detail.

"No one died. I came to see my parents. Life is too short to keep holding this grudge."

She heard a small chuckle. "If it's anyone who can relate, it's me. But, I'm paying you a hefty retainer for you to be here on your A game."

Typical Michael. Everything was about him. "This may come as a shock to you, but my life doesn't revolve around you. If you must know, I have a son. I came to see my parents and I, um, met him," she said.

Silence filled the line. Good. It seemed as if she had managed to shock him. *Percolate on that awhile, Loudmouth.*

Then Michael bellowed, "You have a son and didn't tell me! How dare you keep that from me? Why would you keep your son hidden? Why isn't he with you?"

Without knowing it, Verona raised her voice. "Hold on a minute. As far as I'm concerned, it's the case of the pot and kettle because you have two children, two, who somehow slipped your mind to mention." She laid the sarcasm on thick.

"That's because it really wasn't your business," he shot back. "You're my employee. I'm not beholden to you. I don't have to disclose my personal information to you."

His haughty tone fired her temper. "I'm not some lowly employee. I'm the woman standing by your side even when you're the world's biggest jerk. Which you are most of the time! I'm sick of being your lapdog. You'd better learn to respect me or I'll quit!"

"Don't threaten me, woman! And, didn't you quit already?" he asked.

"I can't remember right now. Come to think of it, it's not relevant to this discussion because I'm here. I'm

holding your purse strings in my hands. I've been busy
keeping your hole-filled sinking ship of a business afloat.
Whenever I'm not spending time with my son or my
parents, I've been on that computer and on my cell phone
handling things. For you. You'd better recognize!" She
yelled at the top of her lungs.

Verona heard a knock at her door. Her mother asked,
"Honey, are you okay?"

She cupped a hand over the phone. "Yes, Mom, I'm
fine." Then she went back to her call. "Now see what
you've done. You've got my mother coming and asking
if I'm all right because, as usual, you're being a moron!"

"Goodness, woman! You will respect me!" Michael
said. She heard three loud exhalations through the line.

"Stop breathing like a stalker on the phone!"

"I'm trying to cool my temper," Michael explained. She
heard him shout, "Lord, help me!" before he continued in
an even tone. "And for your information, I do recognize
all you do for me."

Verona really needed to follow his cue and calm down.
Elijah would arrive in an hour and they were going to the
mall and the movies. She was looking forward to taking
her son shopping. She was not about to let this idiot ruin
her mood.

"Thank you," she said, through gritted teeth.

"No. Thank you," he emphasized. Verona let him
because he should be thanking her.

"I don't know why we're arguing," Michael said. "I
didn't call to fight. I called to check on you. See how the
woman I love is doing. But, instead, my voice is hoarse
and my blood pressure is sky high. You're the only
woman on the planet who does this to me."

Wait. Did she hear right? Verona pressed the cell
phone tighter to her ear. Did he say what she thought he
said? "What did you say?"

She heard some sort of a commotion on his end. "Hang on," Michael said. From what she could hear, it sounded like Trey was asking him to play ball. She heard Michael agree before he returned to the call.

Verona's heart was pumping fast and she gripped the phone with one of her sweat-filled palms. "What did you say?" she repeated.

The man had the nerve to play dumb. "Tiger, I have to go. By the way, I'm going to need you to sign off on a major purchase for me. No questions asked."

Oh, now he was all business. Well, she would die before she asked him again. "I'll wait for the call." Verona swiped the end button and trudged down the stairs in a funk. Both her parents stood at the foot of the stairs. Two pairs of concerned eyes watched her descent.

"Are you all right? I think the entire block heard your conversation," Louisa stated.

"Yes, Mom. I'm all right." In a daze, Verona confided to her parents. "I think Michael told me he's in love with me."

Now they looked confused.

"You think?" her mother asked.

"Well, we were arguing. He said it like he regretted calling . . ." Verona trailed off, knowing her parents must think her plumb crazy. Michael riled her passions. She could not curb her reaction.

"I'm lost. Isn't that good news?" her father inquired.

Verona nodded. She was still befuddled. "I told Michael about Elijah. Well, I didn't get to give him the whole story. We were both heated from sharing our"—she formed quotes with her hands—"good news."

"My word, you two have to come up with a better way to share your good news," her mother noted.

Verona made a rash decision. "You're right, Mom." With sure steps, she zoomed toward the computer in the kitchen. Her parents followed.

"I'm booking a flight for New York. I'll leave tomorrow sometime. I need to work on the case. I must speak with Michael in person."

Louisa clutched her chest. "You're leaving?" Her crestfallen expression tore at Verona's heart. "I know you have to work but I just got you back."

"I'm coming back the second week in January," Verona assured her. "Elijah, I mean, Jah told me he's singing in church that Sunday. I'll be here."

"That's what I want to hear." Noel gave her a pointed stare. "No more running. You've been a prodigal too long."

Verona put her tongue in her cheek to keep from going off. She did not appreciate her father comparing her to a prodigal. She knew he had meant it in jest, but it hit home.

In less than five minutes, Verona had booked her first-class ticket, snagging the last seat on an afternoon flight. Sulky, she went to the refrigerator to grab a yogurt. She plopped a huge spoonful in her mouth. Her father came and pulled a chair out.

"You can't run away from the hard stuff. I taught you better."

"I don't see myself as a runner," Verona said. Just then, she noted Louisa's absence. "Where did Mom go?"

"She's upstairs getting dressed. She wants to come with you and Elijah to the mall. She didn't think you'd mind."

"No, I don't mind. I like the idea of three generations doing something together."

They shared a smile, before her father got serious. "You didn't just leave us. You left the church. You left God. What did He do to you to deserve you dropping Him from your life?"

"I didn't drop God. How do you know I wasn't involved with church in New York? You could be misjudging me."

Noel gave her a knowing glance and called her bluff. "Am I?"

Verona's shoulders dropped. "No, you didn't. I blamed God for not stopping you and Mom for taking Elijah from me. All throughout my pregnancy, I prayed. I prayed and I prayed. But, God didn't hear me. You still plucked that baby from my arms and gave him to the Smith's to raise."

"We did, and right or wrong, I have to stand by my decision. I walk this life by faith. What you don't know is I was praying as well, nonstop. I asked for God's guidance. I felt He was leading me and I acted based on that belief."

"I don't think God would agree with you giving a child up for adoption for no reason," she said.

"The Smiths are wealthy and they were able to give Elijah a good home. We were broke and our home was in foreclosure. For us, the Smiths were answered prayer. By the way, God does favor adoption. What do you think we are? We are adopted by Him."

"I make more than enough money now to provide for a child," Verona declared, jutting her chin.

"Now. Not then. When you ran, I sought God's face. He directed me to talk with the Smiths. They agreed to an open adoption. Elijah has been a part of our lives ever since."

"So, you and Mom could've helped me raise him," she stubbornly insisted.

Her father sighed. "It's in the past. I can't change that. We have to move forward."

Verona finished her yogurt. She could not let it go. She drummed her nails on the table as she gathered her thoughts. "Moving forward is easy when you're not the one who had to carry Elijah inside your womb for months. You didn't stand by helpless as he was ripped from your hands. You could have helped me instead of punishing me."

"You have selective memory. I did help you," Noel persisted. "Even though we could've used that money, Louisa and I didn't touch your college fund. When the time came, we gave you all we had. That money paid your college tuition and shelter. We didn't regret giving it to you, even though you never kept in touch. There were days we had rice for dinner but we were content because you had a better life."

His words pierced her core. Her father told the truth. She had had no problem taking the money and leaving without a backward glance. While others were bogged down with student loan repayment, Verona had graduated debt free. She had been too spoiled and too rebellious to accept her parents' apology and their love.

A Bible verse from 1 Samuel 15 came back to her:

Rebellion is as the sin of witchcraft.

Truer words had never been spoken.

A sob escaped as Verona acknowledged her selfishness. "You're right. I was too caught up in my own hurt. I felt justified cutting you off. I didn't recognize that, whether I agreed with you or not, you did what you did because of love. Honestly, I don't deserve you and Mom."

Noel leaned forward. "Do you know how much it hurt me to not see my only child graduate from Stanford? Your mother cried for days when I told her we didn't get an invitation. Then you left without a forwarding address. We didn't contact the authorities. We knew you weren't missing. We knew you didn't want us."

Her nose ran. Her tears blinded her. Noel went to the counter and ripped a piece of paper towel before coming to wipe her face.

Choked with emotion, Verona lifted shame-filled eyes to her father. "I was angry and I was wrong, Dad. I see that now. If I could go back and—"

Noel held up a hand to still her words. "We can't go backward. However, I accept your apology and I thank you for it."

Verona finally saw his wisdom. He had regrets. She had regrets, but there was no do-over. There was only tomorrow.

"I'm not trying to rub it in, but, Verona, I must ask. If you felt we took Elijah from you as a teen, why didn't you try to do something when you became an adult? We couldn't have stopped you, then," Noel said.

"I don't know," she stammered, trying to recover from the truth-punch to her gut. She had never tried to contact the Smith's or even see her son. Verona could not blame her parents for that.

"I'm only pointing that out because I want you to let the past go. Don't you think Elijah is wondering why, if you loved him, you did nothing to reach out to him? Especially since you're a big-time attorney."

"He hasn't asked," she said, biting her lip.

"Not all children speak their minds, Tiger. Some keep these thoughts bottled up inside them and then poof! It all blows up in your face. If I were you, I'd talk to him."

"Has he said anything to you?"

"Not in so many words, but even if Jah had said something, I wouldn't break confidence. I'm not going to do your job for you. Just as I have to answer to you, you have to answer to Elijah. You've got to sit in the hot seat and take the heat. You can't run from this one."

Her father had read her left, right, and center and she was torn up inside. Verona had gone through her life stuck at seventeen, failing to realize the tables would turn one day. She now had a child who could resent her if she did not communicate.

She squirmed as the difficulty of the conversation she must have with Elijah hit her with full force. "I'm scared," she confessed.

"Good. You should be."

In spite of the tough talk, Verona smiled. "Those were the words Elijah said to me the other day on the phone. 'You should be.' I was saying something and that's how he responded."

"Well, where do you think he got it from? I have a relationship with him," her father bragged.

Checkmate.

Chapter Forty-three

For God hath not given me the spirit of fear; but of power, and of love, and of a sound mind. For God hath not given me the spirit of fear; but of power, and of love, and of a sound mind. For God hath not given me the spirit of fear; but of power, and of love, and of a sound mind.

For God hath . . . What if he doesn't show up?

Mindy popped her gum and looked at her watch. Her stomach was in knots. She knew it was nervousness. She had already been to the bathroom twice.

She eyed the clock. It was ten a.m., the day after New Year's, and she was sitting outside Dr. Forrester's office. If her father knew where she was, he would be furious. She had told him she was on a beauty regimen run and Bill had reinstated her Amex card, saying, "I'm glad you're acting normal. Go get all dolled up. We can go out later since we didn't do anything for New Year's Day."

Mindy wanted to say, "If I have to act, it's not normal," but she was not about to argue with him. And, which "normal" girl her age spent New Year's with her father?

Mindy touched her face running her fingers across the small scars above her lip and on her right cheekbone. Bill had suggested plastic surgery but Mindy had recoiled at the idea. All she needed was time and she'd be good as new. On the outside, anyway.

Where was Pastor Keith? He'd made the appointment and had promised to come to the session with her. This day and time had been the earliest Dr. Forrester could squeeze her in to accommodate them.

She tapped her feet. By chance, Mindy looked down. She cupped her mouth. What was she wearing? Those were her stripper shoes! Mousie!

You might take those pills to silence me but I'm a part of you, Mousie said. *I'm not going away that easy.*

Desperate, Mindy covered her ears. Then two doors opened at the same time. Pastor Keith rushed in and Dr. Forrester opened her door.

"I'm sorry; there was an accident on the road."

"Hello, Mindy, it's good to see you. Come in."

Pastor Keith greeted the doctor and smiled. For the first time, Mindy noticed his dimples and his smile. He was *fine.*

The three of them made themselves comfortable in Dr. Forrester's office. Mindy liked the sound of the small waterfall. The hues of blues and pinks on the walls were comforting. She couldn't resist touching the small bonsai tree.

"Dr. Forrester, do you mind if we begin the session with a short word of prayer?" he asked.

When the doctor nodded, they lowered their heads. Mindy kept her eyes peeled on Pastor Keith.

"Father, we invite you in. Please provide guidance and healing. We pray this prayer in Jesus' name. Amen."

He was not kidding when he said short. Did God hear that? She wondered.

"Mindy?" Dr. Forrester held a sheet of paper in her hand. "Please read and sign this statement saying of your own free will, you agree for Pastor Ward to sit in on the session with us. This is not normal protocol."

Mindy's heart pumped fast as she glossed over the words. Her father would kill her if he knew. But he was not here. With bold strokes, Mindy scribbled her name.

"What do you want to talk about today?" Dr. Forrester asked.

"I want to talk about that night. I need to remember," she said. "But everything's all jumbled inside my head."

"The best possible method is hypnosis. Are you finally ready to try it?"

"Yes," she breathed. She looked toward Pastor Keith.

He recognized her distress and he came over to hold her hand. "I'm here with you."

As fine as Pastor Keith was, Mindy did not feel feminine attraction. To her, Pastor Keith was being the father she never had. It was like God was speaking to her. She opened her mouth to tell him but changed her mind. She would sound crazy.

She giggled at that thought. "Thank you, Pastor." Then she addressed the doctor. "I'm ready."

Keith watched as Dr. Forrester coached Mindy under. Was this of God? He wondered. Unlike the movies, there was no light or swinging stopwatch. Instead, her voice was soothing and calming.

"There's no need to be afraid. I'm right here and we can stop at any time." Dr. Forrester told Mindy.

Within minutes, Dr. Forrester nodded at him.

Keith admitted he was a skeptic. A lot of church folks believed hypnotherapy was a form of enchantment. But what if it worked? Could the human mind really be manipulated in this fashion? Nevertheless, he took out his pad and paper to take notes.

"I see Carl." Mindy's voice held a childlike quality.

Wait a minute. Carl? Keith eyed the doctor. She held her hand up and pointed to her ears. Keith relaxed. He had prayed. He had to let God lead.

"You want to talk about your brother?"

"He's dead," Mindy cried. "I found him hanging in the air and Daddy wants me to pretend I didn't see it. But, I did. I did. He killed himself. He was my only friend. Now who's going to play with me?"

Keith jotted down the word: loss.

"I'll play with you," Baby said.

She was reliving the trauma, which triggered her multiple personalities. Keith felt goose bumps prick his arms.

"How old is Baby?" the doctor asked.

"She's five."

"Is that how old you were when you found Carl?"

"Yes. And there's Mousie. She's the brave one. She makes sure no one hurts me," Mindy explained.

Keith wrote another word: loneliness.

"I was sad when Carl died. I didn't think I would ever smile again," Mindy cried. She looked at Dr. Forrester. "My father didn't let me cry. He told me crying wouldn't help bring Mommy and Carl back."

This time he penned the word "depression."

Loss. Loneliness. Depression. The devil's tools. *For we wrestle not against flesh and blood but against spiritual wickedness in high places.*

Dr. Forrester said, "Today I'm giving you permission. Mindy, go ahead and cry."

Mindy's shoulders shook and she wailed. Keith's heart constricted. He could not remain silent any longer. "I know you feel alone, but God is here. He can fill that void," he said.

Mindy grabbed him and sobbed into his chest. "I felt lonely when I met Michael."

Keith released her and picked up his notepad.

The doctor took over the conversation. "How did you feel meeting Michael?"

"He was nice to me. He spoke to me and treated me like I was a human being," Mindy offered. "I couldn't wait to see him."

"Did he do or say anything you weren't comfortable with?"

Mindy shook her head. "Michael was my friend. He wouldn't hurt me."

Keith's heart rejoiced at her confident words. He knew Michael was innocent but her words were confirmation. *Thank you, Lord!*

"Tell me about that night," the doctor commanded.

"I'd been with Elle G."

Keith wrote the name down. Mindy had mentioned this person before. He tapped his chin with his pen. Was this a real person, or another personality?

"Who's Elle G?" Dr. Forrester asked.

"She's a friend. Well, she's Mousie's friend. Mousie met her outside the club at Finn's," Mindy whispered conspiratorially. "Mousie was a stripper. I think she did it because if my father ever found out, he'd blow the roof."

Keith was no expert but this sounded like resentment and rebellion. However, Mindy had taken it to a whole other level. Now he understood why God had placed him on three days of fasting and prayer. She needed deliverance.

He continued to listen to her recap. "Mousie met up with Elle G at the Ritz-Carlton. She'd brought wine. I don't drink, but Elle G convinced Mousie to try it. Mousie didn't care for the taste either but she had a friend. She only drank one glass to calm her nerves, but it made all of us woozy. It was worth it though. For the first time, Mousie had a girlfriend. Mousie and Elle G talked and laughed, mostly about Michael.

"Then Elle G suggested Mousie e-mail Michael and invite him over. I told Mousie I was scared, but Elle G told us Michael loved me too. He was simply scared to admit it because he was my father's friend."

It sounded like Elle G was manipulating her. Keith noted Mindy had now switched to "I." It was confusing, but he was keeping up. He glanced over at the doctor who was scribbling on her notepad. One thing he knew, this job required patience.

As a minister, he spent hours counseling and talking with his parishioners. He could relate.

Dr. Forrester gave him a warm smile before coaching Mindy to keep talking.

"My legs were shaking. When Elle G saw how frightened I was, she offered to stay with me. She gave me the skimpiest piece of lingerie I'd ever seen. I went into the bathroom to change. I . . ."

Dr. Forrester asked, "Do you need to stop?"

"No, I've got to face this," Mindy said. "I want to continue."

"What happened when you went into the bathroom?"

She grabbed Keith's hand again as if to make sure he was still there. "I cut myself."

Mindy kept her eyes on him as she said it. Keith schooled his expression. There was no way she would know how affected he was by her words. But being a parent himself, Keith was shaken. If that were Epiphany . . .

Mindy continued talking. "So Mousie took over. She cleaned me up and got me dressed and I left the bathroom. I wobbled. I remember vowing never to drink again. I got on the bed. Elle G promised she'd wait in the bathroom."

"What did you use to cut yourself?" the doctor asked.

"I have a small blade. I carry it in my bag sometimes. That's why Elle G didn't see it either. I lay on the bed and waited for Michael to come. He would pick up the extra card at the front desk. Elle G had worked it all out. I got nervous. I reached for the blade," Mindy said.

That explains the blood. It had been everywhere.

Mindy continued, "Michael came in. As soon as he saw me, he said, 'Mindy! Who did this to you? What happened?' By then, I was barely conscious, but I remembered saying, 'Why? Why did you do it? You hurt me and all I did was love you.'"

Goose bumps rose on Keith's flesh for the second time. Mindy had repeated verbatim what Michael had said. He interjected. "Why did you say that to Michael?"

Dr. Forrester intervened. "Pastor Ward, let her—"

Keith continued. He had to know. "Mindy, why did you say those words?"

Mindy's face was flushed and flooded with tears. "I'm sorry. I'm sorry. I was confused. It was Baby who said those words. She was talking to my brother. She was talking to Carl."

Keith excused himself. He rushed outside and stumbled over to his vehicle. Once inside, he released a warrior's cry. He gripped the wheel. All Mindy had was a mere apology for ruining Michael's reputation and for throwing him behind bars. Keith knew she was sick. Mindy was tortured, but he was human.

"Oh, God," he cried. "Her illness put my brother in serious trouble." He knew he should feel relief the truth was out. Instead, Keith grappled to control his anger.

He should be rejoicing but he wanted to . . . he wanted to shake Mindy, to scream and yell some mean words. "Help me, Jesus. Help me see her as you see her 'cause I'm struggling right now."

Keith leaned his head on the dash of his vehicle and communed with God, meditating on His soothing voice.

He heard a rap on his window. It was Mindy. "Do you hate me?" she asked.

Her question tore at him. He could not provide a suitable response without lying.

Keith narrowed his eyes. He could not say yes. He could not say no. He wanted to say yes, but knew he should say no. And so it went.

So, instead, Keith shared a Biblical truth. "God loves you and He forgives you."

"I'm going to the police station to talk to the officer," Mindy said.

Keith wanted to go home and work out the punching bag. However, he was still on God's job. He thought of several young men who were dying to be ordained ministers. If they only knew.

"I'll be right beside you every step of the way," he encouraged her.

Keith watched Mindy trot over to her vehicle. She kept looking back until Keith gave her a reassuring wave. Mindy didn't have anything to worry about. Keith was not going anywhere.

What choice did he have? God had chosen him for this path. He was the vehicle God would use for her healing. Keith started up the truck and followed her out of the parking lot, but he was not done whining to God.

Lord, was all this necessary? I just wanted my brother back home and saved.

I have three souls, not one.

"Three?" Keith voiced. Michael. Mindy. Who was the third? Several possibilities ran through his mind, but then Keith gave up. He was learning to stop predicting what he thought God would do. God did whatever He pleased. He would just have to wait to find out.

"But what about the condom found on the scene?" Nigel questioned. "Did Mindy mention that when she spoke?" The two men were at the coffee shop across from the district attorney's office. Keith had called Nigel to assist in the meeting with the district attorney the next morning. He had called the meeting as soon as Mindy had finished her statement at the police station.

Keith shook his head. "No, she didn't. She's made it clear she never slept with Michael. How his DNA ended up there will remain an enigma. Michael has no clue and I've presented several scenarios but he's holding firm he has never stayed in that room."

"I'll check the hotel records to corroborate his account."

Keith nodded. "That's a great idea. With Mindy's testimony, the DA doesn't have a case. He'll have to drop the charges and we can go about clearing Michael's name."

"I'm impressed," Nigel said. "How did you even get Mindy to talk to you? Bill has her under heavy guard."

Keith shrugged. "Mindy's actions are a result of prayer in effect. She's not as protected as you think. Apparently, she's able to fly the coop anytime she wants."

Nigel returned to his notes. "I'm going back to the condom mystery for a minute. Remember your theory about Michael being set up? Do you think there was another person involved?"

"I don't know. The main witness is a mentally ill patient. Mindy mentioned an Elle G several times. But, I don't know if she is a real or an imaginary person."

Nigel sighed. "What a mess!"

Keith agreed. "I've never prayed so much on a case in my life. I'm going to need some more help from God. I know the charges will be dropped and Michael will be free, but a part of me will never be settled until all the loose ends are tied."

"Someone had to put it there."

"I feel the same way. But the $64,000 question is, who? Who put it there?"

"Should I call Frank? Michael has used him in the past and he does get results."

For a second, Keith was tempted. Frank could find a speck of dust on a shiny surface. That was how skillful he was. But, Frank vetted his information by any means necessary. Keith could not promote evil even if it was for a good result.

"No, don't call Frank," Keith replied. "I can't support him especially since I know he's a strong arm. The truth will come out. It always does." He looked at his watch. "Let's not keep the DA waiting. Hopefully we'll convince him to drop the charges and we can get before a judge tonight."

Nigel waved a hand with confidence. "I do have the judge on standby because without Mindy this is all circumstantial. We'd rip them apart in court. I smell victory." He nudged Keith with his elbow.

Tiredness seeped through Keith's bones. "We'll start the celebration in church this Saturday. I hope you'll accept my invite."

"I might surprise you and show up," Nigel promised. "Tell you what; if we close out Michael's case today, I'm coming and sitting in the front row."

Keith grinned. "It's in the bag."

Chapter Forty-four

Such kissable lips.

That was Michael's first thought when he opened the door and saw Verona standing there. He was alone as both Keith and Gina were out, so he was glad for the company.

"You're here," he said, stating the obvious. "I thought you weren't coming back until next week."

Verona bit her bottom lip, driving him crazy. *Stop it, Michael. You're engaged.*

"I'm here now," she said as she entered. "It's time I stopped running." She looked around. "Where's Keith?"

"I think he's with Mindy at her therapy session."

Verona stopped short. He almost ran into her back. To steady himself, Michael grabbed her arm. Awareness rocked his being. The thought hit: they were alone and there were six bedrooms in the house.

However, her mind had been captured by his words. "He's with Mindy? I haven't been gone that long, have I? What on earth happened?"

Michael led her into the family room and they sat on the largest leather couch.

"Mindy sought Keith out for counseling. He wouldn't disclose their conversation but he did tell me she wanted to go see Dr. Forrester. She asked him to go with her."

Verona's mouth hung open. "How did he get Mindy to agree? Does her father know?"

Michael shook his head. "I don't know. I think this is all happening because Keith, Gina, and I went into fasting and prayer."

"You fasted? You're cranky when you get hungry."

He decided not to share his pizza binge. "I did it though. Keith said God told him it needed to be done and after the past few days, I'm inclined to believe it."

"God's going to solve your case? Do you know how amazing that is?"

Michael did not see it that way. He was afraid to get his hopes up. "Well, maybe God figured He had to step in since my very expensive attorney kept running off and quitting on me."

"You couldn't resist the gibe, could you? Do you think we can ever have a normal conversation without hitting below the belt?"

His eyes darkened. "I like getting you all riled. Your nostrils flare and your eyes flash this weird color. It's exciting. It's hot."

Verona threw a pillow at him. "You're trying to get closer to God. You shouldn't be talking like that. You need to be avoiding temptation."

Michael had another reason why he did not need to be flirting with her: Lauren, his fiancée. But, Lauren was not here and she was not Tiger. "Then stop looking so tempting," he teased.

Verona did a little squirm. Michael gave her a knowing grin. Keith had lectured him that getting to know God meant living a life pleasing to God. At the moment, the warnings were a little fuzzy.

He watched her tongue dart into her mouth. His body reminded him it had been awhile. Verona must have read his thoughts because she was looking at him like the insect in the spider's web.

She stood and backed away. "I came straight here from the airport. Jetlag's kicking in. I'm going to get some rest. I'll be back later."

Michael followed her, keeping his eyes on her delectable mouth. No way was she leaving until he had gotten a taste. He stalked her until he had her right where he wanted her.

"Michael, I'm getting back into church myself and I—"

By this time Michael had snatched her close to him. Verona was saying something but all he saw were her lips moving. He knew he should be thinking of Lauren, but this tiger needed taming and he was the only one suited for the task.

Michael used his other hand to raise her chin, imprisoning her with his strength. Then he lowered his head to suck on her neck marking his territory.

Verona pummeled his back with her fists but he didn't loosen his grip until her skin glistened with his love bruise. She stomped over to the mirror and arched her neck. "I can't believe you! That's juvenile. Which judge is going to take me seriously with this red blotch on my neck!"

Michael moved in behind Verona until his body cradled hers and they were both looking at each other through the glass. He studied his handiwork before smiling with satisfaction. Their eyes met.

Keeping his eyes on her, Michael lifted her hair to kiss her exposed ear. She liked watching, he noted. He loosened the buttons on her shirt. Her eyes darkened. While they faced the mirror, he moved a hand down her chest. Leaving it there to play, he kissed her cheek and twisted her head to meet his mouth.

"Michael!" a voice boomed.

For a split second, Michael froze. Then Verona sprung into action. He had never seen someone button a shirt so fast.

When had Keith returned? Like two teenagers caught with their pants down, Michael and Verona hurriedly adjusted their clothes. He shielded her body with his own until she was presentable. He saw her failure to hide his love mark and Verona elbowed him in the ribs.

"Didn't you hear the door open?" he growled into her ear, turning the blame on her.

"I can't believe you're pinning this on me!" Verona furiously whispered.

"I cannot have this in my home," Keith said. "Verona, please leave. I must have a talk with my brother."

Verona strove to preserve her dignity with professionalism. "I came to get caught up on the case."

Keith arched an eyebrow but said nothing.

Verona's face was beet red. Without another word, she gathered her purse. From behind Keith's back, she flipped him the bird. Michael shrugged. It was not the first time. He had better uses for that finger and as soon as he could, she would find out.

What Verona didn't know, at first, was his brother must have seen her through the mirror. Keith lifted his chin and folded his arms. Her eyes widened with horror when she discovered he had indeed seen her. She bolted through the door.

Wow, what sweet payback. Despite Keith's baleful look, Michael laughed so hard, a tear slid from his eye. He loved that woman.

She just flipped the bird in a pastor's house. Her finger could have wilted or something. Verona hightailed it out of Keith and Gina's house. As she skittered down the steps, Gina's car came into view.

Would her humiliation never end?

"Where are you running off to?" Gina lowered her window to greet her.

Verona skidded on the ice, falling bottom first. It was too much. She keeled over with laughter.

She heard the car door slam. Gina scurried to where she sat and helped her to her feet. "I'm glad I ran into you," she said, giving Verona a warm hug.

"I was going to call a cab," Verona said.

Gina's eyebrows arched. "You should've waited inside instead of coming out here in those impractical shoes. Didn't you listen to the weather? We're expecting snow tonight."

"I was in California visiting my family," she explained. "This was my first destination after exiting the plane. I wanted to see Michael. Keith barged in on us and asked me to come back later." A little fudge on the truth, but Verona would never admit she had been kicked out for bad behavior.

To her relief, Gina did not question her further. Although, Verona thought she saw Gina hiding a smile.

"How about we grab an early dinner?" Gina asked.

Verona nodded her assent.

About twenty minutes later they were being seated at Café Baci. Verona looked around the establishment, admiring the cozy feel of the earthy décor. "What a lovely restaurant."

"Keith took me here when we were . . . dating."

Dating? What a way to pretty up two-timing brothers. Gina had been "dating" Michael then too, but Verona kept her opinions to herself. She was no fool. Verona was not about to let her mouth get her stranded in West Hempstead without a ride.

Once they ordered and their meals arrived, Gina said, "Tell me about your trip home."

Verona gave her a detailed description of the events. She showed her a selfie she had taken with Elijah.

"What a handsome young man," Gina exclaimed.

Verona agreed, grateful the other woman had not commented on his blue hair. Come to think of it, not once did she see any judgment in Gina's face. Instead, it reflected understanding. There was something about Gina that made her open up because forty minutes later Verona was still talking.

The waiter cleared their plates and soiled linens and she kept on talking.

He brought them pies and sherbet and she kept on talking.

And through it all, Gina listened. She should have been a psychologist. She would have made a fortune. For a tiny woman, she had big shoulders, Verona thought as they left the restaurant.

"I'm going back this weekend to talk with Elijah and hear him sing," Verona said, concluding her tale.

Gina studied the ground for several minutes. Then she asked her only question: "Was there another reason your parents didn't help you raise your son?"

What an insightful question. "I don't think so. We were in dire straits and about to lose our home. My parents didn't want Elijah to suffer," Verona said.

"Hmm, sounds logical. But most parents I know wouldn't give up their blood so easy, even if they're dirt poor and on the streets. I think you should ask," Gina advised. "When you mentioned that, I felt a gut reaction. Dig a little deeper when you go home. It may be nothing, but I'd ask the question. Your father is right. You must talk everything out with your son if you want to build a good relationship moving forward."

Of course, Verona could not wait until she was home. Gina had waited with her until her cab arrived. As soon as Verona entered her apartment, she was on the phone. Louisa answered. "Mom, was there another reason why you and Dad pushed the adoption?"

Before her mother could offer a reply, her doorbell rang. Verona kept the cordless to her ear and opened the door.

"Ms. Stachs? I need your signature to okay a future purchase from our store."

Verona waved the courier inside. "Mom, I'll call you back in a minute." She tore open the envelope and quickly perused the contents.

What! She gulped. It was an open purchase order from Tiffany's. Her heart sang. "Yes. Yes. I'll gladly sign on his behalf."

She gave the courier an exorbitant tip though he stressed it was not required. "Go buy yourself something," she said.

When she closed the door, Verona sashayed into her bedroom. She was so giddy she floated. Michael was going to ask her to marry him! She was so excited she forgot all about calling her mother back.

Instead, Verona spent hours planning her wedding. In bed that night, she tried out her new name for size: "Verona Stachs Ward." No, that was too stuffy sounding. "Verona Ward Stachs." That didn't sound right, either. It sounded like a sentence. She could imagine the gibes: "Verona Ward Stachs what?"

"Verona Ward." Now, that was just right.

Chapter Forty-five

"Daddy!"
"Daddy!"
Michael hugged John and Olivia tight. He lifted them in his arms, cracking up at their squeals of delight. "Thank you for bringing them," he said to Lauren. The twins headed to the backroom to visit Epiphany's playroom.

She held up her left hand. "How do you like my engagement ring?"

Michael eyed the bread tie crudely wrapped around her finger. *Oh, no.* That would not do. He opened his mouth to protest, but Lauren was not done talking.

"I was glad when you called, actually. I need to go to Nordstrom and check out their gowns. I'm thinking a champagne color would be suitable for the courthouse. Valentine's Day is clichéd but appropriate, don't you think?"

Lauren was moving with intense speed. Michael waved at her to get her attention. He dipped his head to meet her eyes. "I need to let you know something."

She raised curious green eyes to his. "Are you backing out of the wedding?"

"No, I . . ." He planted a quick kiss on her lips. When he would have pulled away, Lauren gripped his head and deepened the kiss. The old him would have jumped on that invitation and they would be doing more than locking lips. Key words being "the old him."

The new Michael was walking a new path. The new him heard Keith's words beating in his head. The new him did not feel right kissing one woman when he was in love with another.

Whoa! Michael broke the kiss. He took a step back and wiped his mouth.

"Excuse me, but did you just wipe away my kiss?" Lauren asked. Her rapid blinking eyes was a telltale sign of her displeasure. Something else was written on her face. He had better answer right or she would have no problem setting things off.

Michael knew he had messed up big time. "No, I'm distracted. At this very moment, Keith is at the district attorney's office trying to get the charges dropped. Mindy went to the police station to give her statement of what happened that night. Keith was there with her for everything at her request. We expect full exoneration."

Lauren's jaw hung so low he could see her tonsils. "Why didn't you tell me? How did this happen?"

Michael shrugged, still reeling from his own disbelief. "A few days ago, Keith told me and Gina that God had directed him to fast and pray for Mindy. He asked Gina and me to join him. I was reluctant but when it comes to God, what do I know? Keith's the expert."

"God told him?" She sounded a bit jaded. "As in, he heard a voice?"

"Yes, God spoke to him," Michael defended. "I don't know if he heard a voice. I didn't ask him all that as I was too busy protesting giving up my food."

Lauren looked dubious but Michael now believed God had led Keith. There was no other explanation for the quick turn of events. He said, "I thought something would happen the same day. But nothing. Then Keith calls and says he dropped by the church and Mindy pops up to talk with him."

She squinted her eyes. "What did she say?"

"Mindy told him she's mentally ill and Keith offered to go with her to therapy. It was when she visited with her doctor that Mindy was able to piece it all together. Mindy remembered everything from that night."

"Everything?"

Why was Lauren questioning everything he was saying? Irked by her habit, Michael's annoyance grew. He supposed it was from her reporter days, but it was getting on his last nerve. "Yes, everything," he emphasized.

Lauren let out a big whoop and danced a little jig. "Yay! Now we can put the shotgun wedding idea to rest. Forget the gown; I'll get a wedding dress. I'm thinking Olivia can be the flower girl and John the ring bearer. Ooh, maybe your brother will let us have the wedding at his church? I'm sure Keith won't object. Maybe he can announce it to the church."

Without waiting for answer, she rubbed her hands. "And I can replace this bread tie with a real ring!"

Michael lifted Lauren's hand to grin at the twist tie. "It'll definitely be replaced." Once Verona approved the Tiffany's purchase . . .

Oh, no. Verona might think it's for her. Might think? Of course she would think it was for her. He was an idiot!

"Why do you have a look of horror on your face?" Lauren fussed at him. "Wipe that frown off your face. Women aren't the only ones who can get wrinkles."

Michael complied with a wide smile. On the inside, he was already working out making two purchases instead of one. He would buy Verona a pair of earrings to match her eyes. Lauren patted him on the arm and Michael redirected his attention to her words.

Again Lauren was moving ten speeds ahead of him. Michael kept silent as she rambled on about caterers and decorations. He would just show up.

There was something Michael needed to say. He took Lauren's hand to get her attention. "Before you go shopping, I wanted to let you know how grateful I am you were willing to marry me when I was on my face."

She gave a slow nod. "You're the father of my children, Michael. I know I ran from you and I kept them from you, but I was wrong." She waved her hands. "Anyways, none of that matters now. What matters is I have you and everything is working out the way I'd . . . I mean, the way God planned."

Michael was not sure why but warning bells were ringing. Why did he feel something was not right, like a piece of the puzzle was missing? Michael did not understand his gut feeling. He should be on cloud nine, but something about this seemed too convenient. Was he being paranoid?

Why couldn't he give God thanks without doubt creeping in? Maybe he was too jaded to accept God handing him his freedom on a platter.

Michael pushed the negative thoughts aside. "I can't wait to put this nightmare behind us forever. I imagine the reporters will be camped outside my penthouse once they hear about this, but that will die down in time as well." He injected enthusiasm in his voice and told Lauren, "In the meantime, go plan the wedding of your dreams!"

"Don't worry, I know how to handle reporters. And as for the wedding costs, I'll charge it to your account," she said before the door clicked upon her departure.

Once she exited, Michael exhaled. Lauren had so much energy it was draining. He welcomed the quiet before running to check on his children. They had been back there too long without supervision. All sorts of scenarios played through his mind until he rested eyes on them.

They were fine. Epiphany's toy room was another matter. He carefully made his way through strewn toys—cars, dolls, stuffed animals—and stooped to watch his children at play.

"Daddy, come play," Olivia demanded.

Michael's heart expanded. "I'd love to have tea with you." He picked up the pint-sized teacups and squatted next to her.

He had been around several tables with some of the biggest names in construction. He had attended power lunches and deal-making dinners. But, as he drank from a play cup and ate a piece of pretend pie, Michael acknowledged he had never felt this level of satisfaction and belonging as he did straddling a forty dollar plastic table.

Michael's eyes strayed between John and Olivia. He had done the right thing asking Lauren to marry him. Seeing them sealed his decision. Once they were married, he'd have a family.

But, what about love?

Chapter Forty-six

"I don't like being lied to," Bill roared.

Mindy kept silent.

"I don't like being played for a fool," he yelled.

She lowered her head. Her father was right. She had tricked him and played him too many times to count.

"And, I don't like being drugged," he stated, in an ominous tone.

How did he know? She had been careful. Mindy's head shot up. She wondered if he had discovered the other thing she had done. She took a step back and Bill advanced toward her. His face held menace and she knew she was in for it.

"Did you think I wouldn't find out? Do you think me so stupid I wouldn't figure out what my only daughter has been doing to me?" he roared. Bill grabbed her by the shoulders and gave her a vicious shake.

Mindy could not hold her tongue. "Yes, I did it! I wasn't trying to kill you or anything. I wanted, no, I needed to be free. I wanted to get help." She pressed. "What about what you've been doing to me?"

"Wha . . . What?" he asked. "What have I done to you, more than love you?"

"You don't love me," she spat. "You treat me as if I'm a possession, a prized doll. You pretend as if there's nothing wrong with me when we both know I'm sick. I haven't been the same since the day I found Carl. I . . ." She broke. "And, you won't let me talk about it."

This time Bill was the one to back away. He shook his head. "No, I refuse to accept what those quacks, who've never experienced anything in their lives, have to say. You have an active imagination. I only gave you the pills to put your mind at ease, but I know the truth."

Mindy lifted ravaged eyes to his. "I went to see Pastor Keith and we went to see Dr. Forrester."

Bill leaned forward and cupped one ear. "Did I hear you correctly? Did you say you went with Keith? Keith Ward, Michael's attorney and brother?"

Mindy trembled. She rubbed her nose, wiped her eyes, and then grabbed her head. *Answer him.* "Yes, I went to see Dr. Forrester with him. Pastor Keith was nice to me. He listened to whatever I said. He was nice."

"Ha! Of course he was nice, as you've mentioned twice. He was taking advantage of you."

"No, he helped me!" Mindy forcefully replied. She lifted her chin. "I'm not sorry I asked him. And, Dr. Forrester helped me."

Mentioning Dr. Forrester again took Bill's mind off Keith. "Did she spout all that psychobabble so she could take more of my money? The only way to deal with your brother's, um, what happened to him is to move on."

Mindy held her hands out toward him. "Why can't you see you're wrong? Say the word, Daddy. Suicide. Carl killed himself. He was ill and he didn't get help. I'm afraid I'll do the same thing!"

"Don't. Ever. Utter. Those. Words. Again." Bill gritted his teeth. "Going to a shrink is not going to bring Carl back."

"I know. I'm ill, not stupid. And, you're wrong! I spoke about Carl. Then, Dr. Forrester helped me remember that night."

Her father looked at her with pain in his eyes. He did not withhold anything. Mindy knew she had pushed him enough with the subject of her brother's death. Time for a conversation change.

"I was stripping for a while," she confessed.

Bill craned his neck toward her. "What did you say?"

"I've been going to Finn's for a while, off and on. I made good money. He didn't know who I was." Her body shivered with fear, but Mindy felt it was time for full disclosure. She needed to take responsibility for her actions and her alter egos. Pastor Keith had advised her to speak with her father and tell him everything.

Bill studied her like he had never seen her before.

She gulped. "I'm not your sweet little girl. I—"

Her father snatched her hand and gave her a beseeching look. "It's going to take me some time to process all of this. This is the first real conversation we've had in years. I feel like I'm speaking to *you,* if that makes sense. And, I much prefer the ugly truth over being drugged any day."

Mindy gave a wistful smile. "I'm sorry, Daddy. In my defense, I wasn't always in my right mind. I've got a journey ahead of me, but I intend to try God. Pastor Keith has shared some scriptures with me, and I know God can heal. I really believe God can heal me."

For once Bill did not criticize her. He nodded his head.

"Now that I know the full truth, Michael will be off the hook. He can begin to pick up the pieces of his life I destroyed." She jutted her chin to keep from crying but the tears came anyway.

In a surprising move, Bill encircled her with his powerful hands. "You didn't destroy his life, Mindy. You were afraid and confused."

She sniffed. "I did. I almost put an innocent man behind bars."

"Now, he might not have done this, but Michael Ward is no innocent," her father corrected with a pat on her head. "He'll bounce back in no time. He'll come back bigger and better. I'm the one who should be worried."

For the first time since she had known her father, Mindy heard him distressed. She noticed the bead of sweat around Bill's forehead. "What do you think he'll do to you?"

"Ruin me."

Mindy could not believe he had actually answered her. Bill was treating her like she was a real human being. Awkward, she bit her lip and touched him on the back. "Michael's not going to do anything. He doesn't blame you. He knows I'm sick. It will be all right."

"I should've killed him when I had the chance," Bill moaned covering his face with his hands. "Now, he's going to come after me and what's going to happen to you? Who's going to take care of you?"

Mindy could not believe her ears. Her father was fretting over her? "Michael's got religion. He's been going to his brother's church."

It took her a minute to realize her father's shoulder was shaking. Laughter bubbled up within him and Bill clutched his stomach. He landed on the floor, laughing until tears filled his eyes.

"Daddy, have you gone mad? Control yourself," Mindy commanded. Wow, how the tables had turned.

"You really believe that hogwash?" Bill howled. "It's all an act. Michael's pretending until he's in the clear. Then he's going to go back to his scheming ways. You mark my words, Mindy. I give him two weeks max and he'll back to his old self."

What if her father was right? Mindy wondered. He and Michael had been best friends for years. He knew him. There was only one way to find out. She held her hand out to help him to his feet. "I'm going to Pastor Keith's church this Saturday, Daddy. I think you should come with me."

"I don't—"

"Scared?" she challenged. Her heart pummeled in her chest. Who was this new person emerging from within? She was proud of her. She liked her.

Bill brushed his pants. "Never met a challenge I didn't accept."

"You invited Mindy to our church?" Gina asked as they folded back their bedspread. "I don't think that was a good move. Mindy can receive the same Word from Terence and Colleen's church."

"Must we argue over every move I make?" Keith retorted with a heavy sigh. "First of all, it's not my church. It's God's church. I am only his vessel. I can only do what He asks."

"God asked you to invite your brother's accuser to church this Sabbath?" She tossed the pillows on the floor.

"Not in so many words, but Mindy came to me for help. She needs God just like everyone else."

"I agree. I'm not saying that," Gina said.

"Will Verona be there? I remember you said you invited her." Keith undid his cuff links and unbuttoned his shirt.

"She's going back to California for the weekend."

Gina wandered off into their shower. Keith finished undressing and plopped into bed.

Thank God, Verona would not be there. Keith planned to announce Michael and Lauren's engagement and that would have been awkward. Keith shook his head. When Michael informed him of his engagement, Keith had questioned him at length. He had urged Michael to slow down, to take time to be sure of his feelings. Keith reminded Michael about his catching him and Verona in a compromising position.

But Michael was adamant about "doing the right thing." Whatever that meant. There was no way Keith was marrying someone for any reason other than love.

Boy was he glad he was settled with a wife. Keith would not want to be in Michael's shoes. When would single men realize how marriage freed you? Keith had a ready date. He had a friend. He had a lover. He had everything he needed wrapped up in one pint-sized, feisty package.

The next morning, Keith's front lawn was covered with reporters. He knew Michael's acquittal would be big news but he forgot how sensational it would be. Trey and Epiphany had not made it out to school. They were all quarantined inside the house.

Keith waited with the entire family for the press conference. The police commissioner came on and gave a perfunctory speech. He didn't stop for questions, closing with, "The City of New York wishes Michael Ward the best in his future endeavors. If you don't mind, I have six other pressing cases waiting on my desk." With that, the case closed and it was on to the next one.

Everyone gathered in the family room breathed a sigh of relief. Keith pumped his fists in the air. "Hallelujah!"

Gina clapped her hands. E.J. joined in with exuberance, though she did not fully understand what was going on. Trey gave his uncle a hug.

Michael rushed over to Keith. "Thank you, brother. Thank you for helping me."

Keith shook Michael's shoulders. "Thank God. God gets all the credit. He did this for you."

"I say we throw a party," Gina suggested.

"Why not a wedding instead?" Michael grinned.

Chapter Forty-seven

"I'm telling you, Mom. Michael plans to ask me to marry him."

As they strolled the Westfield Fashion Square mall, arm in arm, Louisa gave Verona a wistful smile. "In my umpteen years here on earth, I've learned not to count chickens."

"I'm not counting chickens, Mom. I know he's making a large purchase from Tiffany's. What else could it be? Michael said he loved me. Granted, we were fighting at the time, but . . ." Verona was not about to tell Louisa about her and Michael's passionate make-out sessions. Some things a mother did not need to know.

"Did you speak about when it you were in New York?"

Verona shook her head. "We didn't verbalize our feelings, but I know how he feels. Why do you think he's against me quitting? Michael needs me, and I need him."

Louisa stopped to look at the blouses in Ann Taylor. "I don't want you getting your hopes up for nothing."

"Too late," Verona confessed.

They made their way down to the ice cream spot. Each ordered a cone. Once they were munching away on the cold treat, Verona remembered she wanted to ask her mother a question. "Mom, I wanted to ask you a question. Was there another reason why you and Dad pushed for the adoption? I mean I know things were bad, but I'm still asking."

Her mother's eyes flittered like a butterfly. She was looking everywhere but at Verona, which made her hackles rise. "Mom. What is it?"

Her mother set glassy eyes on hers. "Your father is sick. Noel hasn't been well for years."

Verona clutched her chest. "But, he doesn't look sick." She balked. "What's wrong with him?"

"He has hypertensive heart disease. For years, he had high blood pressure. While he's done everything right, he could still suffer from heart failure. Right when he received the news, you became pregnant. At the time, we weren't sure." Louisa coughed and took a sip of water before continuing. "We weren't sure he'd make it past five years."

"Why didn't you tell me?" Verona asked. "I can't believe you both kept something this big from me. To think I blamed you, I blamed him." She stood. *Oh, Lord.* She was the most selfish human being on the planet. Louisa grabbed her bag for them to go, but Verona held up a hand. "I need a minute, Mom. I'll be right back."

Verona raced toward the bathroom. Her chest heaved. She peered into several stalls before finding one clean enough. She made it into the tiny compartment before she broke.

Her body shook. She put a fist in her mouth to keep from crying out in agony. Her father could die at any minute. She had wasted years shutting her parents out of her life. What if she had never come home? What if she had never reconnected with them?

This was all too much. Verona tilted her head and saw the paint chips in the ceiling. "God, I didn't know. I didn't know," she cried.

She heard a rap on the stall door. "Verona, are you in there?"

Verona wiped her face and pulled several tissues off the roll to blow her nose. How long had she been gone? Ten minutes? An hour? She did not have a clue. Pain filled her heart like shooting darts.

"Verona, please come out, honey," Louisa urged.

She knew her mother was worried, but it still took Verona several minutes before she could command her feet to move. Numb, she opened the door and collapsed into Louisa's arms.

"He's lived with it for all this time and he's still here." Louisa ushered Verona out of the public restroom.

Verona sniffed. "Yes, but he could die."

"He's not dead now." Her mother was firm. "Get yourself together. Noel and I brought you up to have faith and to believe in God. God sent you home. You've rekindled your relationship with your father. Come what may, all is well."

By this time, the two women were seated in Louisa's car. The hymn "It Is Well," came into Verona's head. Though her cheeks trembled, Verona began the refrain: "'It is well, with my soul.'"

Louisa hummed along as she navigated her way out of the busy mall. Verona's voice strengthened with each line and by the end she believed the song. Noel had missed out on her graduation from law school, but he would not miss her wedding. As soon as Michael put that ring on her finger, she would be in major planning mode.

Hold on. Why wait? Verona already knew Michael planned to ask so she was not jumping the gun. "Mom, can we stop by the bridal store before going home?" Verona asked. "I think it's time I go dress shopping."

Verona followed closely behind her mother hiding the gown. She knew she was doing the cart before the horse thing but she could not leave this number in the store.

Verona wondered how Gina would feel about standing in as her matron of honor. She scrunched her nose. She did not care for that term. "Matron" sounded too old, archaic. Lady in waiting. Yes, she liked she sound of that.

Louisa kept her mouth closed. Verona knew she wanted to say something but was biting her tongue. "I know you think I'm moving too fast, but this dress was a bargain. I couldn't let it go. It's chic. It's classy. It's me."

"I'm not worried about the gown," Louisa fretted. "Call me old-fashioned but I certainly wouldn't jinx things by buying a dress when no one has asked me to marry them."

Verona plodded behind her mother up the stairs, holding the gown high in her hands to keep the train from snagging. "He's going to ask, Mom. This purchase is faith in action."

Louisa lifted her hands. "Okay, honey, I'm done arguing with you. You know better than I do, but I for one won't be plunking down a fortune on a gown until I get the official invite."

"Where's Dad?" Verona wanted to show off her gown to someone else. She felt a strong need to hug him and never let go.

"He's in our room. It's his usual rest time. I know you want to talk to him but, sweetheart, please give yourself a day to process." Louisa strolled down to their bedroom and Verona a faint smile.

Verona nodded. Louisa had reassured her that Noel exercised and maintained a healthy diet but she had visions of her father collapsing at her feet. Hearing about her impending nuptials would give her father a boost, a reason to keep well. If only Michael would hurry up and ask her already.

Verona entered her childhood room and closed the door. Her head was filled with wedding cake ideas. Maybe she should go with cupcakes; they were all the rage. She tapped her chin. Her mother was right. She was getting ahead of herself. She needed to secure a location first.

Verona did not want to get married in Keith's monstrosity of a church. But wedding season was upon them and pickings would be slim.

With extreme tenderness, she unzipped the garment bag to gaze at her gown. The silky material felt smooth in her hand. She fantasized about how Michael's eyes would pop when he saw her in this ensemble. Paranoid about damaging or soiling the delicate material, Verona re-zipped the bag and hung the dress in her closet.

She dug into her jeans and pulled out her cell phone. There was a text from Nigel, but Michael had not called. However, Verona was not concerned. Michael was most likely searching out engagement rings. Good, because she could not wait to see her father's face when she told him she was settling down.

No matter what her mother said, all she could think about was her father dying suddenly and not seeing her as a bride. Verona straightened. Her father was not going to miss another milestone in her life. Not if she could help it. Noel would walk her down the aisle. As soon as Michael slid the ring on her finger, Verona was moving full speed ahead with her plans.

Chapter Forty-eight

"Let me look at those again?" Michael asked Raoul, the clerk chosen to wait on him. He was seated in a small room designed for clientele with particular tastes and the money to satisfy them. It was Thursday evening and he wanted to get this off his to-do list.

The young man was quick to do his bidding. Michael marveled at Raoul's patience.

He had already chosen Lauren's wedding ring. Correction. She had sent him a picture of what she wanted. Michael found it ostentatious and borderline gaudy, but he was going to grant her every wish. How much was too much for the woman who had borne his children?

"Let's see if any of these earrings appeal to you," Raoul said, before carefully depositing the tray in front of him.

Michael waved him off. It had been close to an hour but finding the right pair to match Verona's eyes was a challenge. Nope. He did not see anything he liked.

Raoul poked his head in.

"I want you to look at this." Michael swiped the camera app on his phone and searched for a picture of Verona. They had been at lunch. She had been laughing at something. On impulse, he had snapped the photo. Her eyes sparkled. Michael smiled whenever he pulled it up, which was often. He held up his phone to Raoul to see. "Can you match her eyes?"

"Your fiancée is beautiful," Raoul observed. Michael did not correct him. Raoul snapped his fingers. "Aha. I have exactly what you're looking for."

When Raoul returned with his vision, Michael immediately nixed the earrings. In his hand was a tiger-shaped
pendant engraved with golden bronze-colored stones. He
slanted Raoul an eerie glance before clutching it in his palm.
It was as if whoever designed the gem had read his mind
and made this as a custom piece for his Tiger. Well, Verona
was not his Tiger. That would not stop Michael from buying
her this gift. "Wrap it for me. I'll take it."

"Do you want it delivered by messenger, sir?"

He shook his head. "No, I'll do it myself."

Raoul gave him a knowing smile before running off to
prepare the package.

Why are you marrying Lauren? The random thought
attacked his psyche. Michael shrugged away the question.

He exited the back room and meandered his way
through the other customers until he found Raoul. He
did not know what possessed him to scan the engagement
rings on display. His eyes locked onto an exquisite five-
carat yellow diamond solitaire. Like a siren, it beckoned
him over to the case. Michael needed to feel it in his
hands.

Sensing another sale, Raoul hovered. "Our yellow rose
has entranced many but no takers as yet. You want to
take a peek?"

Michael gulped then nodded. Yes. He was looking at
Tiger's engagement ring. He could visualize it flashing on
Verona's hand, getting caught in that wild hair of hers.
Someone needed to buy her that ring.

He accepted the ring with slight embarrassment at his
emotional connection. Michael knew it sounded sexist,
but he thought only women felt that way. Standing there,
though, Michael admitted there was no way he could
leave it behind. His heart pounded.

You realize she'll know it's an engagement ring?
There's no passing that off as anything else.

Who said I cared?

"Ring it up, Raoul," Michael commanded. He massaged his temples. There was no excuse for what he was doing: buying two rings for two different women. He could not live in denial another day. It was obvious who had his heart. Why was he marrying Lauren?

As he drove to his penthouse suite, Michael debated the question. He could not even tell when his feelings for Verona had morphed into love. For years, he had thought Lauren was the one. He had scoured the United States to find her and his children. Now, he had all three and he was undecided. Who did that?

And, what about John and Olivia? Michael wanted to be a full-time father in their lives. No. He had to marry Lauren. It was the right thing to do.

He groaned. But, he could not picture making love to any other woman for the rest of his life but Tiger. He craved her all day long. During the day he could fool himself, but at night his dreams betrayed him. He could not pretend for the rest of his life, could he?

Why couldn't he have two wives? Didn't Adam? No, it wasn't Adam but Abraham. Michael had read about the patriarch in the book of Genesis. Abraham had a killer time managing Sarah and Hagar.

Michael chuckled, picturing Lauren and Verona scratching and mauling each other. There would be no peaceful cohabitation with those two. No, he was not made out for polygamy and neither woman would settle with being a sidepiece. Besides, Michael would land in jail and . . . why was he even entertaining this dumb idea? It was a waste of his brain cells.

The fact was he was already engaged. To Lauren.

He could live with Lauren. He could be the husband she needed. He knew that. But could and want to were not the same. He wanted to be with Tiger. He wanted to be Verona's husband. There was a big difference.

Michael pulled up to the valet in front of his building. His head whipped left and right. There was no press waiting. No cops waiting. In fact, everyone he saw was going about his or her business. He released a deep breath. It would be awhile before he could accept he was a free man.

Michael entered his building with a wide smile on his face. It was good to be home.

"Good to see you, Mr. Ward," Aisha, the front desk clerk, greeted him.

"It's good to be back," he said.

In the elevator, Michael saw a text from Verona saying she was in California. She would be back Sunday night. He glanced at his watch. Keith was going to announce his engagement to the church this Saturday. He could fly to California and back within that time. He could ask Verona to marry him and if she said no, he would marry Lauren. Problem solved.

Disgust filled his being. He was bargaining with two women's lives. Gina flashed before him. When would he learn? He had married Gina knowing deep down in his gut something was wrong. He had ignored that feeling. The same one he was having about Lauren. Michael knew he was marrying the wrong woman even if it was for the right reasons.

Not this time.

He would choose love.

Michael decided he would not wait another day. He was going to California to ask Verona to marry him.

Chapter Forty-nine

"He looks better in person," Louisa whispered peering through the peephole.

Verona cracked up. "Mom, you're a hoot! It's typical Michael to show up here spur of the moment." She rushed toward the stairs. "Let him in. I've got to comb my hair and freshen up."

Her mother turned toward her with wide eyes. "Maybe he's here to ask you to marry him."

Verona's heart skipped a beat. "We'll never know unless you open the door." She hurried into her bathroom to make herself presentable. *Don't get your hopes up. He could be here on business.* Too late. Her hopes were up. Way up. Verona's hand had a slight tremble while she brushed her teeth.

She looked in the mirror. *My goodness!* Her eyes were wide open. She felt excitement and terror at the same time.

Michael must have used his private plane. Of course he did. He did not travel any other way. She thought he would have waited until she returned to New York before popping the question. *Wait.* What if he came to meet her parents and ask their permission to marry her? She had better hurry.

Five minutes later, Verona scurried down the stairs to find both her parents and Michael sitting in the family room. Her parents had enraptured expressions. Michael had obviously managed to charm them, which was no surprise.

"Michael." Her voice sounded breathless. *Calm down. Breathe.*

He had been laughing at something, but whipped around at the mention of his name. "Verona, it's good to see you."

"You're free." She mentioned the obvious, twisting her hands.

Louisa gave her a thumbs-up sign before pulling Noel from the room. "We'll leave you two to talk." Her voice squeaked with excitement.

Verona knew that was her mother's way of telling her Michael was indeed there to propose. Lord, she needed to sit down.

As her bottom hit the cushion, Michael dropped to one knee and took her hand in his. "Verona, you're the most infuriating woman I've ever met. You're stubborn, feisty, but you're loyal. I can't function without you. I value you. I want to spend the rest of my life with you and I'd be honored—"

"Yes!'

"I'm not finished." He grinned. "I'd be honored if you would accept—"

"Yes." She shivered with glee.

Michael gritted his teeth. "Will you shut up and let me finish my proposal?"

Verona nodded.

"Will you be my wife?"

Her eyes watered. She cupped his face in her hands and pulled him until he was seated next to her. "Yes. Yes, I'll marry you. I want that more than anything in this world. I love you."

"I love you too," Michael said, snaking her into his arms and kissing her until her toes curled.

It was too soon for her when he ended the kiss. Michael reached into his shirt pocket and took out a small box.

With a slightly embarrassed look on his face, he said, "I'm messing this up big time. Should I get back on my knees?"

Verona gave him a playful pat. "No, I don't care how it's done. You did it and that's what counts." She whisked away the tears on her face. "I knew you were smart and this proposal confirms it."

He chuckled at her humor. "Ha-ha. Funny. I can see there'll never be a dull day with you."

"Open the box!" she commanded, shaking with glee.

Michael opened the box with slow deliberation. When she saw the solitaire, Verona clutched her chest and whispered, "Michael, it's exquisite."

He slipped the ring on her finger. Verona admired it with silence. All of a sudden, Michael lunged at her, knocking her flat on the couch before lying on top of her. It took a millisecond before his weight crushed her. "Get off!" she croaked. There was only a crack between their bodies.

He would not move.

Verona pushed against him flailing her arms. "Michael!" she screamed, shoving at him. "Get off!"

Her parents must have have been lurking nearby because they both ran into the room.

"What's going on?" Noel asked.

Verona used her strength to turn her head. Seeing the worry on Noel's face made her revolt her imprisonment even more. Not even having her parents in the room made him move.

"I'm never letting you go. This is how you capture a tiger," Michael boasted before releasing her. She sagged with relief. He lifted her hand to show off the carats twinkling there.

"The oaf could've stifled me to death," she fumed. When neither of her parents acknowledged her, Verona crossed her arms.

Michael grabbed her chin and planted a kiss on her. In spite of her attitude, Verona responded. Louisa cleared her throat causing Michael to pull away.

"I take it she said yes?" Noel grinned.

Mortified, Verona covered her cheeks. She was appalled at Michael's antics in front of her parents, although they seemed delighted. In fact, her mother beamed.

"She did, sir," Michael confirmed. "I always knew she was smart, but this confirms it."

Her eyes bulged. "Hey, you stole my words!"

Michael dismissed her remark and continued to thrill her parents with his open display of affection. He could not keep his hands off her and her parents were eating it all up. It embarrassed but stimulated her at the same time. Verona squirmed. She would have to think of a way to make him pay later.

Verona noticed Michael "accidentally" brushed against her in the most sensitive places. Were her parents' blind or pretending not to see? Purposefully, she stood and put some space between them.

"Michael, can you stay to meet my son?" Verona asked.

"I wish I could but I have to go back to New York tomorrow. I would love to meet Elijah—sorry, Jah—when I come back. Or, I could fly him and your parents up to New York next weekend?" He directed the question to her father. "I can have my secretary arrange a getaway of sorts for the both of you?"

Louisa had stars in her eyes. "I've never been to New York. I've been meaning to go."

"Son, if you're trying to bribe us, it's working," her father joked. "We'll come next weekend but we'll pay our way."

Did her father call him son?

Michael waved his hand. "Nonsense. Everything's on me, Dad. I insist."

Did Michael call her father Dad? Verona felt sweat line her upper lip. This was real. The men in her lives had taken to each other. She had to wipe another tear.

"Oh, how generous," her mother exclaimed.

Her father nodded and shook Michael's hand. "Thank you."

"This is my way of thanking you for giving me a woman like Tiger. She's remarkable and I'm complete with her by my side."

Verona bit her tongue to keep any sarcastic comment from popping out of her mouth. Michael was a sweet talker. When he looked at her, she rolled her eyes and he smirked. Deep down, she melted at the effort he made on her behalf.

"I love you," he mouthed.

"I love you too," she mouthed back.

"Come sit with me," he mouthed again.

Uh-uh. She wasn't falling for that. She shook her head. Out of nowhere the words burst from her. "I don't want to wait too long to get married."

His voice dropped. "For once, I agree. Let's get married as soon as possible."

In his private plane, gliding at 30,000 feet, Michael studied the clouds while he thought. How was he going to get married as soon as possible when he had another fiancée waiting for him in New York?

He had had the good sense to put his cell phone on silent while he was at Verona's house. But once he had left and turned it on, Michael was bombarded with messages from Lauren. She had inundated his voicemail with updates of the wedding plans and when she received her ring. Michael eyed the picture Lauren sent with the rock on her finger. That ring would be her consolation prize.

Michael rubbed his head. He was going to have one angry woman on his hands once he broke the news he was ending their engagement.

He stiffened his spine. It had to be done and he was not going to dawdle. He was not going to juggle two women. Michael knew the one he wanted and he was going to marry her. Lauren would get over it, though he did not relish the yelling and screaming he was sure would ensue.

If only he knew. He was dead wrong.

Chapter Fifty

"Put your big panties on and speak to your son," were Michael's words of advice before he left. Verona had recounted her father's suggestion to have a heart-to-heart talk with Elijah. Michael agreed.

Verona tapped the steering wheel as she waited for Elijah to arrive. She had arranged with the Smith's to pick him up outside his school that Friday. She did not want to put off their conversation for another moment. There were things she needed to say.

Once Elijah was inside the car, she decided to drive to the beach. She spread the blanket while Elijah hoisted the picnic basket. Verona packed all the usual suspects—PBJ, turkey, assorted fruit, cakes, chips, water, juice, and sodas—to feed an army or in this case one hungry teenager. In her defense, she didn't know what he liked.

Elijah's eyes popped when he saw the food. "Are we feeding the five thousand or something?"

Verona cracked up. "You sound like your grandfather. That's something he'd say."

"I know. Everyone says I'm not the typical teenager." He grabbed a paper plate and heaped an assortment of foods on his plate.

"I believe you. Honestly, I know I wasn't always in your life, but I'm proud to be your mother. I know I'm not your mom, but . . ." She trailed off, suddenly unsure of what to say.

"It's okay. I know what you mean."

Verona watched as Elijah munched on an apple. She had to ask, "Is this how you are all the time? So agreeable?" Verona did not know teens like this existed. When she was a teen it was all about mutiny and being misunderstood.

Elijah had the grace to blush. "Yes, because I have a bad temper. I try hard not to lose it."

"Now that I can relate to." She chuckled. She toyed with her food. *Lord, help me not mess up this conversation.* "Elijah, I wanted to ask you something and I hope you'll be honest with me."

He nodded.

"Um." She ran her fingers through her hair while she figured out how to ask the big question. "Are you mad at me for not coming back home all these years?"

He set down his plate and could not quite meet her eyes. "I wondered about you. I wondered if you wanted me. Nana told me you loved me but you never called, you never sent a birthday card." He shrugged. "I mean, nothing."

Verona was afraid to touch him though she ached to make some physical contact. "I know my words may sound like air to you but I do love you."

"Then why did it take thirteen years for my mother who claims she loves me to find me?" He broke. In one breath, he spewed all his pent-up emotions. "You are this big-shot attorney and you couldn't have gone to court or something? I don't get it."

She touched his shoulder. "Were you unhappy with the Smith's?"

"No," he declared. "But they aren't you. I'm grateful for them and they've been the best parents in the world, but it's not the same."

Verona tried to hug him, knowing he had to let it out. Elijah shrugged her off. "No, don't touch me right now." His chest heaved as he visibly struggled to regain control.

Never had she felt so helpless and guilty. Was this how she made her own parents feel? Verona pushed her food aside.

Elijah jumped up. "I didn't mean to get upset," he mumbled. "I'll be back."

"Do you want me to come with you?

He shook his head. "No, I need some space."

Verona curled her body, feeling defeated as Elijah stomped toward the shoreline. They had been getting along well before she had dredged up the painful past. Maybe she should have left well enough alone. Now she had a sulky teenager on her hands.

Shielding her eyes against the sun, Verona spotted Elijah kicking the sand near the edge of the water. He dug into his pants and took out his cell phone. Verona saw him clutch the phone to his ear. His voice carried, but she could not make out any words. Elijah was talking to someone on the phone. He chatted for several minutes before trudging his way back to her.

She was dying to know whom he had been talking to but knew it was not her place to ask. She watched him circle his foot into the sand.

"Um, Mother, can we go please?" he asked.

Verona could not tell from Elijah's tone if he was mad, sad, or indifferent and that slashed at her heart. Logically, she knew it would take time to build a relationship with her son, but her heart ached.

Verona nodded and gathered the paraphernalia of their outing. Elijah helped her to her feet. She gave him a small smile when he offered to carry the basket. In spite of everything, she could appreciate his being a gentleman. They meandered their way through the sand and packed the vehicle.

Before she drove off, Verona had to say something. "Elijah, I love you. I've loved you from the day you were born. I'm sorry it took me fifteen years to tell you that. I know it's hard, but I want us to have a relationship. I won't try to take your mother's place but I'd like to be more than your koala bear."

"Koala bear?" He chuckled.

Her odd phrasing lightened the air and her heavy heart. "Okay, it's a poor and corny analogy."

"I called my mom," he confessed in a small voice.

"Oh?" Gripping the wheel, Verona strove to sound normal although jealousy filled her at his loving tone. Elijah's eyes were pinned on her gauging her reaction to his talking about his mom. She knew she had better make him believe she was cool with it.

Keeping her tone neutral, she asked, "What did your mom say?"

"She said I needed to remember you weren't much older than me when you found out you were pregnant. She said I needed to put myself in your place because you were a kid and unsure. She made sure to tell me I must still respect you no matter what," Elijah said.

Verona was surprised at Sister Smith's defense. Nevertheless, she did not show that in her answer. "And, what do you think about her advice?"

"I felt better after I spoke to her. I know if I was to get some girl pregnant, I'd be scared and wouldn't know what to do."

She slanted Elijah a warning look. "And, trust me you don't want to find out."

"Yeah, I guess not. Don't worry. I'm safe. I'm cool."

What did that mean? Was her son having sex? Did he have a girlfriend? Well, whoever she was, Verona did not like her. "You have a girlfriend?"

"No, I don't. I need a job first. Girls are expensive," he said.

She cracked up. "You'll have more women than you'll know how to handle in time. For now, you need to remain in school and focus on your singing."

He chuckled and relaxed his body further in the cushion of the car. "You sound like a mother."

"I am a mother," she said. "I may not be Mom to you, but I am your mother."

"I can deal with that."

She smiled. So could she.

Chapter Fifty-one

How wrong he had been. Lauren was not yelling or screaming when Michael uttered the words to end their engagement. She was staring at him with unblinking eyes and it was unnerving.

The children were already in bed when he had arrived at her place that Friday night. She had flung her arms around him and chattered about their wedding. Michael extricated her arms from around his neck, before saying, "Lauren, we need to talk."

His grave tone cooled her enthusiasm and she eyed him with wary eyes. "What's going on?"

"You're the mother of my children and I love you for that but I can't marry you."

That's what he had said and five minutes later, Lauren still had not responded. It was as if she was frozen. He could not stand the silence. "Lauren?"

She exhaled with a whoosh of air. "Excuse me. For a moment, I thought you were breaking things off with me."

"I was. I mean I am," Michael stammered. What was going on with her?

Lauren poked him in the chest. "No, you're not. You're not tossing me aside again. You're going to marry me and be a father to your children."

Her calmly spoken words freaked him out, but Michael was not going to let her bully him. "I will be a good father to John and Olivia, the best they ever need. However, I will not be marrying you. I don't love you."

She inhaled.

He regretted his harsh words but he owed Lauren the truth. With a tone laced with sympathy, he continued, "You deserve a man who will love you and cherish you. I'm not that person and I don't want to hurt you."

"For someone who doesn't want to hurt me, you're doing a bang-up job," she scoffed.

He needed to leave. "We'll talk later. Once you think about it, you'll appreciate me for saving us heartache in the future."

"Keep your sugary words." Lauren rolled her eyes and tapped her feet.

Michael ambled toward the door. He wanted to see the children but did not want to push his luck by asking her if he could visit with them.

Michael's hand was on the front doorknob when the tapping stopped. Lauren's next words chilled him to the bone.

"If you don't marry me, I'll kill myself. I'll kill myself and the children."

Michael advanced on her until he was up in her face. "Take that back!" he yelled.

Lauren's face remained expressionless. "I mean it," she said. She didn't back down instead she met his gaze head-on.

For a second, Michael entertained visions of wrapping his hands around her neck, but he counted to ten. *Lord, help me.* He would not harm her. He used his hands to undo the buttons on his coat.

There was no way he was leaving Lauren alone after she had said those words. He debated calling the cops but nixed that idea. He doubted they'd believe the potential rapist, even though he had been exonerated. Michael considered calling Lauren's bluff but what if the heifer actually meant it?

Instead, he found himself saying, "I'm sorry, Lauren. I must have a slight case of cold feet. We'll get married."

Instantly, Lauren's demeanor changed and she was happy again. Chipper, she clapped her hands and carried on as if she had not threatened him with a murder-suicide scenario. Lauren presented him with wedding cake pictures and decoration possibilities until his head spun.

Michael only said the words to appease her. He was biding his time until he figured his way out of the situation. He had a restless night. The sun rose and Michael still didn't know how to remove himself from Lauren's clutches.

Sitting in church Sabbath morning, Michael still had not figured out what to do. After positioning herself as close to him as possible, Lauren gripped his hand so hard her nails scraped his palm. Michael pulled on his shirt collar and tried to pretend everything was all right.

People were lifting their hands and praising God around him. They were carefree but he felt trapped. He was replaying the scene inside Lauren's home after she had uttered those fateful words.

Michael had called Keith last night but had not reached him. He planned on soliciting his brother's help. Michael bobbed his head to the praise songs, but inside he had needles lining his stomach.

He could not catch a break. Michael had gotten rid of one cross and it seemed as if he had picked up another. He should be skipping down the aisles like the sister with the banana hat was doing right now. He had been cleared of a vicious crime. He was not going to spend his life behind bars. Nevertheless, Michael was now imprisoned with an invisible noose. And, she had claws.

He watched Lauren under hooded lashes. This time he pulled at the tie around his neck.

"Do you need me to adjust that for you?" Lauren asked him with a sweet voice.

Michael saw her angelic face and creased his forehead. How could Lauren act normal after her outlandish words last night? He shook his head at her, and she went back to her singing.

Lauren raised her hands and shouted "Hallelujah's" at the top of her lungs.

At that moment, Michael knew what crazy was like. Mindy was sick. Lauren was plumb crazy. For some reason, Frank entered his mind. Frank could take care of Lauren for him if he gave the word. Michael would never have to deal with her again.

Let go. Trust me.

He had heard those words before. He knew the voice. *I'm trying, Lord,* Michael answered. Could he trust God? His heart thumped. He thought about Frank. He thought about God. He had to make a choice once and for all.

Keith's voice permeated his conscious mind. It was time for the sermon. "Today, I'm going to talk about choice. Making the right choice."

Chapter Fifty-two

Mindy entered the sanctuary with her head down. The usher led her close to the front and she did not want to attract attention. Mindy received a couple frosty glances for being late, but most of the faces she encountered were friendly.

Pastor Keith stepped up to the podium. She squirmed. Some of the women were wearing some big hats and one happened to be in her direct line of vision. This lady's hat was like a pineapple slice. Mindy angled her head seeking a better view. Her neck was going to hurt in this position. There was only one thing to do.

Mindy tapped the woman on the shoulder. "Excuse me, but can you take your hat off? I can't see."

The lady gave her a wide-eyed stare. A man sitting next to her, whom Mindy presumed to be the husband, guffawed. "I told her she shouldn't wear that boat today. Didn't I tell you, Pearl? It's only good for rainy days."

Several people chuckled and Mindy covered her mouth.

"Shut up, Hugh," Pearl commanded, but removed her hat and smoothed her wig.

"Thank you," Mindy whispered.

Bill squeezed in next to her just as Pastor Keith began to talk about choice. She whispered, "What took you so long?"

"I had to find a parking space," Bill said a wee bit too loud.

Pearl turned to shush them. Mindy gave a sheepish smile. She settled under the crook of her father's arm to listen to the message.

Three souls. He was expecting three souls this Sabbath. Keith's eyes surveyed the crowd. He winked at Gina who was sitting in the front pew with Trey. E.J. was in children's church. Two rows behind her was his brother. Beside Michael, he saw Lauren. Nigel was in the back somewhere. He had texted Keith to tell him of his arrival.

His vote would be on Lauren.

He knew Michael was one.

Mindy was the other. Keith looked through the rows to see if she had arrived. She promised him she would be there. Keith had told the usher to place Mindy a few rows behind the others, if she came. He wanted to be able to see her.

Yup. The third soul had to be Lauren. That would make things right. Excited at the prospect, Keith racked his brain to remember how many other couples he had baptized together. It might be two or three, but whatever the number, it did not happen that often. The fact that it would be Michael and his intended was a coup Keith could not resist. He planned on bragging to the congregation, to the world, when that time came.

He adjusted his tie. God had given him the right message befitting the occasion. Keith smiled, thinking of the outcome.

He stepped up to the podium. Mindy had arrived. *Good,* he thought. All was as it should be. *Wait, did she ask Missionary Pearl Matthews to remove her hat?* Keith stifled a giggle by turning it into a quick praise. He hoped he remembered to tell Gina later.

Keith addressed the congregation. "Before I get into my topic, I'm glad to see my brother, Michael here. Seated next to him is Ms. Lauren Goodman. Some of you might remember she's been here a few times. Please give this couple a Zion's Hill welcome."

Keith emphasized the word "couple." He knew the single sisters would not be too happy. Keith watched as several people hugged and kissed Michael and Lauren before getting back to the message.

"Today, I want to talk to you about choice." Was that Bill Laurelton he saw coming in? Inside, Keith groaned. He hoped Bill did not come to cause any more problems for Michael because Keith would not tolerate it.

He continued, "In our lives, we will come to many forks in the road, where we will have to make a choice. The question is not whether we have a choice, but which choice is best? Which choice puts us on the right path to where God wants us to be?"

Okay, Bill had settled in with Mindy. All was well. Keith relaxed. Now he could close his eyes. "Pray with me," he directed and bowed his head. "Lord, I ask that your Holy Spirit speak through me and direct me so I can lead your people on the right path today. Let every word I speak line up in accordance with your Word. I ask this in Jesus' name. Amen.

"Turn your Bibles to First Kings 18 and verse 21. It reads, 'And Elijah came unto all the people, and said, How long halt ye between two opinions? If the Lord be God, follow him: but if Baal, then follow him.'"

Keith heard several shouts of praise and took a sip of water. "Our Heavenly Father asked us not to have any other god besides Him. In this scripture, Baal was a manmade god of stone but a god can represent anything that distracts you: money, possessions, power, drugs, alcohol to name a few. What is your god? Perhaps, it's none of those. Perhaps it's women or sex. What is it you find hard to give up?"

He paused. Someone shouted, "Preach it, Pastor!"

"Close your eyes and think about what you want most in the world." He waited until most of the congregation had complied. "Whatever it is you're picturing is a god. My question today is, is it worth your soul? What is the point of holding on to that one thing if you lose your soul?

"Elijah presented the people with a question and today I ask the same question. If you're halting between two opinions, today is the day to make a choice. God is asking you to choose Him. Love Him. Accept Him. If you need help making the right choice, come forward today."

Keith gave the signal and the choir stood. The minister of music, Zara Anderson, came forward and she began to sing: "'I come to the garden alone.'"

He saw Michael stalk toward the altar.

"'While the dew is still on the roses,'" Zara sang.

Keith saw Mindy step out into the aisle. She swayed but stayed where she was. Keith spoke into his microphone, "Don't be afraid. Come."

"'And the voice I hear falling on my ear. The son of God discloses.'"

Lauren had her hands held high. Her head was thrown back but she was not budging. Keith watched her for the duration of the song, but she didn't leave her seat. He sagged a little. He had made the call and couldn't force anyone to comply.

Keith gestured to Zara to sing the refrain one more time. He and the deacons and prayer warriors went over to those who came to the altar and prayed with them. Still, Keith didn't lose hope. As he prayed, he watched. Gina went to stand with Mindy. He prayed for another person, however; his eyes remained on the lookout for a certain redhead.

One who was now sitting in her seat, contented.

He sighed. *Lord, give me patience.* He ended his prayer.

Keith returned the podium and everyone returned to his or her seat. It was time for the benediction. Keith paused. He had to try one last time. "I would like to do a special prayer. If you have decided you want to accept Jesus as your personal Savior, please come forward, even if you were just up here."

Michael came forward.

Mindy came forward.

No Lauren. *Maybe it was Nigel?* But he had not spotted Nigel in the throng at all.

Gina slid her finger across her throat telling Keith to quit dragging and close the service. The musicians strummed a tune. All right, he would wrap it up.

After Keith anointed them, he bent his head and began to pray. "Holy Father, I ask that you commit these souls into the book of life. They've made the choice today to put their lives into your hands. They are here to accept the gift of salvation. Lord, I ask you to wash their sins. Heal them from all past pain, hurt, and illnesses. Heal them both spiritually and physically. Bless them with abundant life. In Jesus' name. Amen."

He entered a higher realm and rejoiced for the souls who had come forward. When he opened his eyes, he stepped back in shock. God had a wicked sense of humor.

Bill Laurelton. Bill Laurelton was the third soul.

Chapter Fifty-three

"That's my son," Verona breathed into her mother's ear. They were seated together in front for Sunday morning worship. She cupped her mouth, overcome with emotion. "Why didn't somebody tell me my baby could sing?"

Her mother smiled. "His range is unbelievable. Whenever he sings, we say there's an angel among us today."

Verona nodded. "I can see why."

Elijah wore khakis and a dress shirt and he'd dyed his hair blond. Because of the many colors he'd tried out, it looked reddish brown. She was glad the horrid blue streak phase was over, for now.

The church stood to their feet, praising God when Elijah was finished singing. He lifted his face toward heaven in worship. Seeing a young man standing in awe before God made the church go wild.

Verona jumped to her feet, her chest puffed and her smile wide. This is why she had brought Elijah into the world. He was meant to give God glory. This was her "Hannah" moment. She saw him as the next Smokie Norful or Hezekiah Walker. "Bless him, Lord!" For the first time in her life, Verona was at peace with the Smith's raising him.

Elijah gestured to the crowd to settle down. "Everybody in here knew me from when I was knee high. Now, I've been fortunate to have two of the best parents a boy could want or need. But, I've waited fifteen years to meet my birth mother and see her face. I've heard how she did know me and loved me. But people, I was two. That's news to me."

Several people chuckled at his ramblings.

Elijah continued, "A few weeks ago, my wish came true. My mother, Verona Stachs, is here today with my Nana and Pop Pop." He whipped his head to point to his grandfather.

Elijah then pierced Verona with a look she knew well. It mirrored her own. "Mother, I've been hearing from everyone how you used to sing back in the day."

Oh, no. He was putting her on the spot. Verona shook her head to Elijah hoping he would heed the hint.

"I'm hoping you'd come and sing with me up here. Praising God is how I give Him thanks for giving me you."

When he put it like that, how could she resist? Verona swallowed. It had been years since she sang in front of such a large crowd. Mount Moriah boasted approximately 3,000 attendees for each of its three services. Her mother touched her cheek. "Go on, dear. Go sing with your son."

Her son.

Verona's vocal chords were rusty, but there was no way she would not satisfy his request. His eyes compelled her. She willed her baby deer legs to steady as she wobbled her way up to where Elijah stood. His eyes looked glassy from unshed tears.

He was on the brink of manhood. His intelligence and mannerisms made her proud. She took the cordless microphone he offered and leaned over to whisper, "It's been a long time. Don't sing any of the modern songs."

Elijah mouthed, "I got you," before laying his hands across the keyboard. Within minutes the tune to "His Eye Is on the Sparrow" resonated throughout the sanctuary. Lyrics and melodies came back to her as she cued her son to begin.

When he sang the first word, "Why," tears shimmered against her eyelids. Her hand shook slightly as she joined in the second line. Together they sang the timeless words to the sentimental song. As she sang, it was like God was talking to her. Her memories rolled before her like a vision of how He had been there with her all along. Not once had she been alone. Nothing she had accomplished had been done without Him.

Humbled, Verona stretched her hand toward Elijah, beaming when they blended and harmonized the chorus. Their duet could compete with Mary Mary or any other top artists who had sung together for years; that was how well they sang together. Verona felt joy bubble up within her and closed her eyes. She had forgotten singing had been her secret weapon. A line from Nehemiah 8:10 came back to her:

For the joy of the Lord is your strength.

When they ended with the final note, there was silence. Verona opened her eyes and saw handkerchiefs and tissues wiping faces and noses. Then suddenly, thunderous applause filled the sanctuary. She tilted her body to eye her father, knowing it was time for him to preach.

Her eyes widened when she realized he was stretched out on the floor. Fear leapt in her throat. Verona scuttled up to the podium. The other ministers beckoned that Noel was okay. Knowing her cheeks had to be brick red, Verona made her way to her mother's side.

"I thought . . ."

Louisa gave her a whimsical smile. "It's been awhile since you've seen somebody laid out in the Spirit."

Verona nodded wishing the earth would open up and swallow her. Wait, strike that thought. She was not trying to go down there anytime soon. The musicians started playing a tune and people started stomping and handclapping. Her mother did a praise jig and the brethren around her cued her on. Verona followed suit with an awkward step or two before deciding to sit this praise session out.

She kept her eye on her father, exhaling when he finally took his place at the podium. "Forgive me, church, seeing my daughter and grandson did my heart good. God is good," he choked out. "But, I know you need a Word to take with you. Today, I'm going to speak briefly about the story of the prodigal son."

She should have known, Verona thought in bemusement, crossing her arms. How fitting.

"I know how that father felt when his child left home for parts unknown. I imagine how he must have prayed many nights, worried and concerned. He must've looked out the window, or whatever they had back then, and stood there for hours hoping to spot his child."

Oh, man. Verona lowered her head. This was too much. It would be impossible for her to remain dignified. She imagined all eyes were on her because they were burning holes in her skin. She fiddled with the buttons of her Oscar de la Renta dress and lowered her eyes not trusting herself to make eye contact with anyone.

Louisa shoved several tissues in her hand. "Thanks, Mom," she whispered.

"Imagine at the precise moment he was about to give up all hope, out of the blue, his child returns. Imagine the relief he experienced. Imagine the burden he carried in his heart suddenly being lifted." Noel cleared this throat.

Verona heard her mother sniffling beside her. In fact, she was quite sure there was not a dry eye in the house. She felt a hand grasp her hand on her left side. Elijah. Verona leaned into him, resting her head on his shoulder.

"Brothers and sisters, I know God is pleased when we return home to Him. Angels in heaven rejoice when one person decides to accept Him in their life. Is there anyone here today who wants to come home? Come as we sing 'All to Jesus I Surrender.'"

Verona listened to the words of the song and could not hold her tears. She had made amends with her parents; now it was time to make amends with God. She stood. Inch by inch, she made her way to the front of the church. She lifted her hands. In one smooth motion, Verona fell to her knees.

It was time. She was coming home.

Chapter Fifty-four

Monday had not come fast enough. Michael undid John and Olivia's seat belts from their newly purchased car seats. He had hightailed it over to Keith's as early as he could without arousing Lauren's suspicions. She thought he was taking them to Chuck E. Cheese, and he would after talking with Keith.

Josie opened the door. Her eyes sparkled when she saw the children. She ushered them into the kitchen for some treats. Michael practically sprinted into Keith's office.

"I'm engaged to both Lauren and Verona," Michael announced after knocking and hearing he could enter.

Keith's head snapped up from the book he had been reading. "How did you manage to do that?" Without waiting for a reply, he continued, "I'm glad I didn't open my big mouth and mention your engagement to Lauren in church last week."

"I did ask Lauren, first. However, when I went into Tiffany's to pick up the ring, I saw one that screamed Verona's name. I had to get it. I had to ask Verona to marry me. I've been fighting it, but I know she's the one."

"You can't stay engaged to two women," Keith ordered, stern-faced. He beckoned to Michael to close to door. Michael complied before easing into the chair across from Keith.

"You have to break things off with one of them," Keith reiterated.

"I know. I tried. I went to Lauren's Friday night and told her I couldn't marry her. She threatened to kill herself and the children if I left her."

Keith slid away from his desk. "She said kill? As in intent to harm and you're just now telling me this?"

"I called but it went to voicemail. I've been glued to Lauren's side ever since. I haven't let John and Olivia out of my sight." He rubbed his head. "It wasn't what she said; it was how she said it that has me in torment."

"How did she say it?" Keith questioned.

"She didn't scream or yell. In fact, she growled the words in this low, menacing tone."

"Listen, there's too much going on with people today to dismiss that as a harmless threat. I think we need to alert the authorities. Even if Lauren wasn't serious, those words should've never left her mouth."

"I agree, but I'm not trying to get her in trouble."

"Then she never should have fixed her mouth to say something so despicable. We need you to pursue emergency custody."

Michael wavered. "I don't know, Keith. She's John and Olivia's mother. How would that look if I stole them from her?"

"You wouldn't be stealing them. You'd be rescuing them from potential harm. How many mothers have you heard hit the news for driving their kids into the ocean or something? Too many. Well answer this, how has she been acting? Did she apologize for her statement?" Keith's eyes narrowed to slits.

Michael backtracked over his and Lauren's conversation. He shook his head. "No, she didn't apologize. I did. I backed down with the excuse of cold feet. Once Lauren heard that, she went right back to the wedding planning. She didn't skip a beat."

Keith narrowed his eyes. "Is she bipolar? How well do you know this woman?"

Michael shook his head. When he met Lauren years ago, Michael had been heartbroken over Keith and Gina's betrayal. For him, Lauren had been a tool for his revenge. And she had been a crazy good bed partner. He squinted his eyes. Somehow, he was a magnet for psychos.

"I don't know if she's bipolar. I know her in the biblical sense," Michael said. He pulled out his cell phone and speed dialed Frank.

After a couple rings, Frank picked up. "Frank, I need you to gather all you can on Lauren Goodman. I need it yesterday."

Michael disconnected the line. By then, Keith had grabbed his coat and waited for him by the door. "Let's go to the police station and get an emergency custody order. John and Olivia are safe here. I'll warn Josie not to let Lauren in the house if she comes by."

"I don't think she will. She believes I'm at Chuck E. Cheese."

Keith nodded. "Have you told Verona any of this?"

"No. I was hoping to have it handled before she returns."

Keith stopped and put a hand on Michael's shoulder. "If you love her and she's the one you want to marry, you need to tell her. Lauren doesn't sound stable. She might decide to go after Verona when she finds out the truth."

Michael gulped. He had not thought of that. "I really made a mess of things, didn't I?"

"Hold the remorse," Keith advised. "Lauren had everybody fooled but God. That's why, in my spirit, I believe you should take her at her word."

The brothers entered Keith's vehicle. Michael's heart thumped in his chest. "I hope we're not overreacting."

"Better to overreact than to have regrets."

Keith was right. "Now I feel as if I waited too long," Michael said.

"No point in second-guessing. You did the right thing by not leaving her. I know it may seem as if I'm being dramatic but, believe me, you don't know how many cases there are that don't make the news."

"When Lauren said those words to me, it took everything within me not to strangle her with my bare hands." Talking about it brought Michael's anger back to the surface.

"She'd be picking her teeth up off the floor if those had been my children."

"Pastor Ward, I don't think that's a godly response," Michael teased, although he appreciated Keith's honest reaction. It made him human.

Keith acquiesced. "You're right. God looked out for me by making sure I wasn't present at the time. Once I'm assured the children are safe, I'll try to pray for her."

Michael chuckled at Keith's choice of words. If it's one thing he could appreciate about his brother, Keith was real. "I'm glad you're here with me," he observed.

His brother smiled. "I'm glad you're here. Period."

"Give me my kids, Michael!" Lauren screamed. "I know you're in there. So come outside! I'm not leaving without my children. John! Olivia! Mommy's here."

Keith had been expecting her. He opened the door and stepped outside. He kept his tone neutral and said, "Lauren, I'm going to ask you to leave. You made an awful threat against yourself and your children. It's late and John and Olivia are sleeping. You can hire an attorney and protest the judge's decision, but you need to leave."

She shoved her hands in her pocket. Keith backed up, wary. He should have stayed inside. Lauren could be packing and he was easy target. *Lord, I invite your presence. Keep me safe and from all harm and danger.*

She shivered. "Keith, I love my children. Please let me see them. I need to take them home."

Gently, he said, "I'm sorry, Lauren. I can't."

In an instant, her demeanor changed. Lauren let loose a string of profanity and screamed at the top of her lungs. "I want my children! I want them! I'll come back and blast this place apart if you don't give them to me."

Wow. She was "out of this world" crazy. She was "kill her kids and everyone in his home" kind of crazy.

Keith sprinted up the steps and sailed through the screen door. He needed her to enter his home. After that, anything that transpired would be self-defense. Gina was standing by the door with Trey's bat in her hands. Keith put his hand over his lips, urging her to remain silent.

Lauren picked up some of the stones that lined his driveway and flung them at the door. Keith clenched his fists. This was a woman who would make him fight her like a man. He turned and said, "Lauren, if you don't leave. I'll call the cops. The neighbors are probably already on the phone." Thankfully, he only had a couple of surrounding homes in the vicinity.

The commotion must have awakened Michael for he strode toward the front door. Keith tried to hold him, but he pushed past Keith.

Michael stormed over to Lauren. "It's one-thirty in the morning. Go home. Now. We will talk later on today."

The young woman sobbed. "I miss them," she said. "Please, Michael."

Michael moved to hug her but she reared back and spit in his face. Turning on her heels, Lauren stomped to her car. "This is not over," she sneered flinging the ring off her hand and tossing it in the bushes. "You're going to be sorry you did this to me, Michael. After all I did to be with you. I can't believe this is how you repay me. You wouldn't even have children if I didn't . . ."

Suddenly, she stopped. Jumping in her car, the tires squealed under her outrage as she spun off for parts unknown.

Michael remained rooted in that spot for several minutes. Keith went out to him. With troubled eyes, Michael asked, "If she didn't what? What did she do?"

"Don't take too much stock in the words of that troubled woman," Keith advised.

"I won't rest until I find out what she meant," Michael promised, with a distinct edge to his tone.

Keith sighed, feeling weary. *Lord, I need you.* "Wait to see what Frank finds out before you do anything."

"What if she comes back?"

"If Lauren knows what's good for her, she'd better not." His patience was worn thin. If she did show her face, he would not be as nice like this time.

As they made their way back into the house, Michael tried to defuse the tension with humor. "I'm sure this engagement is over now. She threw a twenty thousand dollar ring into the bushes like it was an old piece of chewed-up gum."

"Cancel her access to your penthouse if you gave her a card. An angry woman makes a vicious, vindictive enemy."

"Tomorrow, I'll get a restraining order." Michael yawned.

"That's a mere piece of paper to people like Lauren. You'll need more than cops in your corner. You'll need the hand of God."

Chapter Fifty-five

"You sure you weren't seeing things?" Bill asked. "I don't want to look stupid when we go see the pastor. He's a busy man."

Mindy wished he would stop asking her if she was sure about this or sure about that. "I'm not sure, Dad. That's why I need to talk with Pastor Keith." She searched through the pile of sweaters on her bed until she found the cardigan that matched her dress.

Her father rushed her out the door. It was one silent ride until they pulled into the church parking lot.

"It's not that I don't believe you," Bill said as they exited the vehicle.

"I know. I understand. FYI, I have been taking my pills. Let's go inside." She lifted the handle and pushed the door to the church open. Now she wished she had come by herself because her father was hovering and it was getting to her. She entered the church office with Bill on her heels.

Mindy sighed with relief when she saw Pastor Keith approach. He must have been looking out for her. Mindy scurried over to him. "Greetings, Pastor. Thanks for seeing us early this morning."

Pastor Keith had bags under his eyes. He looked like he had not slept in days. She felt bad for the early morning call, but Mindy could not rest until she spoke with him.

"It's not a problem. I decided to wait here in the hall to look out for you since Dianne isn't here yet." Keith shook hands with Bill and said, "I have a lot going on but I will always make time for Mindy. I promised and I intend to keep my word."

Pastor Keith ushered them toward his office. He unlocked his door and turned the lights on. "Dianne will be here soon with coffee and bagels."

Mindy and Bill settled into the chairs. Then Pastor Keith zeroed in on her. "Are you still seeing Dr. Forrester? Are you taking your meds?"

"Yes and yes. I'm also reading the Bible, especially the New Testament." Mindy had been enthralled with the scripture of Jesus saving the madman with the legion of demons. She knew she would be delivered one day.

"She lives in that book," her father joked.

"Every time I feel any way out of the norm, I reach for the Bible," she confirmed. "It helps. I've never felt so whole."

Pastor Keith smiled. "Mindy, I'm amazed at your faith. You're teaching me what trust in God really means."

"Tell him why we're here," Bill chimed in.

"I came because when I was in church and it was time for the altar call, I thought I saw Elle G. It wasn't until last night my mind pieced it all together. She is real and I didn't make her up in my head."

She braved a glance at Pastor Keith. He looked interested. "I thought it was only Mousie who had seen her, but I know her. I first met her outside of Dr. Forrester's office."

He pushed his body across his desk. "I'm listening."

Mindy had his undivided attention. She did not feel so stupid now. "She struck up a conversation with me, and introduced herself as Elle G but I saw her sitting next to Michael on Saturday—"

"Whoa. Back up!"

Mindy quailed at his tone.

"What is it?" her father interjected. He, too, must have noticed Pastor Keith was more than interested.

Keith waved his hand. "I'm sorry. I won't interrupt. Please continue."

Mindy nodded. "You were introducing Michael and his friend Lauren Goodman and when I saw her, I wondered why it felt as if I knew her—"

Again, Keith interrupted her. This time there was no denying his jubilation. "Elle G is not a name, they're initials! Not a name. Oh, Lord, you've answered our prayers! LG is Lauren Goodman."

She was not quite following his train of thought, but she would not be deterred. "Then last night, I remembered how I knew her. She was the person I met at Dr. Forrester's office. She was the one who befriended Mousie at the strip joint. It was Lauren who punched me and beat me up."

"What!" Bill roared. "You didn't tell me that!"

"That's because I didn't want you doing anything crazy," Mindy answered. "And, I'm the one who asked her to punch me. I didn't like myself. Sometimes the pain of being alive was too much and I'd cut myself. It was supposed to be one punch. It took me forever to persuade her but once she started, she couldn't stop. She enjoyed it. I was begging, begging for my life and she wouldn't stop." Oh, Lord, the horror of that night was coming back to her. She hid her face as tears poured.

Seeing her distress, her father came to hug her.

"The next thing I knew, I was waking up in the hospital," she sobbed.

Pastor Keith came around holding a box of tissues in his hand.

"Thank you," Mindy said, blotting her eyes and cheeks.

Pastor Keith took her hands in his. They felt small in his larger ones. "Thank you for telling me, Mindy. You don't know it, but you've helped Michael's case."

She sagged. After all the hurt she had caused, this was great news. "How?"

"Lauren and Michael dated. She is the mother of his children. I'm thinking that's why she befriended you. Did you mention Michael at all when you first met?"

Mindy knew her eyes were bulging. "I don't know." She clutched her forehead. "I might have. Because why else would she have been there at the hotel with me that night? I don't have all the answers."

Pastor Keith patted her on the shoulder. "It's okay. You've done plenty, Mindy."

"See, Dad?" Mindy gave her father a tremulous smile. She remembered something else. "Her hair wasn't red, though. She always wore a black wig."

Pastor Keith snapped his fingers. He grabbed her to kiss her on the cheek. "I'll check the camera tapes the police confiscated to see if Lauren was there in disguise. I have a feeling Lauren is the answer to the condom found on the scene."

Pastor Keith excused himself to make a phone call. He was barking orders in the phone to someone. She felt good she had been helpful.

"I'm ready to go, but I need to go to the bathroom, first."

Her father gathered his belongings and hers. Mindy raced into the stall. When she came out to wash her hands, she gasped.

"Elle G? I mean, Lauren. You scared me." Her eyes scanned Lauren from head to toe. Lauren was dressed in a wedding dress, complete with tiara. And they called *her* crazy.

Lauren came over to hug her. "Mindy, what are you doing here?"

Mindy's hands shook as she pretended she did not think it odd Lauren was dressed as a bride. "I was speaking to Pastor Keith."

The older woman reached to touch her hair. Mindy inhaled, scared. She remembered Lauren's vicious beating and trembled. Normally, being this scared would make her switch personalities. Instead, a part of her favorite verse popped in her head. *"For God has not given me the spirit of fear,"* she recited internally.

"I'm here to see the good pastor myself," Lauren said.

"Are you getting married?" Mindy had to ask. It might appear odd if she didn't ask.

"No. Not anymore," came the cryptic response.

Something about Lauren's tone gave Mindy the creeps. She washed her hands and uttered a quick, "Okay, see you later." Her hand was on the door when Lauren stopped her.

"Not so fast."

Mindy faced her with dread. Her chest tightened when she saw Lauren held a gun pointed directly at her. "Wh . . . what are you doing?"

"I'm sorry, friend, but you're my insurance in case things don't go according to plan."

Chapter Fifty-six

Michael ended his call with Keith and shouted, "Thank God!" He threw on a sweater and jeans preparing to meet Keith at the church. His knees weakened when he heard Mindy had identified Lauren as her accomplice that night. Finally, all the pieces of the puzzle were in place. He could move forward.

After Lauren had left the night before, he had taken Keith's advice and confessed all to Verona. She had hit the roof a couple of times. He saw all the emotions on her face as they had used FaceTime to talk. But, Michael kept telling Verona how he loved her until she calmed. He showed her the pendant. He intended to give it to her as his wedding gift. That appeased her, somewhat. He knew their love was strong enough. It was the real deal. She was not going anywhere. Neither was he. He was ready to commit and spend his life basking in the love of a good woman.

John and Olivia were already up. He dressed them. They were now eating breakfast, prepared by Josie. The Jamaican lady was a godsend. She was a substitute grandmother to his children. He wished he could clone her but she had already tipped him off about her cousin, Pat Wilkins, in Jamaica. Michael hired her based solely on Josie's exemplary performance. He had already filed the paperwork for Pat's work visa. The Jamaican Embassy had approved her entry into the United States. She should arrive within two weeks.

Michael headed into the kitchen. "Josie, I have to meet Keith at the church. Would you mind if John and Olivia stayed with you?"

"Leave them. They'll be all right," she said, washing the breakfast pots and pans. He'd never seen a more hardworking woman. She worked nonstop. Gina's house was immaculate.

Walking over to John and Olivia, Michael crouched to let them know he was leaving. "Daddy will be right back, okay? I won't be gone long." John sniffed. Olivia's bottom chin wobbled. His heart melted. "Oh, guys, I promise I'm coming back."

"Okay," they said.

Olivia pulled on his pants. "Daddy, we go to closet?"

What did she say? Michael bent over. He asked her to repeat what she'd said.

"Do we go closet now?"

John wailed. "I don't want to go in closet."

Did Lauren put his children in the closet when she would leave the house? Michael thought of the time Lauren showed up at his penthouse alone. Surely, Lauren had not left them unattended for hours.

Josie stopped her tasks, openly listening to the exchange.

Michael's eyes collided with her horrified ones. "Did you hear that?" he asked.

"Yes." Josie nodded.

Michael was a strong man but his insides mushed up at that thought. Anything could have happened to them. The possibilities crippled him.

He gazed on his children. His love for them overflowed. The world could not contain it. He grabbed a paper towel to wipe their runny noses. "John, Olivia, you won't be going in the closet. You'll be here with Josie."

"Yay! Josie," Olivia yelled and ran over to hug the older woman around the leg. John followed gripping her other leg.

"Go ahead, Mr. Michael, they'll be fine. Go, do what you have to do." He noticed her cheeks were red and knew she had also been moved by the situation.

Michael drove to the church with record speed. The entire drive he replayed John and Olivia's faces as they asked about going in the closet. To children that age, the closet was a dark and scary place. He thought of Lauren and wished her dead. A feeling akin to hate rose within him.

When he sped into the parking lot, Michael noticed the three cars. One was Keith's; one was Bill's; and the other? Wait. That was Lauren's car.

Michael punched the steering wheel. He was going to knock Lauren to the floor when he saw her. He stomped into the church. It was eerily quiet. Michael senses went into overdrive. Something did not feel right.

He made his way to Keith's office and peered inside but it was empty.

His heart rate increased. Where was everyone? He heard a yell and spun around. Cautious, he made his way toward the sound, hating every echo and creak of his shoes on the tile.

When he turned the corner, he stopped. Garbed in her wedding dress, Lauren had a pistol waving it around in the hallway leading to the children's room. She raged, "I have four bullets and I'm not afraid to use them."

Mindy's eyes rounded and her huge intake of breath alerted Lauren to his presence. She greeted him with a maniacal smile.

"Well, bullet number four has found an owner. Come and join the rest."

Her cackle bounced off the walls. Lauren was cuckoo for Cocoa Puffs. Michael eyed the gun. He made up his mind he was not going down without a fight. "Lauren, put the gun away and let's have a conversation."

"No! I'm done talking. You and your brother took my children. All my years of planning are ruined." She gave Michael a spiteful look. "When I shoot you, I'll be sure to watch you bleed out."

Michael blurted out, "We'll see about that, you poor excuse for a mother. You locked our children in a closet? Why did you do it?"

"I . . ." Her face filled with shame. "Nothing happened to them. I . . ."

Keith gestured to him to keep her talking as he inched closer to her.

"What did you mean last night when you said if it weren't for you, I wouldn't have children?"

Her chin rose. "I saved the condoms. I knew you couldn't have children. I collected your tired, slow semen and paid good money for artificial insemination."

Michael glared. "That's illegal and plumb crazy you'd do something like that without my consent."

"Well it worked." She snorted. "Only you didn't believe me. You kicked me out. It wasn't until I watched your brother professing his love for Gina that a plan formed."

A light bulb went off. He jabbed a finger at her. "You planted the condoms at the hotel and in my house!"

"Bingo," she boasted.

"Why would you keep those condoms all these years? They were old and of no use." To Michael that was sheer stupidity.

Lauren shrugged. "I don't know." For once, she seemed a little unsure. Then she squared her shoulders. "It worked, didn't it? They still served their purpose."

"You used me and took advantage of me and my family," Keith hurled.

She lifted her chin. "Yes, you were too in love with your wife and God not to see it. I wanted Michael. I wanted the fairytale. Your God was taking too long. I took matters into my own hands. Imagine my good fortune when you presented me with your home on a platter."

"My daughter was impressionable. Why did you have to include her in your scheme?" Bill stormed toward her. Michael knew from past dealings Bill was not a man to be messed with.

"She was stupid. An easy pawn. It was fate when I met Mindy at Dr. Forrester's. I've been her patient for the past two years and had never met another patient. There must have been some scheduling snafu that day. Whatever, Mindy and I became fast friends. I never met somebody so desperate for attention in all my life." Lauren rolled back on her heels. Looking at Michael, she said, "I had to endure Mindy's childish mooning over you but it was worth it to see your name plastered all over the papers."

"Bill, get back!" Michael shouted.

"Yeah, Bill, you'd better listen to your friend." Lauren snorted. It was only when Mindy grabbed his arm that he retreated.

Keep her talking, Michael told himself. He crossed his arms. "If all this was to get me, why didn't you accept my proposal the first time? Why tell me about a boyfriend?"

"A girl can't appear too eager. She has to play a little hard to get," Lauren said. "And, how did you not miss that Martin Weston has your initials? You should've figured that out but then I forget that underneath those tailor-made suits is an imbecile. You were dumb to let me go."

"No, kicking you out was the smartest thing I ever did," Michael shot back.

Keith gave him the signal. Both men pounced. Caught off guard, Lauren swayed in several directions. The gun fell from her hand and hit the floor with a bang.

"No!" Michael screamed as it expelled a single, fatal shot.

Epilogue

"This is the happiest day of my life. I'm walking my daughter down the aisle." Noel cried, not caring who saw.

Verona wiped her father's cheeks. "Don't start. My makeup is flawless and I'm not about to ruin it with waterworks."

Elijah came inside the house. "Everyone's waiting and Michael is yelling he's coming in here for you if you don't get a move on."

"Tell that mule head this is my day and I won't be rushed because of his impatience," she glared.

Elijah grinned, and left to rejoin Michael and Keith at the makeshift altar in the gardens of what used to be Lauren's home. Verona and Michael would be raising John and Olivia there, as it was the only home the children had ever known. It was traumatic enough their mother had died a few months ago. Uprooting them would be too much. Verona and Michael would tell them the whole sordid tale of how Lauren died by a gunshot wound one day. For now, they told the twins Lauren was in heaven. Which was a lie.

Michael was not selling the penthouse, though. He was having the rooms redone and equipped for young children.

Verona touched her tiger pendant and smiled. Her life was complete. Her son and Michael were building a relationship but it was not without its trials. Elijah bristled when Michael corrected him about something.

Michael felt she had been too generous with the Hummer she had bought Elijah. And, on it went. But, all was well.

John and Olivia entangled themselves in folds of her gown. Her mother came running after them.

"I can't keep them still," she fussed, though she laughed at their antics.

Verona bent to kiss them. God had given her children. She now understood what her father meant about adoption. Olivia was the cutest flower girl and John was taking his job as ring bearer very seriously.

Taking Noel's hand, she said, "I'm ready."

Gina came and smoothed her Badgley Mischka gown. "I have to do my job as the matron of honor and let me just say you are stunning. Michael won't be able to keep his eyes off you."

Mindy rounded the corner. "I hear the music playing. We have to go." She served as Verona's only bridesmaid. The young woman had been floored when Verona asked her. Mindy was so intent on not missing a step during rehearsal Verona had to tell her she needed to relax and have fun.

As Verona focused on Michael, calmness seeped through her being. She was on the right path to the man God had perfected for her. He was obstinate and stubborn, but he was hers. She could live with that.

Reading Group Questions

1. Keith and Michael were estranged. Keith spent years in prayer for Michael to return home. God answered, though not in the way Keith expected. Have you ever sought God's help for something but were unprepared for how He responded?

2. Michael held on to past hurts, which made him bitter and distrustful. Forgiveness frees us. Is there a past situation in your life which you need to let go of? Share with your reading group.

3. Recall how Michael felt when Gina touched him of her own volition. How did it make him feel? What did that touch tell Michael about Gina's feelings even though she hadn't said a word? Share a time when a touch brought you comfort.

4. Keith called for a time of fasting and prayer. How did that help Michael's case? Give other examples from the Bible where God fought man's battle for him. Share a time when you may have fasted and prayed about a matter and the results.

5. Mindy battled mental illness. She sought both psychiatric and spiritual help. Do you think it should be one or the other? Is it possible to be saved and still struggle with a mental illness?

6. Verona felt God was punishing her when she learned she was unable to have more children. Does God punish women in this way? For instance, some women who have had abortions feel God punishes

them by closing their womb or by giving them sick children.

7. Verona was in love with Michael for years but kept it hidden. Share an experience where you had feelings for someone who may not have returned your feelings. What did you do about it? Do you regret your actions or inaction?

8. Do you agree with Noel and Louisa Stachs's reasons for giving up Verona's son for adoption? In your opinion, is there ever a good reason for adoption? What do you think of the idea of open adoption?

9. Lauren brazenly stole Michael's sperm and used it in artificial insemination to get pregnant. This was entrapment and highly unethical behavior. How do you feel about women who trap men into marriage and/or relationships through children?

10. Michael felt the honorable thing to do was marry Lauren because she was the mother of his children. Other than being in love, what are the necessary ingredients for a healthy marriage?

11. Keith stated that there was no way he would marry someone other than for love. Do you share his belief? Would you marry a poor man you loved or a rich man who could provide you security?

12. Looking at the title, *The Fall of the Prodigal,* explain how both Michael and Verona were kinds of prodigals. Talk about their journey "home."

About the Author

Michelle Lindo-Rice enjoys crafting women's fiction with themes centered around the four "F" words: Faith, Friendship, Family, and Forgiveness. Her first published work, *Sing A New Song,* was a Black Expressions featured selection. Originally from Jamaica West Indies, Michelle Lindo-Rice calls herself a lifelong learner.

She has earned degrees from New York University, SUNY at Stony Brook, and Teachers College, Columbia University. When she moved to Florida, she enrolled in Argosy University where she completed her Education Specialist degree in Education Leadership. A pastor's kid, Michelle upholds the faith, preaching, teaching, and ministering through praise and worship.

For more information about her other books, or to leave an encouraging word, you can reach Michelle online at Facebook, LinkedIn, Tumblr, Stumbledupon, Twitter @mlindorice, Pinterest, Google+. To learn more about her books, please join her mailing list at www.michellelindorice.com.

UC HIS GLORY BOOK CLUB!

www.uchisglorybookclub.net

UC His Glory Book Club is the spirit-inspired brain-child of Joylynn Ross, Author and Acquisitions Editor of Urban Christian, and Kendra Norman-Bellamy, Author for Urban Christian. This is an online book club that hosts authors of Urban Christian. We welcome as members all men and women who have a passion for reading Christian-based fiction.

UC His Glory Book Club pledges our commitment to provide support, positive feedback, encouragement, and a forum whereby members can openly discuss and review the literary works of Urban Christian authors.

There is no membership fee associated with UC His Glory Book Club; however, we do ask that you support the authors through purchasing, encouraging, providing book reviews, and of course, your prayers. We also ask that you respect our beliefs and follow the guidelines of the book club. We hope to receive your valuable input, opinions, and reviews that build up, rather than tear down our authors.

What We Believe:

—We believe that Jesus is the Christ, Son of the Living God.

—We believe the Bible is the true, living Word of God.

—We believe all Urban Christian authors should use their God-given writing abilities to honor God and share the message of the written word God has given to each of them uniquely.

—We believe in supporting Urban Christian authors in their literary endeavors by reading, purchasing and sharing their titles with our online community.

—We believe that in everything we do in our literary arena should be done in a manner that will lead to God being glorified and honored.

We look forward to the online fellowship with you.

Please visit us often at:
www.uchisglorybookclub.net

Many Blessing to You!

Shelia E. Lipsey,
President, UC His Glory Book Club

ORDER FORM
URBAN BOOKS, LLC
97 N18th Street
Wyandanch, NY 11798

Name (please print):_____

Address: _____

City/State: _____

Zip: _____

QTY	TITLES	PRICE

Shipping and handling: add $3.50 for 1st book, then $1.75 for each additional book.
Please send a check payable to:
Urban Books, LLC
Please allow 4-6 weeks for delivery

ORDER FORM
URBAN BOOKS, LLC
97 N18th Street
Wyandanch, NY 11798

Name (please print):_____

Address: _____

City/State: _____

Zip: _____

QTY	TITLES	PRICE

Shipping and handling: add $3.50 for 1st book, then $1.75 for each additional book.

Please send a check payable to:
Urban Books, LLC

Please allow 4-6 weeks for delivery